One Shot at Love

Annette Mori

Also by Annette Mori

Heart Strings Attached with Ali Spooner
The Panty Thief
Pleasure Workers
A Window to Love
The Book Witch
The Book Addict
The Dream Catcher
Free to Love with Ali Spooner
Unconventional Lovers
The Organization with Erin O'Reilly
Captivated
The Termination
The Review
The Ultimate Betrayal
Locked Inside
Out of This World
Asset Management
The Incredibly True Adventure of Two Elves in Love
(Affinity 2014 Christmas Collection)
Love Forever, Live Forever
The True Story of Valentine's Day
Vampire Pussy…Cat
Nicky's Christmas Miracle X3
(It's in Her Kiss, Affinity's Charity Anthology)

One Shot at Love

Annette Mori

Affinity
Rainbow Publications

2020

One Shot at Love

Affinity E-Book Press NZ LTD
Canterbury, New Zealand

1st Edition

ISBN: 978-1-98-858877-3

Editor: Angela Koenig
Proof Editor: Alexis Smith
Cover Design: Irish Dragon Design
Production Design: Affinity Publication Services

ACKNOWLEDGMENTS

A huge thank you to all of my beta readers: Gail Dodge, Erin Saluta, LJ Reynolds, Ali Spooner, Ameliah Faith, Dana Holmes, Danna Micoletti, and Maria Siopsis who made great suggestions to improve the initial draft. As always, I have to acknowledge Erin O'Reilly who is a constant support and encouragement to me. I am honored to call her a friend and have her support me in my journey. I would also like to express my gratitude to Affinity Rainbow Publications and the wonderful trio (JM Dragon, Erin O'Reilly, and Nancy Kaufman) who continue to provide feedback to tighten up manuscripts that need assistance and publish my unconventional work. I am eternally grateful for the opportunities they give me to let my stories see the light of day. My other family members, who are also very supportive, include my nephew, Aaron, and his wife, Chelsea, my older sister Val, and my father who struggles to read my books with one eye. I always enjoy working with the beta editor, Nancy Kaufman, who helped tighten my story. Thanks to Angela Koenig for her magic as the final editor to tighten the story even further. She is a delight to work with. Inevitably, there are those pesky final errors that slip through and I am thankful that the final proof editor, Alexis Smith, caught those before the book went to print.

Thanks to Nancy Kaufman for the final cover. Nancy is also a promoter extraordinaire. A huge thanks to all the other readers and fellow writers who have sent personal emails, written reviews, and posted nice things on Facebook (you know who you are). The Affinity authors are an especially supportive group and often share posts or send words of encouragement. Finally, my wife, Jody, continues her support even when it interferes with our time.

Extra Special Recognition and Thanks: Not only did Nancy Ann Healy generously offer to allow me to use her character, Emma Bronson, from the *Off Screen* series, but she wrote the speech that Emma gives at the rally. I needed a high-profile lesbian character to include and none of my characters fit. Emma Bronson was beyond perfect. If you have not had a chance to read this wonderful series, I highly recommend it. Thanks to Nancy Ann Healy who continues to be a shining star in lesfic and WLW fiction and romance.

Dedication

To all the young men and women who get involved and tirelessly fight for meaningful gun legislation. And, as always, to my beautiful wife whom I love with all my heart.

TABLE OF CONTENTS

PROLOGUE

The man with sandy blond hair and chiseled features leaned against the rotting wood fence and watched with pride and a little awe. His hair danced in the wind as the impending storm grew. He'd walked to the overgrown field to tell Maribel to come inside but had been caught by her poetry in motion. Her small body held the shotgun with ease and each shot hit its mark when the clay discs spun in the air only to disintegrate in a cloud of dust as the tiny markswoman held steady.

Pop pop pop. Not a single miss. She was a natural. A shooting virtuoso. Not many would describe a markswoman as a child prodigy, but that was exactly what Maribel was.

Every day she began to look more like her mother, and the beautiful agony of it all created tiny slivers in his heart. She was a constant reminder of all he'd lost and all he'd gained in that one fateful moment.

He was twenty-five at the time. He hadn't known the first thing about taking care of a squiggly helpless infant, but somehow, they'd muddled through together with the support of his mother, and then she'd left him all alone to finish the job. He'd done the best he could.

It would have been better to have a boy. The town folk gave him disapproving looks at the way he was raising his little girl. They begrudgingly admitted that it was clear he adored her and she him, but taking a girl hunting at age five elicited frowns and shaking heads. Where he went, so did she, and so began her fascination with shotguns.

"That steady aim of yours is gonna make you famous someday," Ray shouted above the wind to his daughter.

"I'm gonna be like Annie Oakley." Maribel set her shotgun next to her side and posed, grinning as she showed Ray the gap in her teeth.

"Come on in. Storm's fixin' to blow you off your feet. You can practice again tomorrow. Okay?"

"All right, Papa. Will you shoot with me tomorrow?"

"We'll see. I got a lot to do around the farm and can't be wasting my time having my little girl keep showing me up as the better shooter." Ray smiled and waved his hand.

Maribel picked up her shotgun and scrambled after her father. She let the screen door to the old white farmhouse slam, barely managing to remain standing as the strong wind pushed against her small body. She started helping her father by setting the table, looked over her shoulder and asked, “Pa, how am I gonna be famous if they don’t have the Wild West show anymore?”

“The Olympics, Maribel, you’re gonna be in the Olympics someday, and you’re gonna bring home the Gold for the US.”

“They got skeet shooters in the Olympics, Pa?”

“Yup, and double trap, too. They’re allowing women to compete again. Boneheads stopped letting women in the games in ’96, but it’s back now. Thank God too many people raised a ruckus. Tomorrow I’ll teach ya how to change your style. No more holding the shotgun against your shoulder. Ya gotta learn to start from your hip ’cause that’s the way they do it now. You can’t move your shotgun until the clay is released.”

“Oh Pa, I can’t wait to learn a new way of shootin’. It was getting boring, ya know?”

Ray chuckled and patted his daughter’s head. No matter how much she started looking like her mother, he wouldn’t let the pain creep in again. She was and would always be his pride and joy.

CHAPTER ONE

The skinny kid with greasy black hair skulked into the grade school wearing his heavy trench coat. He was a walking billboard for what he was about to do. *Stupid school officials. How they don't realize the terror I'm about to rain on their papier mâché projects is a fucking miracle.* Bright cardboard cutouts peppered the pastel-colored walls, a contrast to his dark colored clothing.

In the stillness of the morning he was cat burglar quiet. The absence of sound would not last forever because soon their screams would fill every pocket of air.

He thought he was telegraphing his intentions with every menacing step he made into the bright hallway. They could have stopped him. They should have ended the madness, but they didn't because nobody had ever targeted a grade school. He was the first. That made him feel powerful. If he made it through this first test, the first chapter of his manifesto, he would progress to the next stage. He had a list and knew where to go first. The high school wasn't that far away. It was entirely possible to hit both targets before the inevitable conclusion.

The feelings bubbled to the surface hot and dangerous like lava. Excitement. Anticipation. Shoving aside the dark coat, his hands gripped the solid handle of the two automatic weapons. Fingers molded to the grips and power surged from deep inside. He began sending his message loud and clear, he was not a nobody, he existed. *Look at me now, Mother, my fifteen minutes of fame should make you proud, you'll be the talk of the town.*

He emptied both guns into the screaming children and desperate teachers attempting to pull them into the safety of locked classrooms. His head cocked to the side. The sirens sounded far away, and he lamented briefly that he wouldn't complete his plan. All the bullets were discharged, and he contemplated reloading, but the sirens were close now. Walking slowly down the hall, he surveyed his masterpiece. The blood created interesting patterns. He could almost hear the thud of his heartbeat, slow and steady over the increasing awareness of the police sirens that he knew were mere feet away on the other side of the door he was walking toward. With each step closer to the outside he heard the dull clomp of his boots on the floor. He pushed open the door and grinned as he squinted at the sunshine above.

It didn't matter it was over in a matter of minutes, and the death toll was worthy of recognition. He pulled the handgun from the front of his pants and stuck the barrel into his mouth. He would rather take matters into his own hands. Suicide by police was not in the cards for him. His last thought before he pulled the trigger was, *when I die, I'll know that I must have existed.*

†

Aretha Franklin's rich vocals blared through the speakers in Blair's practical Ford Fiesta. She'd wanted to buy a Prius, but that was out of her range.

Blair was singing along to the CD, no Bluetooth for her. She knew that most of her friends preferred a different style of music, Katie Perry or Beyoncé, or some such other pop music, but she didn't care because Aretha was the queen in her mind, and the new music did not hold a candle to the classics. She'd never bend to the pressure to fit in. She liked what she liked. To hell with other people's judgments on what was hip and what was not.

Her phone didn't connect to the car in any way, but when she heard the buzz, she couldn't help herself and glanced at the text message from her mom of all people.

Don't turn on the news, come home.

Like a moth to a flame, Blair pushed the button on the radio to switch her to an FM station. She needed to hear the news, because the hairs at the back of her neck suddenly stood up like rigid soldiers. Blair knew life would never be the same again and it wasn't.

Through the tinny speaker she heard a male voice report on breaking news: "A shooting at Cedarbrook Elementary—"

Screech.

Blair slammed on her brakes, pulled to the side of the road and called her mother's cell phone. She angrily punched the button on the radio.

"Blair?" her mother's anguished voice answered.

Blair was already crying before she managed to push out the words. "Trina? Please tell me that she's okay," Blair pleaded.

The silence on the other end of the small cell phone was deafening. "Come home," her mother said.

She pushed the button to end the call and sat in the car with her head in her hands, sobbing for ten minutes before pulling herself together enough to be the shoulder her mother needed. Her little sister was the light in both their lives after her father had abandoned them for the second time. This might be the final straw that would break her mother's back. Mothers are not supposed to outlive their children. That's the rule. How dare someone break it? The world hardly made sense to her before this happened. Now it was just one, big, fucked up mess. If she believed in God, she would curse him right now, but she didn't even have that in her favor. Who would be the recipient of her anger now?

†

Maribel hopped out of her truck and was heading to the feed store when a microphone was shoved in her face. She glowered at the prissy blonde woman smiling at her with a fake-expectant expression plastered on her face. That's what it looked like, a plaster casing, all rigid and void of depth or color.

"Maribel, what is your opinion on the school shooting? You've talked about the gun regulations in California and how hard it was for you to prepare adequately for the Olympics when you had to complete a background check every time you bought ammo, but don't you think they're needed? Especially now. Is that why you moved back to Washington? Because the laws here are so lax?"

Maribel blinked. Why had she needed to spout off a few months ago when that reporter had interviewed her? Now she was the poster child for the NRA, again. She'd literally been that for them when she'd first started out. Her pa had explained how sponsorships worked. Recently, she'd started distancing herself. Although she was still a card-carrying member and believed in her Second Amendment rights, that didn't mean she wanted to get in the middle of the controversy.

"Um…I don't know your name, but did you guys ever interview Michael Phelps every time someone drowned and ask him about pool safety regulations?" Maribel ground out.

The walking Barbie stared at her for a second, a small frown appearing on her face before recovering and pushing on.

"I suppose you haven't heard, or you wouldn't be so cavalier with your response. Twenty children under the age of nine died today, Ms. Sanders. Do you still believe we should stop looking for ways to reduce this senseless violence? Is a gun-toting Olympian the kind of role model you believe we should be trotting out for little girls to follow?"

Maribel's eyes opened wide, and she barely managed to control her emotions. "Have you no decency? Preying on those families and their grief for your next sensational story." Maribel pushed the mic away from her face, brushed away a tear and turned back around to fold her tall body into her truck. She rolled down her window.

"Don't bother to follow me or this gun-toting Olympian might exercise her rights to shoot anyone who has the balls to trespass, and my nine gold medals prove that I don't miss whatever I set my sights on."

The Barbie Doll's mouth flew open, but she took a step back and watched as Maribel spit gravel leaving the parking lot. Maribel couldn't ever remember her anger getting the best of her. Somehow what that reporter said had touched a raw nerve, and her very long, slow, fuse sparked to life. She'd felt that same anger after the hundredth time a reporter had asked her the same question about her support for the NRA. Lately she'd been second-guessing her views, and the lingering questions reporters kept tossing her way was getting to her. First, she'd popped off at the reporter a few months back, and now she'd angrily responded to this woman who had the humanity of a shark.

†

Maribel was too rattled to make the long trek home to her lonely ranch. Ever since her father had died, she felt more than a little lost. Thank God for Sandy, her friend and for a brief time, her lover. She needed to see a friendly face. When she approached the door to the coffee shop Sandy owned, her shaky hand pulled open the door.

Sandy was carrying a new batch of cinnamon rolls to put inside the glass case. As soon as her eyes met Maribel's, she directed the young clerk to finish filling the case.

"You look like you just saw a ghost. Sit," Sandy directed. "I'll get you a cup of tea and take a short break. I wish you didn't live all the way out in bum-fuck Egypt. How am I supposed to make sure you're doing fine all by your lonesome if I only see you when you come in for tea?"

Maribel shoved her hands in her pockets and shuffled over to an empty seat by the fireplace. "Thanks," she whispered.

Sandy set a cup and cinnamon roll on the table in front of Maribel. "What happened?"

"Same old, same old. A reporter stuck a mic in my face and asked about the latest school shooting like I'm personally to blame for the tragedy."

"You're a hermit and an easy mark. Shrug the viper off. Better yet, get yourself a girlfriend and join the human race."

"It's not that easy."

"Yes, it is. You've had plenty of opportunities. Women flirt with you all the time. Start paying attention. Ask one out for a change. You've been alone licking your wounds for long enough. Having someone special in your life isn't the worst thing that can happen to you."

"Fine. I'll take that under advisement and start paying attention. I'm not too proud to admit that a solo life on the ranch sucks. Ever since Pa died, it's like I've lost my passion for life. I don't even enjoy skeet shooting anymore. Maybe finding someone with passion is the ticket to getting my own back."

"Good, now eat your cinnamon roll, and promise me that you'll give me all the details when you take that enormous step to put yourself out there again."

"Who else am I going to call for advice? Thanks, Sandy. Too bad we didn't work out."

"I'm allergic to miles and miles of open space and chicken shit."

Chapter Two

The small coffin looked all wrong. Blair wondered how anyone could choose a profession where they had to make caskets specifically designed for children. She didn't want to look. Damn her mother's insistence on an open casket. She thought it would help Blair achieve closure. It didn't. How could Blair ever come to grips with this kind of tragedy?

The fabric surrounding Trina looked soft. Blair wasn't sure how she knew that. Maybe she hoped it was. She wanted Trina surrounded by comfort even if Blair didn't believe it mattered anymore. Somehow that notion consoled her. Everything she'd heard about a viewing did not coincide with the stark reality. Trina didn't look like she was peacefully sleeping. Not at all.

Blair turned away, and a sob erupted from her throat. Raw and animalistic. "I can't do this." Nothing would entice her to touch her sister. She couldn't bring herself to place one last kiss on her forehead. Knowing she would feel the cold waxiness of her skin was enough to send her running from the room. As her mother reached out to touch her, maybe to keep her from leaving, Blair roughly pushed her arm away and kept on running. She knew she shouldn't have done that. Her mother was only trying to make a connection—to give her a small amount of reassurance that everything would be okay, eventually. It would never be okay. No amount of time could pass that would make this acceptable to Blair.

Bursting into the sunshine, the warmth of the golden rays was a stark contrast to the cold dark feeling making a home for itself in the pit of her stomach. Hate. Blair felt hate toward anyone associated with guns. Her bottom hit the pavement as she sat on the cement sidewalk, shaking from both anger and sadness. She pulled her knees up, wrapping her arms around them as she continued to cry.

A soft voice interrupted her grief. "Um, are you okay?"

Through bleary eyes, Blair looked into the concerned gaze of the stranger. Sandy blonde hair fell across the woman's brows, and Blair saw the compassionate moss-green eyes peek out under the manicured arch of her brows. The contrast to her natural appearance was glaring. Not a stitch of make-up adorned her chiseled face. Blair had the ridiculous thought that it seemed terribly incongruent for this woman to spend so much time waxing or plucking her eyebrows to obtain such perfection. She blinked away the sense of absurdity.

"Sorry, yes. Funeral." Blair relayed the information as if it were obvious why she would be folding into herself, crying on the sidewalk.

The woman shuffled her feet in discomfort. Warring emotions flashed across her face. Finally, she sat down next to Blair. "Anything I can do to help? Sometimes talking with a stranger helps, one who isn't going to give meaningless platitudes."

"You ever lost someone who never should have died?" Blair swiped at her cheek.

"My mother died in childbirth. I'm not sure if she should have died or not. That's up to God to decide, not me. I wish I'd had the chance to know her. Although my papa did a good job raising me."

"I don't believe in God, and even if I did, I'd call him a cruel monster." Blair dropped her head back to her knees and turned her face to the stranger curiously waiting a reaction from the woman who was probably a Bible-thumping conservative.

"I suppose that is a normal and justifiable reaction. I'd feel the same way right about now if I lost someone I cared about."

"She was seven years old. Seven." Repeating the number as if that somehow made all the difference in the world, the anger bubbled to the surface giving a hard edge to her voice.

Something crossed the stranger's face before she looked away. "Shit."

"What?"

"Nothing. I have to go."

"Yeah, I get it. Hard dose of reality. No one can handle it. Not even strangers."

"I'm so sorry for your loss," the woman mumbled almost mechanically. She scurried away so quickly that Blair thought she might have been a figment of imagination.

Shaking herself from believing she had hallucinated the whole conversation, Blair watched the woman get into her truck and bang her head on her steering wheel. Strange. Then it hit her. Maybe the woman had her own tragedy, and stupid Blair had just opened a wound. She hadn't mentioned losing someone to the shooting, but the whole town had been affected. It was certainly possible, even probable, and Blair had questioned her faith. A faith that was perhaps the only thing keeping her together.

†

Maribel couldn't run fast and far enough away from the haunted woman who was so achingly beautiful. After the conversation with Sandy about how she needed to open herself to possibilities, she could not resist coming to the stranger's rescue, even if it meant pushing herself to start an awkward conversation. Learning the funeral was for a child made the harsh words the TV reporter shouted at her rise to the surface. Had she been cavalier with her response? Seeing the woman in pain had been too much to handle, and Maribel did what she usually did when having to interact with anyone but her pa. She was able to joke around with the guys, but she never quite got the knack of talking to women. High school had been a terrible time for Maribel. She didn't have anything in common with the girls from high school. It became a habit to hang with the guys. To hunt and fish. She knew how to do that.

Placing her heavy boot on the step of her truck, she climbed inside and rested her forehead on the steering wheel. That wasn't enough. She lifted her head and brought it down again with precision two more times in rapid succession. Maybe beating social graces into her head would work. Finally, she kept her forehead pressed against the hard leather and waited to gain her senses again before attempting to back out and head home. Hopefully to a home without a swarm of reporters. Shooting her shotgun into the air might not have been the best way to tell them to get the hell off her property.

The subtle rap on her window startled Maribel, and when she looked up, the crying woman was standing there with her brow furrowed. She motioned for Maribel to roll down her window. Cautiously, Maribel pressed the button to lower the window in her truck.

"I'm so sorry. I wasn't thinking. The whole world does not revolve around me. Was…"

The woman choked and did not finish her question, but Maribel knew what she wanted to ask. She shook her head no.

"No, I didn't lose anyone to the uh…no, I'm just shitty with people, and I didn't know what to say to make it better."

"Oh, okay. Sorry to interrupt you. I wanted to make sure you weren't in distress. As disturbing as it seems, there was a part of me that wished you could relate, but then that would mean you'd lost someone to the tragedy as well. That's so…sick, I suppose." The distraught woman scrubbed her face with her hand.

"No, no it isn't. Um, do you want to get coffee or something? I, uh, will try to act like a normal human being, versus a social misfit."

She looked back to the brick building, and Maribel wondered what answer the distraught woman was looking for. Perhaps there was someone inside she was hoping would give her permission to leave. It sure looked like the woman needed a break. Maribel was like that as well when things got too real, she needed to put distance between herself and whatever was causing her pain.

"Yeah, okay. I need to let my mother do what she needs to do, and I hope she understands why I can't join her."

Maribel didn't think the statement was intended to elicit an answer, so she nodded and reached for the door handle. The woman took a step back and allowed Maribel to climb from the truck.

"There's a good place about a block away. Is that too far?"

A half smile turned up, but the woman's eyes remained shrouded in sadness. "Yeah, I know it well. The Percolatte Bean. An old friend of mine owns the place."

Maribel squinted at the woman. "You know Sandy?"

"Yup. We went to college together. Actually, we roomed together starting junior year. We had similar, uh…never mind. We joined the same clubs on campus. She earned a business degree, and I got my degree in social work. We didn't stay in touch as much as I would have liked. My fault. I got too involved in my new job and didn't make it back home as much as I should have. Plus, I went away for my master's degree before I took the new job. Why am I telling you all this?" She started in the direction of the shop, and Maribel fell in next to her to keep pace.

Maribel shrugged and grinned. "I don't know, but the more you talk the less I have to. Although it would be rude not to introduce myself before you reveal your entire life story. I'm Maribel."

The woman playfully bumped Maribel's shoulder. "I'm Blair, and I wasn't giving you my life story. I'm waiting until I get one of Sandy's special lattes." A new set of tears sprung to Blair's eyes.

Maribel didn't know what to do but took a chance by touching her arm in a fleeting connection. "Um, I'll buy," she added awkwardly.

"Sorry, it's just that I used to take Trina with me, and Sandy would make her a special drink without coffee. Trina thought she was all grown up, drinking coffee with me. We never told her the latte was really a vanilla steamer. She liked her drink, but it was Sandy's famous cinnamon bun that made her day."

"Yeah, those are my favorite as well. I don't drink coffee, so I always get the chai tea."

"Then why did you ask if I wanted to go for coffee?"

"I've heard that's an acceptable thing to offer and most people drink coffee. It makes my hands too jittery and then I don't…um, never mind. It's not important. You can talk more about your sister if you want. I mean if it helps."

"At this point, I'm not really sure what helps. I don't want to forget her or to let her memory fade, so right now, I desperately want to remember everything about Trina, even if it hurts so bad, I feel like I'm going to explode from the inside."

Maribel stuck her hands in her pockets and kept walking. Letting Blair talk might be the best way to help her, and Maribel wanted to make things better for Blair. She wanted to see her eyes lose the dullness because the one flash of lightness she'd seen was worth waiting for. It was so quick, if Maribel hadn't been paying attention, she would have missed it.

Chapter Three

The petite brunette steaming milk at the fancy industrial espresso machine turned around when the tinkle of the bell announced the new customers. Maribel had pulled open the door and waved Blair inside. The gesture had always felt chivalrous. Blair had been on a few dates where the women had tried an old-fashioned butch maneuver to impress her. On those occasions, it was all wrong, but today it seemed natural to her.

"Hey, Maribel. Want your usual?" the brunette asked.

"Um, yeah and a…" Maribel looked at Blair.

"I'll have a vanilla latte with two shots of vanilla and two shots of espresso. Is Sandy around?"

"She's in the back pulling out the cinnamon rolls."

Sandy emerged from the back and rushed around the counter. She grabbed Blair in an embrace and kissed her forehead. "Hey, trouble. How ya doing? I'm so, so sorry…" She glanced to Blair's right and furrowed her brow. "Maribel?"

"We met during my first but not last meltdown. She offered to buy me coffee. I mostly needed to put distance between me and…oh, God, Sandy. My mother insisted on an open casket. I can't…I just can't. I don't want to remember her that way. They fucking lied. She doesn't look peaceful. She looks dead. Dead," Blair repeated as her lip trembled.

Sandy pulled Blair close to her again and began rubbing her back. "I know, hon, I know. Want me to call your mom and say you aren't going back?"

Blair nodded.

"Done. You two, go sit down, and I'll bring you both your drinks and a roll each. Okay?" Sandy pointed to the plush sofa perpendicular to the fireplace.

Maribel reached around to her back pocket and pulled out a thin wallet. Removing one of the credit cards, she handed it to Sandy who promptly pushed her arm away. "Don't even. Put your damn card away, please."

"How ya gonna stay in business if ya keep giving away your product," Maribel grumbled.

"Psht. I'm doing just fine." Sandy waved her hand in the air, pushing any arguments away as if they were crumbs on the table from one of her famous cinnamon rolls.

"I've learned not to argue with her. She's more stubborn than anyone I've ever met." Blair grabbed Sandy's hand and squeezed. "Thanks, Sandy. Will you come sit with us for a bit?"

Sandy nodded before hurrying back to gather the drinks.

Maribel sat rigidly on the sofa, and Blair got the impression she was trying to avoid direct eye contact. It was certainly kind of this stranger to get her away from the funeral home and the ghastly viewing, but she wondered why the offer for coffee was made when Maribel was clearly uncomfortable.

"So, how do you know Sandy?" Blair asked.

Maribel looked up, startled by the question. "Um, I moved here a few years ago and came in for a chai tea. You know how Sandy is."

Blair smiled. She did know how Sandy seemed to wrap her arms around the lost ones and bring them into the fold. She could easily see how Maribel appeared quite lost. Moving to a new, small town where you didn't know a single person was hard for anyone, but for a person who was a bit socially awkward, it had to have been terrifying.

"Why did you move here of all places?"

"It's where my pa and I grew up." No additional information was attached to the short answer.

"Okay…" Blair might have to pry the answer from Maribel using a crowbar the size of Texas. "And? Care to finish that explanation?"

"Not really. Tell me about your sister."

Blair felt the tears resurface and looked away as she talked. "After college, I moved away. Trina would get so excited whenever I visited because I always brought her a present. It wasn't ever much. She liked pretty bows. And flowers. She would press them inside her books. She loved to read. She was smart, too. Really smart." The tears began to flow more rapidly.

Maribel leaned forward and patted Blair's hand. "Maybe she's in a better place now."

Blair's head shot up, and the anger returned with such force she didn't have a chance at tempering her response. "Don't you dare say that, and I don't need your fucking prayers either. What we need is common sense, reasonable gun control. I'm not going to stop until this stupid country gets it and does the right thing. The NRA are a bunch of white supremacist terrorists, breeding more little terrorists."

Maribel winced and moved away. "Not everyone who owns a gun is a terrorist."

Sandy approached the two women and set down the hot drinks. "Whoa, what the hell is going on with my two most favorite people in the world?"

"Well-meaning offers of prayer," Blair bit back.

"Oh. Maybe you two should avoid talking politics. I wouldn't want to have to kick you out after a heated brawl. People come here to relax and sugar up for the day. Speaking of which, I need to get those five thousand calorie cinnamon buns." Sandy walked away shaking her head.

Maribel lowered her head and mumbled, "Sorry. See, I'm no good with people. I shouldn't have asked you to coffee."

Blair sighed. "No, it's okay. I have a hair trigger temper right now." She laughed without humor. "I guess gun analogies are rampant. We can't get away from guns in our everyday sayings. Earlier, I almost had the thought that I would have to pry information out of you from your cold, dead hands. But I could not bring myself to think of that asinine spokesperson for the NRA. My thought went to a decidedly less gun-happy analogy. He's ruined all the Planet of the Apes movies for me now."

"I better not say anything in response. I'd rather not incite verbal violence." Maribel half smiled.

"Fair enough." Blair glanced up as Sandy approached with two of her famous cinnamon rolls. "Sandy to the rescue. Here comes the gooey sugary goodness. I don't have much of an appetite right at this moment, but normally I'd be too busy smashing that roll into my face to talk right now. I can try self-restraint instead."

†

After the disastrous hairpin turn in the road regarding their conversation, Maribel had wisely kept her big trap shut and simply nodded and smiled at Blair. She didn't seem to notice, and she sobbed quietly as she talked about her sister, whipsawing between rage and profound sorrow. Her diatribe on gun control kept Maribel quiet about her own relationship with guns, which had been a large part of her upbringing and success. Guns were a central part of her life and had been for a very long time. Blair did not need to know that. It wouldn't help her grief. In fact, it would send her over the edge, and Maribel did not want to do that.

Despite this major difference in philosophy, Maribel found herself drawn to the small-in-stature but large-in-personality woman. Blair was confident, passionate, and vulnerable, something hard to resist. Damn Sandy, who just had to prod her to think about the possibilities of letting a woman into her world. Maribel couldn't help notice everything about the woman. Her tousled sable hair framed a delicate heart-shaped face with enormous dark-brown eyes that at times looked almost black. When she half-smiled, Blair's right side showcased a deep dimple. Maribel had never seen teeth so white, except attached to a movie star who had undoubtedly paid through the nose to have their teeth bleached. Maribel didn't believe for one second that Blair bothered with that. She didn't seem the type.

At one point, Maribel had stared a bit too long at Blair's naturally red lips, and Blair had asked if a crumb managed to catch a ride on her lips, failing to let go. That was another thing about Blair, she was funny even while grieving. Effortlessly funny and charming.

After nearly an hour of conversation, Blair reluctantly returned to the funeral home. She'd announced her intention to muster the fortitude to face her mother without returning to the casket. Maribel had surprised herself when she gave Blair her phone number in case she wanted to talk again or visit the Percolatte Bean.

Shuffling back to her truck, Maribel climbed inside and made the long trek back to her ranch. Her lonely ranch.

She thought the ranch had a beauty atypical to most people's assessments of the high desert in Washington. Nothing would compare to the wide-open space where a person could see for miles. The Cascade Mountains loomed large in the distance. The fact that she saw the white tips made her ranch on the edge of the changing flora more special than the other pieces of land only a few miles away. She wondered why all that beauty wasn't ever able to distract her from her loneliness.

She sighed after slamming the door to her truck and walking up the mostly dirt path to her log cabin. In reality, she couldn't call her home a cabin because the size was massive compared to a small home. Skeeter, her half golden, half chow companion came barreling toward her. His tail wagged frantically as her hand landed on top of his head. She patted him first before running her hand over his grimy fur.

"What did you get into while I was gone? You're a silly beast who is itching for a bath."

He continued to wag and added a pant, before punctuating his greeting with a soft woof. He started to follow her into the house before she held her hand up. "Stay. You are not tracking whatever you rolled in, into this house. I'm getting the shampoo and hosing your ass down."

Skeeter obediently sat, tail still wagging on top of the stone patio while the glass door slammed shut. Maribel went swiftly to the half bath on the lower level and retrieved the sweet-smelling dog shampoo she'd bought at the farmers' market a few weeks ago.

Shaking her head and mumbling to herself, she retrieved the hose and spray attachment she'd bought. "Damn spoiled dog." She'd already popped out the screen in the small window so she could run the hose outside and give Skeeter a bath without subjecting him to only cold water from the outside spigot.

After screwing the spray nozzle to the hose and then turning on the water, she tossed the hose through the now opened window. Maribel chuckled to herself when she realized that besides Sandy and the people she delivered food to, all of her conversations lately were with Skeeter.

She walked back outside and commanded Skeeter to follow. With his tail tucked underneath and head hanging down he walked beside her to where the hose lay on the ground.

Skeeter sat obediently while Maribel hosed him off using the warm water. She was covered in soapsuds as she scrubbed his muddy fur when the buzz in the back of her jeans pocket alerted her to a call.

"Shit." She sprayed her hands to remove the soap and then wiped them dry on her T-shirt. Pulling the phone from her pocket, she squinted at the screen.

"Hey, Sandy. What's up?"

"Trina's funeral is tomorrow, and I thought if you weren't doing anything, you should come with me. Blair could benefit from seeing more than one friendly face. None of her other close friends live here, and I just think…"

"Of course. I'll make the trek to town. What time?" Maribel asked.

"Why don't you come around nine thirty. The funeral starts at ten. Thanks, Maribel. She likes you. I can tell."

"Humph. No, she doesn't. I'm a big stupid clod without a formal education. A simple chicken farmer who only has money because I can shoot straight. Nothing else about me is straight except that."

Sandy chuckled. "That's a fact that could very well work in your favor with Blair. And, you are not a clod. You're an incredibly sensitive, sweet, and funny woman who happens to have a rockin' body, and you have that whole sexy, androgynous model look going for you. Ambrosia to someone like Blair. Hey, I also offered to host the celebration after the funeral. I'm closing down my place so that everyone can gather afterward. Honestly, I'm more worried about her mother than Blair. Blair is Blair, she'll handle it with action and rage. Her mother, I don't know. I got the sense that planning a celebration would have literally broken her in two, never to mend."

"I'll help you with that. Give me detailed instructions and I'm sure I can at least handle that."

"Thanks, I was counting on another pair of hands." Sandy laughed.

"That's why you want me to come with you. You're devious." Maribel shook her head and smiled.

"I'll be honest, that was a factor, but I know Blair and she's intrigued. I'd bet my coffee shop on it. And you know I don't make bets I don't keep."

"You're not gonna tell her about my…"

"Are you frickin' crazy? Of course not. She needs to get to know you before she learns about your Annie Oakley talents. Guns are not at the top of her list of things to embrace right now."

"I know, I know. See you tomorrow, okay?"

"Thanks again."

Maribel shoved her phone back in her pocket after ending the call and contemplated the dilemma of how and when to share that huge part of her life. She'd recently resumed her training for the next Olympics. If she developed a friendship or more with Blair, there was no way she could hide that. Maybe she was getting ahead of herself. They'd just met and already she was planning a deeper connection. Loneliness and Sandy's suggestions were causing her brain to play tricks. Forcing her to dream about something that would probably never come to pass.

"Woof." Skeeter brought her back to the task at hand. Squeezing the nozzle, Maribel proceeded to finish the bath. Skeeter continued to shake every time she paused. By the time she was done removing the remaining soapsuds, both Maribel and Skeeter were completely soaked.

"I don't suppose it would do me any good to shake my body like yours, huh? But I sure would like to see you drenched for once."

Chuckling to herself, she commanded Skeeter to stay while she retrieved a towel. She should have thought to grab several before she began his bath. Stepping into the house, Maribel left a trail of water as she made her way to the bathroom.

On her way, she pulled the wet T-shirt over her head and grabbed a dry one straight from the dryer along with several towels. After removing her wet jeans, she retrieved a pair of cotton shorts and padded out to the back patio. Skeeter waited patiently, but when he saw his mommy, he stood and shook one more time, sending a spray of droplets once again onto Maribel's dry clothes.

"Dammit, Skeeter." She tossed one towel on his head and laid the other one on the ground. Vigorously rubbing him until the first towel was soaked, she then picked up the second towel and dried him enough to allow him inside. Even though she didn't particularly enjoy that wet dog smell, he was her only companion and kept away the loneliness she felt all too often lately. Maybe that would change. Sandy hadn't worked out because they were so different in too many ways to make it work, but she had gained a good friend.

Skeeter made a beeline for his mat in front of the fireplace. Maribel smiled as she settled into her favorite chair. She had only been to one funeral in her life and the memory of that time was difficult. It had taken her nearly a year to pick up a gun again after her father died.

CHAPTER FOUR

Blair did not want to be here. The panic started to rise inside. As her heartbeat quickened and sweat formed on her brow, she reluctantly glanced at the front of the church. The gleaming rectangle of blond wood taunted her and made her perspiration continue along with the pounding of her heart. The service hadn't started yet. Maybe she still had time to collect herself.

"I need a few minutes," she whispered to her mother and then ran down the aisle. Before she burst into the sunshine to collect herself and gather her emotions, she noticed Sandy and Maribel sitting in the last pew. She was surprised to see Maribel. Their eyes met. Blair wasn't sure what it meant when a small measure of comfort flooded her system.

She continued her path to the outside, needing the fresh air to offset the heavy stifling feeling that threatened to overwhelm her with each step, despite the mini reprieve earlier when she'd looked into Maribel's soft, moss-colored eyes. She gulped in air. She was suffocating. Her head felt light, and the panting continued to no avail. She was going to pass out.

A light touch to her shoulder startled her until she turned her head to see Maribel and those eyes. The ones filled with concern and something else she couldn't pinpoint right now.

Maribel guided her to sit and took her hand, gently stroking it. "Can you take a few slow, deep breaths?"

Blair put her head between her knees and struggled to suck in air in a long breath before slowly exhaling. She almost stopped taking in deep breaths when Maribel let go of her hand, but then that same hand was now making small circles on her back.

"That's it. Keep taking deep breaths." Maribel's soft words penetrated her panic.

"I'm okay now. I better get back inside before my mother sends out someone to fetch me that I don't want to talk to. My snooty aunt is not staying the night. She had plans that couldn't be changed. I'll never forgive her. I would have told her not to bother to come but that's me. My mother cares too much about keeping the peace." Blair lifted her head to face Maribel. "Not one single person is staying tonight with Mom. Not one. So much for close-knit Catholic families. I hate them all. Bloody hypocrites. You don't know me and you're at the funeral."

"I'll be wherever you need me whenever you need me."

Blair could not believe this woman, whom she barely knew, had made such an enormous declaration. In her grief she lacked the energy to dissect any possible motive. A new round of tears started, but the panic had subsided for now. Blair stood and walked back into the church, Maribel's arm protectively around her shoulder. Maribel didn't let go until Blair was safely seated next to her mother. A quick squeeze on her shoulder and Maribel returned to her seat at the back of the church.

Blair had turned to watch Maribel and almost begged her to sit beside her until her mother frowned and glanced at Blair with that disapproving look. Then her aunt pursed her lips from the next pew over. Blair scoffed at the notion of her perfect family seated in the row with their rigid bodies turned to the front waiting for the service to begin. Impassive faces, devoid of any emotion. Had they cared about the unnatural death of their cousin or niece? Nope. Blair didn't think they did. Their presence was pure obligation. Nothing else.

†

The sunglasses would not only protect her eyes from the bright sunshine, but they would also hide the swollen red rims and dark circles. Even with the glasses, the bright sunshine hurt her eyes, as Blair used her hand to shield the glare. Blair didn't believe it was appropriate for the sun to shine on such a dark day. She looked at the row of shiny black vehicles waiting to take her family to the gravesite. It wasn't exactly a row. There were three. One for her mother and herself, one for her aunt's family, and one that was too large for the tiny coffin.

Reluctantly, Blair ducked into the back seat and joined her mother. The slow-moving procession took ten minutes to arrive at the gravesite. She'd had every intention of walking beside her mother. She'd be the support her mother needed. An arm to hold on to in case she faltered. Then Blair had unfolded herself from the car and taken a step into the too bright day. The final straw was a glance in the direction of the covered pile of dirt. She'd had a vision of a shovel and a blob of dirt being haphazardly tossed on top of the gleaming wood. Her beautiful little sister suffocating beneath the earth. She couldn't do it.

Blair refused to look her mother in the eyes when she declared, "I'm not going. I'll stay in the car."

Her mother had not responded, but she could feel her presence. She hadn't moved an inch from where she stood. Finally, Blair couldn't handle the silent reproach. She looked up. The pain in her mother's face was almost too much for Blair to retain her resolve not to have a lasting picture in her mind of that blasted dirt covering the tiny coffin.

"Okay," her mother answered and simply turned her back to walk away.

Blair climbed back inside the vehicle and waited. Would she get a lecture? She didn't think so. She laid her head on the supple leather and tried not to obsess over her own thoughts about this whole unreal experience. She desperately wanted this to be a nightmare that she would wake from. Any minute, her beloved cat would lick her face and wake her up. *Please let him stick his gross tongue on my lips.* That always did the trick to startle her out of dreamland. Even that was impossible now, since he'd passed away two months prior.

Maybe it was thirty minutes or more likely closer to an hour, time was irrelevant at this point. The click of the car door caused Blair to move her head in the direction of the noise. Her mother was dabbing her eyes as she returned to sit next to Blair.

"I'm sorry," Blair managed to choke out.

"It's okay. I understand."

Her mother's face revealed anything but understanding. Blair could not quite pinpoint the lines across her face, but she knew for sure it wasn't empathy, sympathy, or any form of acceptance. Blair didn't blame her mother. Not one bit. Her mother didn't have the energy to mask her expressions.

†

What a crock of shit. A celebration of life. A dedicated time to tell stories and remember the loved one who had passed. That's what a gathering was intended to do.

Blair could do that when a life was long. There was a lot to celebrate about the life of a person who had lived eighty or ninety years. The stories were robust when her gram passed. Now, people shuffled about the coffee shop mumbling their platitudes about loss and grief. There were offerings of prayer and apologies. Why did people say they were sorry for her loss? It wasn't like they'd been the one to hold the gun. Blair wondered where that came from. What were they sorry for? Blair didn't know half of these people. Churchgoers. She hadn't stepped foot in a church in many years.

Blair was hiding in the corner, trying to avoid the strangers with their banal messages of apology. They'd left her alone after she scowled at every single one. Sandy was busy making sure the food was laid out for everyone to partake in the celebration. She didn't blame Sandy for not being by her side. She was alone, so utterly alone until a quiet presence spoke from beside her. Maribel.

"What do you need from me right this minute?"

Blair didn't know the answer. She only knew what would set her off.

"I don't need or want an apology. Do not say you are sorry for my loss. That would send me over the edge." She pierced Maribel with a rebellious stare.

"I hadn't thought to do that, so I'm glad I didn't." A tiny smile appeared on her lips. "Good to know what not to do, but—"

"I honestly don't know. Maybe keep these do-gooder fakeazoids away from me. Especially my aunt and her smarmy husband."

"Two o'clock?" Maribel asked.

"Huh?"

Maribel gestured with her head in the direction of her aunt and the rest of her family who were chattering away with one of the church ladies. "Over there at two o'clock. The younger members too?"

"Yes. Don't care for my cousins, either. They're all worshippers of the current administration, and I can't stomach any of them."

"Consider it done."

Blair's aunt stiffly hugged her mother leaving a gap that a dump truck could drive through. Her solemn expression and sympathetic nod followed as she carefully engineered the perfect look for whatever words she was speaking to her mother. Blair could almost hear her. *We're here for you, I'll come back as soon as...*

"A, the kids settle a bit more. B, work calms down. C, my health improves," Blair muttered.

"What?" Maribel scrunched her face in confusion.

"Oh, I was just filling in the blanks on why they have to leave." Blair jerked her thumb in the direction of her aunt. "None of them are staying tonight. They're all scurrying back to their upper-middle-class homes in their cookie-cutter neighborhoods. Shit."

Maribel looked up, and Blair followed her eyes as her aunt began to make a beeline in her direction. Maribel stepped in front of Blair and headed her off, whispering something in her ear. Aunt Carol huffed and stiffly walked to her daughters who promptly glared in Blair's direction, shaking their heads. The small group huddled together frantically whispering while sneaking glances at Maribel who returned to Blair's side.

"What did you say to her?"

Maribel shrugged. "What needed to be said. I did my job, that's all you need to know."

"Clearly you pissed them off. That wasn't part of my ask, but…" Blair lifted her fist in the air for a bump. "I'll definitely take the bonus reaction. I would have said something to piss them off too. It's so much better that you did it because now Mom won't rail on me for being rude." Blair leaned in and kissed Maribel on the lips. "Thanks, I owe you."

"Wh…what did you do that for?" Maribel stuttered. Her eyes were wide and frozen in place.

"I don't know. Sometimes I'm not very rational and I just act. It gets me in trouble all the time."

"Let me get you something to eat."

"Honestly, I don't think I'd be able to keep anything down today." The tears began to pool once again in Blair's eyes.

Maribel looked around the coffee shop and apparently didn't find whatever she was looking for. The place was barely large enough to hold the mourners and nearly every inch was filled with people either milling about or sitting in the comfortable seats around the fireplace.

Maribel tentatively placed her arm around Blair's shoulder and leaned in to ask, "Would you like to take a little time and get some air? If I'm feeling claustrophobic, I can only imagine what it's like for you."

"I shouldn't. It might upset my mother. I've already let her down today."

Blair watched as Maribel caught Sandy's eye and gestured for her to go to Blair's mother. Before Blair could raise another protest, Sandy was distracting her mother, and Maribel was leading Blair into the sunshine.

Maribel's solid presence was exactly what Blair needed. Words weren't necessary. Blair didn't know what she'd say, anyway. Apparently, Maribel wasn't the chatty type either. Sitting on the wood bench with Maribel's thighs touching her own, Blair sucked in the fresh air and gathered her strength. The simple gesture of taking her hand and squeezing was just the right amount of connection.

†

Maribel sat in front of her upstairs fireplace, absently petting Skeeter. He'd managed to stay relatively clean after she'd given him a bath. She ran through her mind the pertinent events at the funeral, especially the spontaneous kiss. Sure, it wasn't a passionate lip lock, but it also wasn't an entirely chaste kiss to the cheek. She supposed her lack of social skills worked when she'd bluntly told Blair's aunt she wasn't fooling anyone with her fake sympathy. She'd warned her that it wasn't going to be pretty if she tried to get within five feet of Blair.

Maribel picked up her sketchpad and began drawing from memory. Blair's grief-stricken eyes haunted her. She absently captured the emotion without realizing she was drawing the woman she could not get out of her head.

The timing was all wrong for her to ask Blair out, even if that was something she ever had an easy time doing. Which, for the record, was never. Maribel wasn't very good with people, but for some reason she'd managed to be a tranquil presence for Blair at a time of need. She could count on one hand the number of times she'd asked a woman out on a date. Feeling a buzz from her back pocket, Maribel lifted her butt cheek and removed her phone.

The text message jarred her from her thoughts and surprised the hell out of her.

Blair: Any chance you would like to meet for coffee tomorrow morning?

Staring and blinking rapidly at the message, the text had caused an almost frozen reaction. A minute later she was reading a new message that had popped up.

Blair: Sorry, probably the last thing you want to do is have coffee with a blubbering grief-stricken woman you barely know. Forget I asked.

Maribel fumbled her phone and tried to stop her hands from shaking as she typed and re-typed her message. The tiny phone keys were not cooperating, and it took her agonizing moments to write back a simple message.

Maribel: No, I would love to. What time?

Blair: Nine too early?

Maribel: Not for me.

Blair: Great. It's a date.

Blair had ended her final text with a smiley emoticon. Maribel couldn't help the smile that overtook her face. Skeeter had cocked his head and decided he'd try to climb in her lap. At nearly one hundred pounds, Skeeter was not a lap dog. Half on and half off, his large paws rested on her lap. Usually she'd push him down and make him lie back on his mat, but just now she didn't care one bit. She had a date. Or at least maybe it was a date. The kiss earlier made it all so confusing. Maribel shook her head and Skeeter finally gave up, settling back on his mat.

She'd have to call Sandy and grill her before tomorrow. It wouldn't matter if Sandy teased her. She always poked fun at Maribel's lack of social graces anyway, so what did she care if Sandy gave her a hard time about this. Deep down, Maribel knew it was coming from a place of care. Sandy had developed into a good friend. Her only real friend since she'd moved here. Sure, she loved visiting the families, especially Danella and Lucritia, but other than taking a special interest in Lucritia, she couldn't lay bare with them.

Sandy had been the one to call her very connected father who had stopped that nasty blonde reporter from continuing to harass Maribel. Sandy's father apparently had a considerable amount of pull with the Seattle news station. He'd put pressure on the executive producer who in turn had reeled in the aggressive reporter looking to make a name for herself. Sandy had seen Maribel's reaction after the reporter had found her and cornered her for a quote. Despite Sandy's different perspective on gun control, she was always able to parse their differences. True friends did not always share every single political stance.

With one last pat to Skeeter's head, Maribel set the sketchpad on the floor. She stood and began pacing in front of the fireplace. She prayed that Sandy was not too busy to answer her call. Methodically punching in the number she knew by heart, she waited for her friend to answer.

"Hey, hermit girl."

Maribel cleared her throat. "I'm not a hermit. Um, I…uh…was…"

"Spit it out Mar. Wait, let me guess. Yes!"

"Huh?"

"Yeah, Blair is a lesbian and single last time I checked with her." Sandy's loud laughter exploded from the phone.

"Don't say anything to her, okay?"

"About what? That you're a socially awkward hermit, waiting for a princess to save her ass from a lifetime of loneliness and despair?"

"Sometimes I hate you."

"She likes you, despite all your efforts to put your worst foot forward. One piece of advice."

"I'm all ears."

"Stay away from politics. She shares my views, and she's a lot more passionate about them than I am. She was like that before this…God, I can't even say it out loud."

"Yeah, I know. Do you think she will judge me for, you know…"

"I'd like to think she wouldn't, but you can't blame her for going off the deep end with this one issue. She's always worked for the far-left causes, and now that she's taken a leave from her job, she's planning to jump in with both feet. Organizing rallies, raising money, getting people riled up, that's what's she does. It's kind of who she is at her core. It doesn't matter that gun control hasn't been a favorite soapbox for her in the past. At this moment her singular focus is gun control. God help anyone who gets in her way."

Maribel groaned. "How can I possibly hide who I am and who's been my sponsors for the last ten years? Not to mention the first sponsor I ever had."

"I don't know, Mar, but let her get to know the real you behind your misguided views on a few things." Sandy chuckled.

"I've come a long way on many other issues. Thanks to you. This is the one area, I can't. You know I can't. I'd be shitting on the memory of Pa."

"I know, hon, I know. Honestly, I get it. I really do. I don't agree with you, but I understand. Hell, I'm a vegetarian. I don't believe in hunting, but I get that I always had the luxury to choose. You didn't."

"Not one of my finest moments…you know, serving elk steak. I thought you'd be impressed with my cooking and the freshness of the food. I'll never forget the look on your face. It went downhill from there."

"No, it didn't. We made it to the friend stage, didn't we? Besides, it wasn't just about our vastly different views on politics, we were never a match. It's weird because I can see you and Blair together. You would complement one another in ways we never could."

"Really? You think so?" Maribel didn't have the same level of confidence. Sandy had always been an easy person to talk to, and she'd been attracted to how Sandy had managed to get Maribel to interact without the intense amount of awkwardness she was known for.

"I do. You are a real softie underneath all that butchiness. She'll bring that to the surface. Goodness knows, somebody has to continue educating you on the correct way of thinking. If anyone can turn you into a tree-hugging liberal, it'll be Blair."

"I seriously doubt that, but I like her. There's something about her, besides her stunning looks, that I'm drawn to." Maribel settled back in her chair. Sandy was the only person she had long conversations with and didn't feel the need to run and hide.

"Yeah, Blair has always been effortlessly attractive. Everyone falls in love with her. You wouldn't be the first. Maybe you'll be the last."

"Stop being such a lesbian and promoting your lesbian ways. We aren't going to fall in love and move in together after two dates."

"Bwa ha ha. You've discovered my evil plan. Don't diminish my abilities. I get you to talk with me like a normal human being, why wouldn't I have other super powers."

"How about unleashing the super power to allow me to interact with Blair in the same way as I talk with you? Minus my typical lack of charm."

"Don't serve her elk steak and you should be golden." Sandy laughed.

"I have a date, or at least I think it's a date, tomorrow for coffee. She kissed me on the lips at the funeral as a thank you to keeping her aunt away," Maribel blurted. "Is it a date? Did she tell you anything?"

"It's a date. Just listen to her right now. What she needs most is someone who will let her talk out loud and work through the pain. Her mother can't do that for her. You can. One more word of advice, be open to anything even something casual. Sometimes you are far too serious with relationships. I'm not the one that fits the lesbian stereotype of falling madly in love on the first date. That would be you."

"Okay. Thanks, Sandy."

"You're a good egg, Mar. Don't ever let anyone tell you you're not. I know better."

Maribel was smiling after she'd ended the call with Sandy. Even though they hadn't worked as lovers, they worked as friends. Sandy knew there wasn't a single thing that Sandy could ask Maribel to do that she would refuse. She'd given up elk hunting for God's sake. That was a big deal to her, and she still felt guilty sometimes. Her pa had taught her to hunt and shoot. She wasn't giving up her sport, but she had given up killing mammals. At least Sandy didn't have the same aversion to fishing.

†

Blair paced the guest bedroom of her mother's house. She wondered if her mother could hear her. She hoped not. The last thing she needed was a conversation with her mother. *What the hell was I thinking?*

Blair knew she shouldn't have sent that text to Maribel. She should be talking with her mother. Helping her mother through the grief. She couldn't do that right now. Refusing to go to the gravesite had been the last straw for her mother.

After the disaster of the funeral, Blair had shoved her emotions back inside in an effort to calm herself. Her mother wasn't happy with her choice not to go to the gravesite, but she'd said she understood. She hadn't. Blair knew that much from the grimace on her face. She'd hung back waiting for the service to end, and her mother had folded herself into the car without saying a word. Then Blair had gotten Maribel to play interference and had practically refused to speak with her aunt and cousins at the gathering.

When they'd returned from the gathering, several television vans were parked in front of the house. A birdlike woman with perfectly coiffed hair turned her focus in the direction of their car, and Blair's anger and anxiety had come back full force. The time spent with Maribel and the quiet introspection as she'd driven home, were erased in an instant.

Her mother couldn't face the hordes of media that stalked her family. She had implored Blair to be civil with the petite blonde because she could not deal with her right now. Why her mother thought Blair was a better choice was beyond any rational thought.

The reporter had been waiting not more than fifty feet from her mother's front door. She was not unlike a stalker. Aggressive. Unwelcome. After ushering her mother into the house, Blair turned her rage on the vulture. The sympathetic look she tossed in Blair's direction was so transparently forced that Blair wanted to smack her until her real expression returned. Hungry. Opportunistic.

"I understand this is a difficult time for you. Is there anything you'd like people to know about your sister?" The manufactured crease above the reporter's brow appeared after the question. The presentation to the world was her deep concern for the issues.

Blair gritted her teeth. "This is not the time, nor the place. Can't you please leave us alone for one minute? Go bother the politicians who refuse to pass any meaningful legislation and leave us the hell alone. You can save your false sympathy for someone else who doesn't see through your façade. Who did you vote for in the last election?"

"Has your father's stance changed on gun control?"

"Figures. That's the real story here." She stared at the pretty blonde who narrowed her eyes but remained mute. "What? You get to ask questions but I don't. Did you vote for my father who has the backing of the NRA? My guess is, yes, so don't pretend to care one bit." Blair turned her back and slammed the door, punctuating her anger.

When she stalked into the living room, her mother glanced in her direction and frowned. The disappointment in her eyes was evident before she looked away and stared at the wall. Her posture remained rigid. Blair opened her mouth to explain, but no words would come. Instead she climbed the stairs and retreated to the bedroom.

She'd been hiding in her room for several hours replaying the recent events. Never one to proceed cautiously, Blair's rash response and actions usually came back to haunt her. She'd needed a balm and had typed the message before she had a chance to dissect her motives. Eventually, she would begin to unpack every single interaction, and the delayed analysis would cause her emotions to spiral.

Panicking, she called the only other person who might help her unravel those emotions and allow her to think more clearly. "Sandy, I think I did something incredibly stupid."

"Blair? Slow down. What? What happened besides blowing up at the twatwaffle reporter?"

"Shit." Blair grabbed the remote and turned on the television in the bedroom. When she flipped to CNN, she groaned.

The heavily edited clip was running on the local stations and had made it to the national channels. They'd cut out the reporter's reaction because that would never do. Too much was revealed in the split second after Blair had fired the question at her.

"It's not that bad. I could tell the bitch deserved what you said."

"I texted Maribel and asked her to go to coffee tomorrow. She thinks it's a date."

"Well, is it?"

"Maybe," Blair hedged.

"I know your gaydar is finely tuned. She's obviously gay. You know that, right?"

"Yeah." Blair sighed. "So…what am I going to do now?"

"You're going to meet her for coffee and it better be at my place. Maribel is good people. She's an exceptionally reliable listener, and she'll let you rant all you want, unlike me who has had quite enough after the first hour."

"You're such a liar."

Sandy chuckled. "You could do far worse than having a date with strong and sexy Maribel. She's hot and a really good kisser."

"I knew it. You two had a thing." Blair stopped pacing. "She's a good kisser?"

"Old news. We were definitely not right for one another. You need to give her a chance even if she doesn't share every single one of your passionate views on, oh…every fucking thing in the world."

"Yeah, I already know she's religious. That's a big thing to forgive."

"No, that really is not, other things, maybe, but not that. Look, all you need to know is that she is sweet, kind, intelligent, and a great kisser." Sandy laughed. "Hey, I have to go, there's another call coming in."

"Bye, rebel."

"Bye, crusader."

CHAPTER FIVE

The next morning, Blair bounded down the stairs. When she reached the living room and saw her mother staring off into space, a blanket wrapped around her knees, her momentary lightness quickly left the building. Guilt curled around her edges, and Blair approached cautiously.

"I was going to get coffee, but I'll cancel, okay?" She patted the blanket that kept her mother in a cocoon.

"I don't need a babysitter, Blair. I'm not a two-year-old." The words lacked any emotion. Simply spoken as if the message should have been known all along. Her mother didn't even glance in her direction as she delivered the message and continued to stare at the blank wall.

"I didn't say you needed a babysitter. If anyone requires looking after, it's me. I'm the one prone to temper tantrums. Speaking of which, if those reporters are still camped outside this morning, they're going to see a hissy fit of epic proportions."

"How long are you planning to stay?"

"I took a leave. Indefinitely. Well, sort of. Nonprofits are all about fundraising these days, and I agreed to continue to write their grants. Fundraising and grant writing were all I did as the director, anyway." Blair shook her head. "I wanted to make a difference in the lives of those kids, and now I barely get to interact with them."

Her mother's head turned in Blair's direction, and she looked at her with dead eyes. "Go home, Blair. I need time to myself. Running away is what you do best."

"That's not fair. You said you understood. I'm not leaving. That is the last thing you need. And, more importantly, that's the last thing I need. I lost her too."

"She would have grown up so nicely. Just like you. Did you know she said she was going to be the Director of Planned Parenthood when she grew up?"

"What? Why Planned Parenthood? That seems a little too adult. I could see something like the Girls Club or a big wig in the Girls Scouts of America, but did she even know what services Planned Parenthood provided?"

"She listened to every single word you ever spoke. All your rants. Women's right to choose. Does that ring a bell?"

"Damn, she is way too smart." Tears sprung to life as Blair realized what she'd said. Trina *was* way too smart. She swiped at her cheek. "A tiny sponge, huh?"

Her mother nodded. "Go have coffee. Tell Sandy hello. Work out your grief with her. I won't be any good to you. I don't have the energy, Blair. I can't muster enough to help you right now."

"You don't have to, Mom. I'm not expecting that. I'm canceling."

"Stop. Please don't. I need a little space. I have something to do, and I can't have you here when I do it. Besides, I haven't decided yet…" Her words trailed off, and she returned to staring at the white wall.

Wiping her sweaty hands on her jeans, Blair stood and placed a comforting hand on her mother's shoulder. "I'll bring back a cinnamon roll."

"No, don't. It will just go to waste. I promise I'll eat something later. You should do the same."

The tiny amount of excitement for her date had dissipated. Blair turned around and watched her mother slowly climb the stairs. She was sure her mother was heading to Trina's room. What she didn't know was whether her mom intended to remove every last item or planned to create a shrine. It was a crapshoot. Blair would not lay any bets on either possibility. What she did fundamentally understand was that her mother needed to do this alone. She was compelled to face the demon unaccompanied because Blair suspected she did not want to bring her only other living child into that hell. That might hurt her nearly as much as the loss of her youngest daughter.

Blair ran away. She had a desperate craving for a distraction. It wasn't right. She knew that. But it wasn't wrong either. There was not just one way to grieve. Stepping into someone's shoes was difficult when that particular pair of shoes was unlikely for most people. The least of Blair's worries was how others might judge her actions.

†

Maribel stood at the counter with her hands shoved deep in her pockets. She had arrived ten minutes early and wanted to have the latte ready for when Blair arrived. She mumbled the order to the young woman, "Vanilla latte with two shots of syrup and two shots of espresso, a chai tea, and two cinnamon rolls, please."

Sandy poked her head out, smiled, and waved. Removing one hand, Maribel waved back and smiled at her friend. Sandy moved her eyes up and down Maribel's body and left the back room.

"Nice duds for a date." Sandy shook her head.

"What's wrong with what I'm wearing? I have chores later on, and I don't think my cocktail dress will provide enough give to bend over and feed the chickens. Besides, the stilettos get caught in the soft dirt," Maribel deadpanned.

Sandy began clapping. "Your sense of humor and social skills have improved. Sarcasm is the first step. You could have put on a clean, button-down shirt and a pair of jeans with a few less stains. Ew, what is that brown mark? Please tell me it's not chicken shit."

"No, of course not. It's dirt. I must have kneeled in the garden to, uh, pick some flowers."

"So, where are they?"

"Um, I left them on the table over there by the fireplace." Maribel pointed to the bouquet on the pocked wood table in front of the couch.

"Okay, that's pretty sweet. You get a huge pass on your outfit. Can I give a bit of advice to you?"

Maribel vigorously nodded. "Yes, please."

"Blair's emotions are going to be all over the place today. Up. Down. She might make your head spin with how fast she shifts gears. It's always been the way she works through things. She can't settle on one emotion for too long. Let her talk. I know you're good at that. You'll be perfect. Just be your normal awkward self, where you don't say much. You have a lot more in that insightful, intelligent head of yours. You certainly can contribute easily to any conversation when you want but no need to do that today."

"I can handle that." Maribel smiled. "Thanks, Sandy."

†

Blair sucked in a large amount of air trying to catch her breath after jogging the two blocks. The Uber driver was being an asshat and wouldn't double park long enough to let her out. There wasn't one single parking space close to the coffee shop, and she was already running late, so she had yelled at him to pull over. Yanking open the Percolatte Bean's door and breezing through, she noticed Maribel's rigid posture as she kept rubbing her hands up and down her jeans. *Nervous. She's nervous.* A smile blossomed on Blair's face when she saw the bouquet of freshly picked flowers. The bunch was void of store-bought wrapping with the piece of twine surrounding the stems holding the flowers together. It was an incredibly sweet gesture, along with the hot drink and a cinnamon roll already waiting for her on the coffee table.

Blair approached the table, and Maribel promptly stuck the bouquet in her face. "These are for you."

"Hey. Sorry I'm late. Seems like every person in town had the bright idea of coffee this late in the day. Usually I would have already had my morning jolt. Who knew the whole town was a bunch of slackers with bankers' hours?" Blair continued to ramble as she accepted the gift from Maribel. "Thank you. These are lovely. I see you've already ordered. How did you know what to get?"

"Um, vanilla latte with two shots of espresso and two shots of vanilla."

"What if I was in the mood for a caramel latte instead?"

Maribel stood. "Oh, uh, I'll get that."

Blair lightly smacked her shoulder. "I'm kidding. Sit your ass down and relax. I don't bite." She winked. "Unless you want me to."

Maribel coughed. “No, uh. Is the roll okay? Want me to get you something else? The chocolate croissants are exceptional.”

“Nope.” Blair grinned. “Nothing beats cinnamon. Although, lately, I haven’t even been tempted by Sandy’s famous rolls.”

Maribel was wiping her hands against her pants again. After Blair sat and then picked up her drink, Maribel followed suit. “Thanks for asking me to coffee. How are you today?”

“Other than the hiccup with my mother this morning and blowing up at a reporter last night?” Blair quirked her eyebrow and then continued without waiting for a response, “Dandy, just dandy for someone who refused to see them toss dirt on top of a tiny coffin.”

“Reporter?” Maribel frowned.

“Yeah. I know I should not say this since I’m a feminist, through and through, but she was this irritating little blonde bimbo with the empathy of a dictator. Probably took lessons from our dear president.”

“I know who you’re talking about. She’s from King 5 News, right?”

“Yeah, that’s the one. How do you know her?”

“Never mind. What’s happening with your mom?”

“I can’t tell if she’s disappointed in me and my utter lack of decorum with all things funeralisque. Yeah,” Blair waved her hand in the air, “I know that isn’t really a word. I’ll go to the grave eventually, just not yet. I want the grass to grow. I want to see flowers and life, not the fake ones on top of the plot. I can't do that right now."

"You didn't go to the gravesite?" Maribel asked in obvious surprise as her voice lilted at the end of the sentence.

"No, I didn't. Stop judging me." Blair glared at Maribel. This was the last thing she needed. Another person believing that she wasn't grieving in the correct way.

"I…uh…sorry…I wasn't. I'll go with you when you are ready if you need someone to lean on or something."

The offer seemed so genuine and real it settled Blair for a brief time. She sipped her coffee, contemplating how she would apologize for biting the head off this genuinely nice person. "Sorry, I'm just angry. Really, really, angry and my emotions are all over the place. You don't deserve my rage. I can't yell at my mother, she's too broken now. I've no one to direct this rage toward. I should probably direct my anger at the NRA and gun manufacturers."

"You can yell at me anytime you want. S'okay."

Blair grabbed her hair and pulled. "Arghhhh. No, it is not. Stop being so perfectly wonderful, sweet, and kind. Oh, and sexy, let's not forget that."

Maribel's eyes widened. "Sexy," she repeated.

"It is so wrong of me to be thinking what I am thinking the day after I buried my seven-year-old sister. I want to get lost in something that will take the pain away. Alcohol and drugs have never done it for me."

"I can be or do anything you want. Okay?" Maribel answered softly. "No judgment. Like I said before, everyone handles grief in their own way. There aren't any right or wrong answers."

Blair lost herself in Maribel's pale green eyes. She hadn't noticed before how calming they were. Like the rolling green hills where the spring grass grew tall. She always loved to twirl and dance in those sweet-smelling blades. Putting distance between herself and those intense eyes, Blair leaned back and settled her head against the cushion. Sex would not resolve anything. It would only make it worse. She decided a different distraction might work just as well, without the guilt. Getting to know Maribel was a lot safer and more acceptable. Especially in her mother's eyes. No amount of explanation would work if Blair decided to turn this date into a three-day fuck-fest as she was prone to do when upset.

"Tell me about how you spend your days and how come you have that huge stain on your knee."

Maribel blushed. "Didn't realize the dirt was so wet when I picked the flowers, and I didn't want to be late."

"Is that how you spend your days? Picking flowers for women? Because you haven't told me what you do all day."

"Take care of my chickens, garden, and prepare for the next games."

"Games?"

"You mentioned that you got your degree in social work or something. Is that what your job is about?"

Although Blair noticed how Maribel had shifted the focus and redirected the conversation, she didn't have the energy or motivation to call her on it.

"I'm taking a break. Well, sorta. I can do most of what is needed from home or anywhere. Even if Mom is angry with me, I still want to be here for her. We can be dysfunctional together as easily as separate from one another."

"Grief and dysfunction are not the same things."

"They are in my family. So…chickens?"

Maribel smiled. "I like eggs. Fresh eggs. The chickens keep me company along with Skeeter."

"Skeeter?"

"My golden chow mix."

"Do you get to play with the baby chicks?"

Maribel nodded.

"I'd love to come see them. Baby chicks, honestly baby anything, are hard to resist."

"Anytime you want to come over, I'll show you around the ranch. I shouldn't call it a ranch, it's more like a farm because I don't have cattle, but I also don't have many crops either. I have a small garden, that's all. The wide-open space is tranquil. I like that."

"I could use a bit of tranquil right now. I get a calm feeling whenever I'm around you. It must be a rub off from your ranch, farm, whatever you call it." Blair picked up her coffee and took a small sip.

"Why don't you follow me home today? I'll show you around. I could grill something for dinner," Maribel quietly offered.

"Will you show me the baby chicks?"

Maribel's shy, sexy smile appeared. "It'll be the first thing on the Maribel Ranch Tour."

"Deal, but I need to check back with my mom first. Why don't you give me your address, and I'll plug it into my phone?"

"My place isn't easy to find. I doubt you'd be able to plug in an address. I'll draw you a map." Maribel awkwardly stood and carefully made her way to the counter. She had a short conversation with Sandy, who handed her a pen and laughed when Maribel grabbed a napkin from the counter.

Smoothing the napkin on the table in front of where they were sitting, Maribel began to draw. She pointed to the line. "Right before you make the turn here, you'll see a big tree on the right. My place is nearly at the end of the road. The driveway is long and winding, but you can't miss it because it's practically the only place around for miles. I own all the land surrounding the place."

Blair raised her eyebrow. "I'll bet it's impressive. What are you, a ranch heiress? I don't even know your last name."

Maribel coughed in apparent embarrassment. "No, hardly. I just like a bit of privacy."

"Owning a lot of land takes money. What exactly do you do for a living? You're not like a huge chicken factory, are you? Draper farms?"

Maribel chuckled. "No, my chickens are only for eggs."

"Bootleg whiskey?"

"I wish." Maribel continued to laugh.

"You're not going to tell me how you came into all your money, are you?"

Maribel shook her head. "Nope, that is a story for after we spend a bit more time together."

Blair grinned. "So, are we planning on hanging out, then? How many times will we have to meet up before I can pry anything out of you?"

Maribel looked away, avoiding Blair's eyes and shrugged.

"A woman of few words hidden beneath an air of mystery. That is far too irresistible to stay away from. Okay, I'll play your game for a while considering I desperately need a distraction besides jumping with both feet into rallies and other activities designed to wake this fucking state up. You'd think with Washington being a liberal state, the laws on gun control would be much stricter. God, I fucking hate the NRA and their slimy tactics to sway politicians."

"What time do you think you can make it out to my ranch?"

"Nice diversion away from a topic that always riles me up. I don't know. Can I call you after I've talked to Mom? I want to make sure she's okay. I hate leaving her alone. At the same time, I'm struggling with her disapproving looks. I am a despicable daughter."

"No, you're not."

"Yes, I am. I really am." Blair abruptly stood and gathered the flowers in her hands. "I better go. I'll call. I promise." She turned away from the hurt look that Maribel failed to hide.

†

Maribel rested her head against the couch and looked at the ceiling, noticing the single silky strand dangling with the tiny spider hanging on. The air from the ceiling fans caused the strand to sway side to side as Maribel watched. She worried about the fate of the tiny spider hanging on for dear life. That's how Maribel felt. Completely out of her element and ready to fall from the end of a rope she desperately clung to. She contemplated what had gone wrong earlier. With the conversation on rewind in her head, she wondered if Blair would call.

The shove against her shoulder caused Maribel to turn her attention to the source. Sandy shook her head.

"What did you do to send Blair running? She's a wily one." Sandy plopped down on the couch next to Maribel.

"She was starting to get worked up again about the NRA. I felt guilty. So, I kinda tried to change the subject. She pegged my misdirection and then thought about how she'd left her mom alone. I invited her to the ranch."

"Mm." Sandy grinned.

"Mm, what? You are acting know it all-y again."

"I've known Blair for a long time. She gets passionate about causes, not people. She's not the type of person to be in touch with her own strong feelings. Can't handle them. I suspect you are reaching a part of her she doesn't want touched."

"Should I back off?"

Sandy laughed. "I don't think you've really backed in. Isn't she the one who texted you?"

"Yeah, but then I brought the stupid flowers." Maribel let her head fall to her chest.

"Mmhm, that was super thoughtful. Nah, you should keep doing what you're doing. It's not like she's a nuclear power core that'll overload with too many emotions."

"I don't know about that. Emotional overload is a real thing. She's clearly overwhelmed with everything right now. My timing sucks. Even if I was any good at courting a woman. Which I'm not."

"Courting a woman? Geez, you sound like you just arrived from the 19th century." Sandy waved her hand in the air. "Never mind, stay exactly the way you are. It's all part of your charm. That, and your uh, physical appearance sure helps. You are so effortlessly sexy, and you don't even know it. Have a little faith."

"She said she'd call me later. I offered to make dinner. Do you think she'll call?"

"If she said she'd call, she will. I'm not sure if she'll go to your ranch, but I'd hedge my bets and get something to grill. Just in case, ya know." Sandy patted Maribel's knee.

"How did you know I was going to grill something?" Maribel asked.

"Easy. You can't cook but you're one hell of a griller. Typical butch."

"Now you know that is a big fat lie. I am a very proficient cook," Maribel retorted.

Chapter Six

Blair didn't understand why she needed to leave. Maybe it was because she couldn't worry about how she might have hurt Maribel when the overwhelming feelings of guilt besieged her. But she was more apprehensive about how Maribel got to her. The pull was inexplicable. Her heart didn't have room for anything but profound grief. Not guilt and certainly not attraction.

The television crews were still camped out in front of her mother's house. Blair did not have the patience or temperament to deal with them head on today. She'd snuck out earlier and carefully made her way through the neighbor's backyard until she was several blocks away, and then she'd called that asshat Uber driver. She was surprised to learn that Uber drivers had arrived in Ellensburg. She couldn't be too picky, so when the same driver picked her up again, she tried to keep the irritation at bay.

Leaning forward, Blair ordered the driver to stop several blocks from her mother's house. Resisting the urge to tell them off again, she held the flowers close to her body and put her head down before ducking behind a tree and moving swiftly to her neighbor's yard. Flipping the lever on the gate, Blair snuck inside the fence.

"Blair? What are you doing in my yard?" Her neighbor, Mrs. Crenshaw startled Blair, and she turned in the direction of her kindly neighbor who had her hands on her hips. Blair was tempted to laugh at the elderly woman who was wearing a Jane Fonda workout leotard straight from the 80s. Her blue hair was pulled back into a long ponytail, and the frown deepened the network of lines on her face. Her passion for gardening coupled with her failure to cover up over the years had left her with more wrinkles than her seventy years would normally have revealed.

"Why aren't you with your mother?"

"Sorry, Mrs. Crenshaw. I needed to avoid the circus out front. I went for coffee."

"Didn't you have any in the house? I can get some for you, dear. I have Folgers in a can. I'd be happy to bring some over. I've wanted to come and check on Rhonda, anyway. I didn't get to spend much time with her yesterday."

Blair put her finger to her mouth. "Um, can you keep your voice down? I don't want the vultures to know I'm back here. I can't deal with them right now."

"Oh, right, right," Mrs. Crenshaw attempted to whisper. "I'll bring the coffee right over."

Blair started to protest and then thought better of it. Having a cushion between her and her mother right now might help her get through the next few hours. Her mother would never venture into rudeness, and Mrs. Crenshaw did not have the capacity to understand when she was overstaying her welcome. If only she had an appetite, because her mother's meddling neighbor did make the best baked goods on the block. They were almost better than Sandy's mouthwatering cinnamon rolls.

The little white lie that flowed from her mouth created such a bitter taste. "That sounds very nice. I'm sure Mom would appreciate that."

†

Blair had been so busy sneaking into the back door as she tried to avoid the melee ten feet from her mother's front lawn that she hadn't noticed any extraneous vehicles. Opening the door, she announced her return, "Mom, I'm back."

Skidding to a stop, Blair's shock turned to rage as she saw the familiar profile. He had his hand casually resting on her mother's back while she cried softly. He didn't look very different from the last time she'd seen him. He sported a bit more gray at the temples but his trim frame remained. The fact that he looked good and had aged extremely well only added to her irritation.

"Sperm Donor, what the hell are you doing here?" She placed the flowers on the counter.

"Blair…" Her mother adopted a warning tone.

"Don't tell me I need to be civil. I asked you a question." Blair crossed her arms and glared at her estranged father.

His dark brown eyes narrowed and hardened. "She was my daughter, too. Neither of you thought to tell me about the funeral. I had to find out on my own. How dare you leave me out of this? Even though I was in the woods on a fishing trip, my staff managed to track me down after connecting the dots. I noticed there weren't any missed calls from you."

"Fuck you. I believe you gave up your parental rights when you left and never looked back. Have you even once sent a card, called, given one shit about anyone but yourself?" Blair failed to control her rising voice.

"You need to calm down. Your mother doesn't need your attitude right now." His voice had a steely edge.

"Get out. I'm not some frightened little girl you can smack around or bribe with an ice cream cone. You are the last person that belongs here. Don't let him worm his way inside. I doubt another unplanned pregnancy, that he'll run away from—again—is advisable at your age."

"That's enough, Blair." Her mother's quavering voice caused Blair to look in her direction. Blair did not have the capacity to control her temper, so she did the next best thing. She prepared to run away. Like father, like daughter. She hated she shared that personality trait. She could not handle the fragments that were left of her mother as her mother allowed her father to be the one to keep them from blowing away. The inadequacy regarding her inability to be the glue was far too painful to handle.

"Fine, do whatever you want. I have a dinner date." Blair fled from the room. Maybe she could find a way to visit Maribel's several hours early. Blair was running out of places to land. Everywhere she turned there was discomfort.

Out of the frying pan and into the fire: Blair burst into the cacophony of media. She'd forgotten about them in her distraction resulting from the shock of seeing her father after so many years. He hadn't stayed long after finding out about her mother's pregnancy.

The perky blonde stuck a microphone in her face and asked, "Can you tell us why Senator Chadwick arrived at your house today? He's on record as a strong supporter of Second Amendment rights. Did the latest tragedy sway him?" Obviously the reporter wasn't going to let go of that line of questioning.

Blair pushed the microphone away. "Get that fucking thing out of my face or I'll stick it up your twat and turn it into a sex toy." The culmination of her anger had reached a peak.

The reporter blinked rapidly, and Blair took a small amount of satisfaction over the fact that she'd rendered the vulture silent with her outburst. Jogging down the side road she made her way to her neighbor's back yard again just as Mrs. Crenshaw came into view with a casserole dish in hand.

She was thankful the reporters had not tried to follow her. As much as her neighbor was a busybody, she was harmless.

"Mom has a visitor right now but knock yourself out. I'd rather you be there with Mom than him." Pulling her cell phone from her pocket, she searched for Maribel's number and poked the screen until the call connected. She didn't have to wait long to hear Maribel's soft, calming voice on the other end.

"Hello."

"Hey, Maribel. It's Blair. Any chance I can see your ranch earlier than we originally talked about?" Blair hated how her voice trembled. Her anger abated, she was left with that all too familiar feeling of vulnerability.

"Oh, um, sure. I'm at the store picking up food for tonight."

"Shit," Blair mumbled into the phone.

"Oh, sorry, are you on your way and I won't be there?"

"No, no, it's not that. I'll have to navigate the chaos again to get to my car. I avoided that earlier today by calling an Uber. I can call one again. How far out is your ranch?"

"Tell me where you are and I'll pick you up," Maribel offered.

"You don't mind?"

"Of course not."

A smile appeared on Blair's face, and the anger that had erupted earlier took a backseat to the pleasant feeling of anticipation. Maribel had a way of smoothing down Blair's raging emotions. Usually Maribel did that by changing the subject or listening to her rage until she'd expelled her anger enough to calm down. Blair had the sense that Maribel's perspectives on a few things, religion for one, were much different from her own. *That should make for an interesting relationship. Whoa. Relationship?*

"Blair?" Maribel interrupted Blair's thoughts.

"Uh, yeah, sorry. I'm in my neighbor's backyard. Let me put a bit more distance from the news crews. I'll walk to the end of the block, and you can pick me up on the corner of Ash and Cherry. Do you know where that is? It's the residential area by the University on the north side."

"I know where you're talking about. I'll be there soon, okay?" Maribel answered gently.

†

Maribel tossed the steaks and chicken into the cart along with the fresh greens and other items for a salad. She'd picked clean most of the arugula and tomatoes in her garden and needed to add to what remained. On her way past the produce section she grabbed fresh corn and strawberries for dessert that she would add to freshly picked blueberries and blackberries. She was in a rush to pick up Blair and didn't have time to plan for a more impressive treat to top off a good meal. Fresh fruit on top of vanilla ice cream would have to suffice. Ice cream was a staple in her house. She always had several pints in her freezer.

Tossing the bags into the back of her extra cab truck, she peeled out of the parking lot. Blair was sitting on the curb, head in hand, as she made the turn to reach the corner of Ash and Cherry. She looked more defeated, and Maribel wondered what had happened in the short time since they'd had coffee.

The second that Maribel pulled her truck to the side, Blair jumped up and flung open the door. Wordlessly, she climbed inside and offered Maribel a weak smile.

"Thanks."

"Anytime." Maribel hesitated. She wanted to lay a comforting hand on Blair but second guessed herself and remained frozen. She didn't know whether the gesture would be welcome or cause more anxiety. Turning back to the road, she eased onto the side street and headed in the direction of her ranch. It was going to be a long, awkward drive if she didn't say something. Anything to break the silence. Would she be prying to ask what happened?

"Um, I don't want to overstep…" Maribel began.

"Sperm Donor showed up," Blair interrupted.

"Sperm Donor?"

"You've heard of the runaway bride. Let's just say my father has perfected the runaway dad. His sperm is potent, only took one try to make Trina. If they hadn't been together twelve years earlier when he'd hung around long enough to celebrate my fifth birthday, I'd have labeled it a one-night stand."

"Oh, I didn't know your father was still in the picture."

"He's not, or at least he hasn't been. He's a despicable man who supports atrocious policies and people.

A politician that stands for everything I am opposed to. I'd hate him even if he hadn't left all those years ago." Blair's jaw clenched as she turned to look at Maribel.

"Does he live here?"

"Nope, he lives in Spokane which is a large enough city with a conservative bent to satisfy his base. He hates Seattle. Too many progressive people live there for his taste. Ironic that his own daughter is the collateral damage of his efforts to stall or obliterate any reasonable gun control. I doubt he gives a shit or feels any remorse," Blair answered bitterly. "He was at my mother's house playing the hero, trying to comfort her. It was disgusting." Blair rolled down the window and spit.

"Maybe he was more affected by this than you think. Tragedy tends to change people."

Blair turned her eyes toward Maribel and the cold, hard, glint caused Maribel to cringe in response. "Not a chance in hell. He's a bastard through and through. A sociopath without a conscience. For once, I hope the vultures in the media dog him until the end of his days on this earth. He had to come, play to the media. It would not have looked good for him to ignore his daughter's funeral. That's the only reason he's here."

"But he wasn't at the funeral, was he?"

"No." Blair shook her head. "I should have known. Of course, he found out. It was all over the news. A few simple phone calls would have given him the information. Frankly, I'm surprised he didn't show up at the funeral home. But then, he wouldn't have been able to control the narrative. I'm the wild card here. He knew I wouldn't have cared about making a scene and he could not have that playing on the five o'clock news."

"I see." Maribel didn't, but she could hear the pain and anger in Blair's rendition of her father and the recent events. The animosity toward her father was incomprehensible to Maribel, especially because her own papa had been her whole world until the day he crossed over.

He'd done an exemplary job of being both mother and father to her, even during the awkward moments when he was clearly uncomfortable. Those moments were frequent during her puberty when she was coming to some very hard realizations about herself. Despite his views of the world, including his deeply religious nature, he'd ultimately come to terms with the fact that Maribel was a lesbian through and through.

There was no hope she'd find a nice man and settle down. At first, he'd blamed himself for treating her like he thought a man would treat a son. He'd taken her everywhere with him. Teaching her to hunt, fish, and handle a shotgun had been some of their most treasured moments when she was growing up. She'd convinced him it wasn't his fault she was gay by presenting him a slew of education about how she was born this way. God did not make mistakes. She wasn't a product of her environment or upbringing.

"Do you? See? Understand? Your father stuck around and raised you. I saw the admiration on your face when you spoke of him."

Maribel furrowed her brow. "I told you about my papa?"

"Yeah, the first day we met. You said you never knew your mother because she died in childbirth and you were raised by your father. I could tell by the look on your face that you practically worship the ground he walks on."

Maribel focused on the road and didn't glance in Blair's direction. Even after all this time, it was still a little raw. She missed her papa and his wisdom. "Worshipped."

Blair's hand gently rested on Maribel's thigh and Maribel glanced down. She felt the small measure of what, she didn't know. Empathy? Sympathy? Reassurance? Blair didn't say a word, just a small gesture to give permission to fill in the blanks. There was a question attached to the end of her fingers as the warmth penetrated her jeans.

"Yes, worshipped as in past tense. He died eleven months ago after a long fight with cancer. The cancer won."

"I don't know what to say. I know that sorry seems inadequate and all wrong. You already know how I feel about that stock phrase, but maybe you don't share that sentiment. I could ask you the same thing you were intuitive enough to ask me. What do you need from me right now?"

The sincerity in Blair's words, especially in the midst of her own grief, seemed to remove the sadness that had erupted without warning. Eleven months should have been ample time to work through her grief and so that was her answer to Blair.

"It's been eleven months. Plenty of time to feel okay. I'm happy at my ranch, and now I get to share that with you."

"Okay, but I'm also a good listener when I put my mind to it and when I'm not wrapped inside the same tragedy. I might not be much of a support for my mother, but I think I could manage that role with you."

Maribel let her right hand drift to Blair's which had not yet taken leave of her thigh, and their fingers intertwined in mutual encouragement of one another. Their hands remained clasped together for the remainder of the trip, even on the curvy gravel driveway where Maribel should have used both hands to navigate.

Chapter Seven

Blair wasn't expecting the gorgeous vista that lay before her. The trees multiplied the farther they drove to Maribel's ranch. This was like a completely different landscape than where her mother lived even though it was less than a half an hour away.

A fluffy golden-haired dog bounded to Maribel, furiously wagging his tail. Blair assumed this was the infamous Skeeter who kept Maribel company. She leaned down and patted his head and a soft woof erupted from his mouth.

Blair exited the truck and stuck her hand out for Skeeter to sniff. "You are a handsome boy, aren't you?" Not an ounce of aggressiveness emanated from his demeanor. He didn't make her feel uncomfortable like some dogs who were extremely territorial when a new person entered their space.

"He's only handsome when he doesn't roll around in the mud."

Blair halted a few feet from the large vehicle to take in her surroundings. She sucked in a mouthful of warm air and breathed in the hint of pine. Shading her eyes with her hand, she looked at the mountain range in the distance. There was still a tiny bit of snow creating a perfect cap at the top. A little white hat for the mountain. Her mother used to say that it got so cold in the mountains they needed that hat almost year round.

Her mother's neighbors always kept their lawns trim and beautiful with frequent watering, but when Blair had ventured a small distance from the cookie-cutter neighborhoods, the dry grass looked dead and unappealing. The only place that had lush greens and plants with color was around the university and in various neighborhoods that encircled the college town.

"It's so green. The pine trees are huge," Blair noted with awe.

"Haven't you ever ventured west? The closer we get to Seattle, the more vegetation. I like this pocket of paradise because I still have the benefit of warmer weather in the spring and summer, along with the trees but not as much rain. Sure, we get all four seasons and a fair amount of snow, but that adds to the charm. I'd get bored with only two seasons. Sometimes I think Seattle only has winter and summer."

Blair looked at Maribel with curiosity. "Wow. I believe that is the largest amount of words you've strung together in one breath since we met. You must love your ranch."

"I do," Maribel answered wistfully. "I'm only missing one thing."

"What's that?"

"Someone to share the utopia with."

"Utopia, huh? That's a grandiose descriptor. I'm going to hold my final review until I see those adorable chicks. Can we look in on them first? I can't wait. Throw in a few kittens and I'm yours for the taking." Blair grinned after making the half-joke.

She could almost see herself living here even though it was so very different from her current life. If she were honest with herself, where she lived hadn't seemed to fit, and she'd never been able to put her finger on the exact reasons for that. She knew she wouldn't fit in a large city, but she assumed an in-between location of not too small but not too large, would be perfect. It wasn't. The crowds were starting to get to her well before she took her leave of absence to return to her childhood home.

Maribel smiled that genuine look of pride. Blair thought she was more in her element, and the confident shift in her posture was a sign that Blair might catch a glimpse of the other Maribel hidden inside.

"There's probably a few semi-feral kittens around. I don't usually let them hang out with the chickens for obvious reasons. I made friends with them a few years back, but mostly they keep a polite distance. On occasion, they let me pet them. I don't think any of them want to exchange their freedom for a nice cool house in the summer and a warm one in the winter. I built a structure next to the chicken coop for them. Keeps them out of the elements but away from my chickens."

"Wow! Look at you. All chatty now that you're in comfortable territory."

Maribel blushed. "Sorry. I'll shut up and just show you the baby chicks and the cat house."

"Cat house? You know that has a double meaning?" Blair winked.

"Um, I didn't mean it that way," she mumbled.

Unbelievably, Maribel's shade of red deepened as she stuck her hands in her pockets and started walking toward the carefully maintained wood structure that Blair assumed was her chicken coop. Blair didn't know much about chicken houses or coops, but this one had to be the Taj Mahal of places to raise chickens with the adjoining structure a veritable cat palace. The wood had a natural stain that brought out the beauty of the patterns in the grain. The structure seemed to match Maribel's large house that was set back in the trees several hundred feet from the stone path leading to the front door.

"Damn, if I was feral or a chicken, I'd want you to adopt me. That's the most beautiful chicken coop I've ever seen. Do you give them massages every night, too? I heard that in Japan there is a breed of cow they give massages to and feed the very best food, only to kill them and sell the meat for outrageous prices. It's called Wagyu."

"Yeah, I've heard of it. I like elk better."

"Oh, please, tell me you don't shoot elk and deer."

"Can I plead the fifth?"

Blair groaned. "I'm going to try hard not to hold that against you because you have other admirable traits."

"Growing up poor necessitates a lot of things. We didn't have the luxury of buying expensive meat and vegetables at the market. Growing our own and hunting for meat was the best Pa could do for me to make sure I had healthy food in my belly. People with money have the luxury of making choices." Maribel's voice had a tiny edge to it.

"Whoa, hey. You're right. I never had to worry about that, and I shouldn't judge. I've gotten the same lecture from people I worked with regarding boycotting the large discount stores. I can understand their perspective but can't bring myself to shop there. I prefer to support local economies and the small shops that are struggling. But, they're right, I can afford to do that. I can be a pretentious ass sometimes."

"No, I'm sorry. I might get a little defensive about some things. People are entitled to their view of the world. I even understand a big part of it. It's hard for me because I'm such an animal lover, so I get it. I also don't much like big corporations. It's a quandary for me. There are competing principles that are hard to mesh together."

"Exactly!" Blair exclaimed.

"I don't hunt anymore. Mostly because Pa isn't here to go with me. And I still eat meat. I'd miss not having meat in my diet."

"I eat chicken and fish and that's probably not any better. I'll especially feel guilty after spending time with your baby chicks. Of course, I don't eat the babies, but still…"

"Don't worry. My chickens are strictly for the eggs. I don't kill any of them unless you think life starts at conception." Maribel grinned mischievously. "I think the pro-chick movement claims that by snatching the eggs we're eating the baby embryos."

"Hmm, there's hope for you yet. Espousing sarcastic liberal rhetoric couched within that country charm." Blair grabbed Maribel's hand. "Lead the way."

†

Maribel reveled in the feeling of Blair's fingers intertwined with her own as she led the spunky woman to her hand-crafted chicken coop. She was smiling as she steered Blair inside to the sectioned-off area where she kept the brooder. The cacophony of cheeps filled the space. Blair released Maribel's hand and squealed in delight.

"They are so adorable. Can I pet them?"

"Sure. You can pick them up if you want. It doesn't hurt them. They like the attention. Make sure you don't keep them out of the brooder too long. They'll cheep loudly if they get cold and then you know it's time to put them back. The temperature inside the brooder is carefully regulated."

"Is that what you call this—a brooder?" Blair pointed to the square wooden container lined with cedar shavings.

Maribel nodded. "Yeah. It's not very fancy, but it isn't too hard to raise baby chicks. All you need is a place for them to snuggle with each other, a feeder, and a heat lamp to regulate temperature. They can get too cold or too hot easily. I try to keep it the right temperature, but without air conditioning, there are a couple of weeks in the summer when I don't have the babies, in case I can't cool it down enough."

Maribel had done the research and, along with the help of her father, had lovingly created the structure. After hearing the tiny meows and coming across a litter of kittens, she'd added the feral cat wing. She'd started feeding the cats, and soon she had plenty to keep the mice and rat population down. Knowing there were coyotes around that not only were attracted to the chickens but would grab other small animals, she'd hoped the new addition would provide more protection than a place to escape the elements.

Skeeter was a fierce protector but coyotes were smart. Maribel had to use her shotgun on more than one occasion to keep them away. Rather than having to run back to the house to grab a shotgun, she always kept one loaded in the section of the coop she'd created for the baby chicks.

Blair picked up one of the chicks and was cooing to it as if the chick were a baby.

"Ooh, you are the softest little thing." She brushed a single finger over the top of the chick's head. Placing the chick back in the brooder, she picked up another one. "I need to make sure I give every single one of you attention. I don't want any fighting to occur. I heard chicks will pick on outsiders, ones that are a little different. Is that true?"

"It hasn't occurred with my chicks, but yeah it happens." Maribel sighed. "You've probably been in stores and places where the chicks are stressed. They're hatched with a thousand of their distant relatives, sorted and unceremoniously packed into a box, endure a bumpy chilly ride to God knows where, and then placed in another crowded box and have to fight for food and water. Now, I'm not saying touching them is wrong, but in those stores random strangers and kids that aren't very cautious ogle and handle the chicks before they're boxed up again. It's a miracle they all don't peck and pick on each other."

Blair groaned. "I've been one of those random strangers ogling the chicks before. I feel horrible now." Blair glanced at Maribel and then seemed to stiffen as her eye zeroed in on something behind Maribel.

She turned around to see what had caught Blair's eye. Maribel hadn't considered how Blair might react to the shotgun she had stored on the wall of the coop.

Before Maribel could explain, Blair's wobbly voice asked, "Why do you have a shotgun in your chicken coop?"

"Coyotes. They are not friends with my chickens or the feral cats. Skeeter can only do so much."

"I've never been comfortable around guns, and now…" Blair's face lost all color and her voice trailed off.

Maribel rushed to the gun, plucked it from the holder on the wall and frantically looked around for a place to keep it from Blair's line of sight. There wasn't much to choose from. She settled on the stack of cedar shavings in the corner and set the shotgun behind them.

"Sorry about that. I forgot I had one here in the coop."

Blair set the chick back into the brooder. "Can I see the cat house now? Maybe I'll catch a glimpse of one of the feral kittens. They like to sleep during the day, right?"

Maribel caught the quiver and hesitancy in Blair's voice and wanted to smack herself for being so careless. Maybe the kittens would be a welcome distraction to the latest trigger causing Blair unnecessary stress.

"Okay." This time Maribel took Blair's hand, hoping the touch would both be welcome and calming. "We have to exit the coop because I didn't think to build a door between the structures."

†

The minute the two women entered the attached building that was the size of a large shed, Blair heard the loud hiss. *Uh oh, Mama must be awake.* The hiss was followed by a chorus of tiny meows. The kittens were screaming about being interrupted from their late morning meal. Mama cat had shifted, her bright green eyes angry slits glaring at the intruders.

Blair looked around at what she would label a cat paradise. Not only were there bowls of food, but a gurgling fountain of water was plugged into an electrical outlet in the wall. The inside of the house for the feral cats had drywall. Blair would have bet an entire year's worth of paychecks that behind that drywall was insulation. Toys were strewn about, along with several dishes of food. The only thing missing was a litter box. Blair wondered how feral the cats really were. For all intents and purposes, they were indoor pets. Maribel had set up several scratching posts, soft cushy cat pillows, and gigantic climbing condos covered in what appeared to be high quality carpet.

The tiny mewls continued, and Blair cautiously took a few steps toward the complaining voices. Five squirming balls of fluff were trying to reattach themselves to their mother's teats. After another glare, the mama cat gave each of them a lick or two. She laid back down and kept her eyes focused on Maribel and Blair.

"It's okay, Mama, we only want to say hello." Maribel crouched down and did a slow half crab walk, half scoot toward the happy family. When she was only a couple of feet away, she gestured for Blair to sit next to her. "Approach slowly."

Blair decided to sit several feet away from Maribel and then began to inch her way closer. When she reached the spot that Maribel had patted earlier, she began her own reassuring declaration. "I promise. I'm not going to hurt you or your babies. Will you let me pet you?"

"Hang tight for a second," Maribel advised, while she moved her large frame cautiously until she was practically lying on the floor of the cat house mere inches away from the family. "Consider how intimidating it is when we're towering over them. They usually let me eventually pet them if I sort of lay on the floor and then snake my hand out slowly."

Following suit, Blair joined Maribel on the floor. She reached out and let two fingers brush the closest squirming ball of fur. She kept herself from squealing in delight lest she scare the skittish mama cat. The kittens seemed more inclined to let her touch them as long as Mama wasn't reacting.

Maribel was a calming presence and managed to pet the mama cat without her reacting in defense of her babies, and that allowed Blair her moment of bliss with the kittens. She wasn't about to disturb the magic by attempting to pick up one of the tiny balls of fluff, although she wanted to.

"Do they ever let you pick them up?"

"Sometimes." Maribel continued to stroke the mama cat.

"You're like the cat whisperer, huh?"

Maribel grinned. "Oh, I don't know about that. I've been bribing them with tuna fish and cream."

"Does that work with feral cats?"

"Mmhm. Food has a way of taming most any beast." Maribel chuckled. "Although, I wouldn't recommend using food with larger predators. They're a lot more unpredictable. When I was little, I tried to tame a wild cougar. I thought if I left food for him, he would be eternally grateful. He wasn't. Papa had to shoot him, or I wouldn't be here right now. I cried for days. But I learned a valuable lesson. Some animals shouldn't be caged. I don't go to zoos because I can't bear watching the most majestic animals in the world confined to those tiny spaces."

"I suppose keeping chickens doesn't fall within your definition of animals that shouldn't be caged."

"They're birds," Maribel corrected.

"A technicality. Shouldn't birds be allowed to roam free?"

"They do. If I wanted, I could sell them as free-range chickens. You've seen the area they are allowed to peck around in. It's huge. If I removed the fencing, I'd be worried about predators. The fencing is intended to keep the predators out, not contain the chickens. By now, they are so comfortable with me, I doubt they would roam off my property."

"So, no exotic pets for you, huh?"

"Nope." Maribel slowly removed her hand and sat up. "Had enough of the kittens yet?"

"Not really, but we should let them be as long as we can visit again." With one last stroke on the tiniest kitten, Blair pulled her hand away. "Can't wait to see what other treasures you have in store for me."

"I should have showed you the house first after putting away the groceries, but I saw your excitement about the chicks and couldn't resist holding off on taking care of the food. Is it okay if we do that now? I wouldn't want the food to spoil."

"Uh, yeah. Me neither. I'll give you a hand, and then you can show me your inner sanctum."

CHAPTER EIGHT

Maribel juggled the bags of groceries as she opened the back door leading into the mudroom. She was racking her brain for a way to close off her trophy room lest her secret get out too soon. She didn't even want the damn thing, but her papa had been so proud. When they'd built the house together, he had insisted she should showcase her accomplishments by putting them in a place of honor. Over the years, she'd won too many competitions to count, easily filling the large space. When she began to exceed her papa's expectations, trophies weren't the only rewards. Her skills with a shotgun ended up pulling them out of poverty. Money was far more valuable than what she considered useless trinkets. She silently chastised herself for not gutting the room after her papa passed.

Setting the groceries on the granite counter, she began putting away the meat and vegetables. Before Blair could do much, she'd managed to take care of the food and store the paper bags in the cabinet below the sink to the left. Maribel watched Blair politely take in her large kitchen. She wondered if she was impressed.

The cathedral ceiling had a skylight in the center designed to bring in natural light. The wood beams contrasted nicely with the off-white walls. The cabinets were solid wood with a clear glossy coat engineered to bring out every nuance to the rich wood grain. Maribel had opted for a butcher-block island versus the granite that covered the rest of the counter space. Although she supposed the large cutting board built on top of the island was intended for use, she couldn't bear to mar the smooth surface and kept it oiled, showing off the beauty of the wood. The open-floor plan led seamlessly to a large living space where her handcrafted stone fireplace commanded attention.

Maribel's home was a far cry from the rickety farmhouse she had lived in for most of her childhood. She almost felt guilty for what she perceived as opulence. She wasn't sure she deserved this luxury because she was good at shooting a gun.

"Wow! Your home is gorgeous. I can't wait to see the rest. What are you? Admit it, you *are* a bootlegger. Oh, I know, you own a marijuana store, the modern-day equivalent. Except, marijuana is now legal."

Maribel chuckled. "Um, no. I have a special skill taught to me by my papa. There are a few professional sports for women that can result in a decent living."

Blair raised an eyebrow. "Do tell. I would have settled for having my college paid for. Alas, I suck at pretty much every sport."

Maribel shrugged. "Prize money adds up when you enter every contest offered and people underestimate you. Sponsorships help."

"Sponsorships? You sound like you're an Olympic gold medalist. Now I'm really intrigued and impressed."

"Don't be. I doubt you would be impressed. Come on, let me give you a tour of the house." When Blair's head was turned while inspecting a sculpture in the entryway, Maribel closed the door to her trophy room and proceeded to walk by the room on her way to the stairway that would lead to the bedroom suites, guest and master. Maribel thought she had almost escaped the inevitable questions, when Blair halted in front of the closed door.

"Don't I get to see this room?"

"No." Maribel continued up the stairs. She didn't have to turn around to know that Blair had a puzzled expression on her face. She wondered how she would react to the clipped, one-word response. She knew it sounded rude, but that would be the least of her concerns if Blair saw a room filled, not only with trophies but enough guns to be considered a domestic terrorist, if one was so inclined to make a snap judgment.

Once Maribel reached the top of the stairs, she waited for Blair who was tracing the handcrafted ironwork that made up the rails. She wondered if Blair was impressed or the style was opposite of what she might select for her own home.

"This is the coolest thing I've ever seen. The trees, mountains, and what I presume are elk go perfectly with the beautiful surroundings."

"I thought so too. I commissioned these when I saw his craft. The guy's a local artist that did a bunch of work for the multi-million-dollar homes in Suncadia."

"That's the famous mountain resort with the world-class golf courses, right?"

"Mmhm. I've been there a few times but not for golf. There are three excellent restaurants worth going to. I could take you to one sometime," she offered hopefully. There was a big part of Maribel that wanted to wine and dine Blair. She was a bit old fashioned sometimes, and the thought of taking Blair to a nice restaurant had a certain amount of appeal. She'd even pull out her good clothes and try to make an impression.

"Are you asking me out on a proper date, Maribel?" Blair grinned and began fanning herself. "I do declare, I'm so flattered," she joked.

Maribel couldn't tell if Blair was teasing her in a good way, or if she was completely unimpressed with Maribel's lame attempt to ask her out. "Um…"

"Relax." Blair playfully smacked Maribel's arm. "I was teasing you. I'd love to check out the place. Although, I don't usually treat myself to expensive restaurants. In my line of work, salaries aren't designed to bathe me in luxury. I'm not poverty bound, but I also wouldn't dream of plopping down a hundred dollars on one meal unless it was for a special occasion. Even then, once a year is about all I can justify."

"I asked, so of course I would treat you."

"I think I'll let you. After getting a good look at your place, clearly you can afford it."

"I can. God blessed me with a talent I probably don't deserve, but since my pa always had faith in me, I wasn't going to squander it."

"Whatever that talent is that you've been so evasive about, I'll bet it was paired with a healthy dose of hard work. Raw talent only takes a person so far. It's the elbow grease that makes things happen. Even virtuosos have to practice like eight to ten hours a day, every day. I'm sure it isn't a picnic for them."

Maribel wanted off this topic, so she began making her way to the master bedroom. "Come on, let me show you the master suite. I probably went over the top with the bathroom. In my defense, I use that whirlpool tub almost every day."

"Ooh, I love decadent bathrooms."

†

Blair's mouth hung open, as she took in the generous space. She'd never seen anything like it before. Cedar stairs led to the marble, enclosed, semi-heart-shaped forest-green tub that was so beautiful she wanted to climb in and try it out. She could see multiple jets where the water was intended to soothe various parts of a person's body. The bronze waterfall spout, shaped like a crescent moon, was the most unique faucet she'd ever seen. Her eyes traveled to the shower, and Blair was sure the delight was evident in her smile.

"Wow, I can't believe you have a dragonfly on your shower wall. That's stunning. I've never seen anything like it."

"It isn't all that complicated if you find an artist that creates special tiles. Pretty easy, really, to embed the art work into the rest of the wall."

"Do you need a roommate? I'll just put a bed in this room and live here. Although, I'd never want to leave."

"I'd be happy to have you stay here. Sometimes it gets lonely on the ranch."

Blair couldn't quite put her finger on why Maribel seemed different from all the women she'd dated. For one thing, Maribel didn't seem the type to enter into casual relationships, and that should have worried her. But there was something so reassuring about having a stable, compassionate woman in her life, even if nothing transpired between the two of them. She had almost forgotten what precipitated the visit to Maribel's, several hours before she had intended to come, when her phone buzzed in her pocket and she spied the name.

"Shit, I have to take this," Blair announced as she pushed the button to connect the call. "Everything okay, Mom?"

Blair could hear the strain in her mother's voice when she answered. "Yes, I thought I should tell you that your father has decided to stick around for a few days. I didn't want you to be surprised when you returned home."

"You've got to be fucking kidding. In that case, enjoy your time with the Sperm Donor. When he leaves and you're still falling apart, call me. Until then, I'm sorry, but I can't be in the same room with him."

"He's trying, Blair. He wants to be here for both of us."

"No, he doesn't. This is all about optics. He has to play the part of the grieving father because I'm sure the press has looked into his background. I can't talk about this. You do what you want, but don't expect me to participate in this farce. Bye, Mom." Blair punched the button to end her call. She looked at Maribel. "That offer still open for a roommate? It seems like I might need a place to stay for a few days. I don't think homicide is the answer. I look awful in orange."

Maribel was nodding. "Of course. I haven't showed you the guest suite yet. The bath isn't as nice as this one, but it's comfortable."

"Oh, I have no doubt of that. Hey, are you sure? God, I'm just barreling my way into your peaceful life. I can always crash with Sandy. Forget I asked. Sometimes I don't think before speaking."

"No, really. I want you to stay."

Blair sighed. "I guess I will have to endure the gauntlet to retrieve a few items, including my car. I know I want to spend my time here doing something that matters. I should not have been so rude to the press before, but my head was not in a space to capitalize on the exposure. Something seems so wrong about doing that. And yet, bringing awareness to important issues around gun control has to be worth selling my soul to the devil. I know the press doesn't care one whit about the issue, but this isn't an opportunity I can afford to pass up. Is it? What do you think?" Blair began to pace in a small circle.

"I don't think I am the best person to answer that question. Do whatever your gut tells you is right, and don't worry about what others think."

"Yeah, everyone leverages whatever they can for the greater good, huh? It's not like I'm advocating violence to further this cause. I need to do a bit of research later and find a group where I can lend a hand and get involved in a meaningful way. Spewing hate against Second Amenders is not very effective."

"Come on, let me show you the guest room. I want to make sure it'll be comfortable for you. I turned the third bedroom into a library, so if it's not acceptable, the only other option is the master suite." Maribel blushed then looked away.

Blair recognized Maribel's attempt to steer the conversation in a different direction. She wondered if it was the topic or if all political activism made Maribel uncomfortable. That might be a big red flag, given Blair's propensity to jump into the fray on the myriad issues she had a passion for. Blair despised individuals who would not take a stance. Apathy often led to tragedy in her humble opinion. People permitted things to happen in small increments, until the cruelties were impossible to ignore. Often it was too late when that happened. She decided it wasn't the time or place to confront Maribel.

Opting for a flirtatious response instead, Blair answered, "I don't think that would be a huge hardship for me, but considering the shade of red on your face, I'm sure the guest bedroom is lovely."

Blair didn't think it was possible for Maribel to turn a deeper shade of red but she did. "The guest bedroom is across the hall from mine, so if you need anything..." Maribel's voice trailed off as she started walking out of the master bedroom.

Blair chuckled to herself as she followed Maribel to the large room with the window facing the mountain range. The view was breathtaking, and Blair wondered how she hadn't noticed this view when they'd walked through the master suite to the decadent bath. She figured the blinds had most likely shielded the view. The sun shined brightly inside the light and airy room. Blair decided she would leave the blinds open so she could wake up and start the day right. Modesty had never been something she'd been concerned about as she often paraded around in the nude. Preferring light over dark, opening and closing shades wasn't anything she ever bothered with. Besides, Maribel's place was literally in the middle of nowhere. Who would see, anyway?

"This is a spectacular view. How come you don't have the blinds open in your room? I'd give my left titty to wake up to this every day." Blair pointed to the mountains.

Maribel shrugged. "I take things for granted. Skeeter gets grumpy in the morning when the sun wakes him up too early."

"So, you let your dog sleep with you. Do you let anyone else in that big bed of yours?"

"Are you asking if I've had a girlfriend before?"

"Have you?"

"I've dated but never had a serious girlfriend. My papa taught me a lot. Courting a woman wasn't anything he passed on, though. After he lost the love of his life, he gave up on love. Old movies were my teachers. That hasn't impressed too many women." Maribel stuck her hands in her pockets and swayed.

Blair leaned in and kissed her on the cheek. "I think your old-fashioned ways are almost irresistible. Don't change a thing. Jumping into bed on the first date is overrated."

†

Maribel wasn't sure what to do after she'd completed the tour of the house, including the guest bedroom a few short steps away from her master suite. She'd never invited a woman to stay at her house before, and the death of her father forced her to rattle around in the huge space alone. Well, not alone. She had Skeeter to keep her company.

Skeeter would even warm her bed. But that wasn't the same as entwining her life with someone and sharing her bed.

"Um, we have a lot of time before dinner. You'd probably like a snack to tide you over, right?"

Blair shrugged. "I'm okay. I'll need to head back to my mom's house to grab a few things, including my laptop if I'm going to start my research on how to get involved. I'm so sorry, I keep leaning on you to come to my rescue. I'll take another Uber so you don't have to play personal chauffeur to an unstable, grief-stricken parasite."

Maribel chuckled. "Parasite? I like being the person you can lean on. I have a lot of free time. It's nice having someone to talk with. It's no problem to drive you there."

"I feel bad having you make the trip back into town again. It's not like we're two miles down the road. Are you sure you don't mind taking me to my mom's place? I'll probably be in a foul mood if I run into the Sperm Donor while grabbing my things. Plus, I need to face the media and use the platform to make a statement. I'm just not sure what that will be at this moment." Blair frowned.

Maribel was the last person who should help Blair with a statement to the press, but that did not stop her from blurting out, "I can help you work through it before we go to your mom's place."

"Not that I want to copy what others have said…Maybe if I go online and do research, something will resonate, then I can make the statement my own. Do you have a computer in this mansion?"

"It's not a mansion and, yes, I have a computer. Come on, I forgot to show you the library. I left my laptop there."

"You're an angel." Blair followed Maribel as she led her down the hallway to the third room on the second floor.

The wall originally intended as a large closet was filled from floor to ceiling with books. Maribel had looked at the architect's designs and asked him to alter the room. She'd asked around for a specialty carpenter to build a solid cherry-wood library. The result was a spectacular handcrafted work of art with a built-in stereo system. Although it had been tricky to add the small fireplace to the second floor, she insisted on this special feature. This room was Maribel's sanctuary, and she spent many hours sitting in her recliner, reading everything from light romance to the best sci-fi with complicated world building that transported her to a sparkly new fictionalized existence.

"Holy shit! This room is amazing. If I hadn't asked for a computer would you have kept this from me like that secret hideout downstairs?"

"No, I was gonna show you this room after the tour of the guest bedroom."

"I was kidding." Blair lightly smacked Maribel's arm. "I need to amend my previous declaration. Roll in a cot, add a mini-fridge, microwave and porta-potty if you can't build me a bathroom, and I'm all set. I'd never leave. Permasquat."

"Permasquat?" Maribel furrowed her brow.

"Yeah, you'd have a permanent squatter in your house."

"Should I install a hand-held shower wand to a sink, like in a tiny house or RV?" Maribel joked.

"Great idea. But you'd have to keep stocking the fridge and add a hot plate. Microwave dinners will get old."

"It's only a few steps to the guest bathroom. Don't you think you can make a tiny exception for a real shower or a bath?"

"I suppose. If I have to." An exaggerated sigh caused Maribel to giggle. "Are you sure you don't mind if I do a little internet research? I don't want to come across as an ignorant hack. Do you think I'm being cold and unfeeling by deciding to turn the media stalk into a platform for social change? There's a big part of me that feels…oh, I don't know…just as slimy as them. I might have to use that shower after I come back."

"No, I don't. God puts opportunities in our path. We shouldn't squander them. I never have."

Blair wrinkled her nose, and Maribel suspected her mention of God had generated that reaction. "Is that what this is, an opportunity? It doesn't feel like an opportunity. It feels like a tragedy begging for something to trigger the masses to action. Fuck, that was an unintentional pun that is literally making me sick right now."

Maribel noticed Blair's pallor had changed, and she reached out to calm her by rubbing her back. She led her to the recliner and directed her to sit. "I don't know what pun you were referring to."

"Trigger," she pushed the word out on a puff of air.

"Oh." Maribel reached for her laptop that was lying on the side table and handed it to Blair. She was desperately trying to redirect the conversation to stable ground. It seemed like Blair's intermittent bouts of anger and righteousness were better than when she was second-guessing her motives or remembering the tragedy that spurred her need to take action.

"Thanks. Is there a password to get in?"

Maribel cringed. She wasn't about to tell Blair that her password was skeetshooter25. The color in Blair's face started to appear again. "Um, I'll boot it up for you. Then I'll make us some snacks for lunch. I have a decent variety of cheeses I can cut up with apples or grapes." Maribel was babbling because she was nervous. She hoped Blair didn't notice.

"Hmm, do you have stuff on this computer that you don't want me to see? Is your password racy or something?" The corner of Blair's lips turned up in a teasing challenge.

Maribel retrieved the laptop, flipped the lid, ran her thumb over the touchpad to activate the screen and then typed in her password before handing it back to Blair. She mumbled a quick response, "Uh no, nothing that interesting to see."

Blair held up her hand mimicking the girl-scout-oath gesture and declared, "On my honor, I promise not to snoop around and look at your browsing history lest I find out all your deep dark secrets, like what porn sites you may have visited." She began to laugh.

"Funny." Maribel nearly ran down the stairs as the blush took over.

CHAPTER NINE

Blair was curious about Maribel. She was hiding something. Although it was tempting to do what she swore she wouldn't do, Blair exercised restraint and stayed clear of clicking onto Maribel's browsing history. She also resisted the urge to click onto her documents and look for any pictures that might uncover something, hell anything, about the tight-lipped woman. It wasn't that Maribel hadn't revealed anything personal. She'd simply been cautious about something. The closed room she wasn't willing to show Blair was like a blinking red light. Blair shook her head and opened her favorite browser to begin her search for a local group she could join. Quickly immersing herself into the various options and the more memorable speeches, she was ready to begin composing her statement.

Looking around the room, she couldn't find a pen or a notepad. Her eyes landed on a large sketchpad. Since the oversized drawing pad was out in the open, Blair couldn't resist checking it out. Keeping the laptop open, she gently set it aside and then walked over to retrieve the pad.

Blair began flipping the pages, finding a series of sketches of Skeeter, as well as numerous landscapes that she recognized as the panoramic views surrounding Maribel's land. As she was turning the page, she heard Maribel's tread on the stairs and turned in the direction of the sound, preparing to greet her new friend.

Maribel had a panicked look on her face as she entered the library. "What are you doing?" The strained words came out of her mouth barely above a whisper.

"I was looking for a pen and paper and saw your sketch pad. You're quite the artist. Living where you live, you have plenty of inspiration. The drawings are outstanding, Maribel."

Maribel set the tray of cheese and fruit on the side table by the recliner and reached for the pad. Blair only caught a quick glimpse of the last drawing before Maribel closed the sketchpad. There was no mistaking the picture of the woman on the last page. It was a remarkable rendition of Blair's face. Prominently depicted on the drawing pad were Blair's grief-stricken eyes.

Blair blinked at Maribel in confusion. "Why am I in your sketchpad?"

Maribel looked down as the pad hung limply in her left hand. "I'm sorry. I draw to relax. Sometimes it helps me regain my focus before a practice session. I…I…haven't been able to get your face out of my head."

"Why?"

"I don't know. It isn't just that I'm attracted to you. I can't really explain."

"Try."

"You bring out something in me that no one besides my papa ever has. I tell you stuff about myself sometimes before I realize I'm doing it."

"Seriously? You know that you're an enigma. I don't know hardly anything about you. I blabber on, hiding nothing, but you… Well, let's just say I'm sure I've only seen the tip of the iceberg. Not that you're a cold fish. Bad analogy."

Maribel shuffled her feet. "I know. I'm not trying to be mysterious. I'm afraid if you know too much about me, you won't like what you see."

"Doubtful. I might not know all your deep, dark secrets. What I know is that you're kind, compassionate, and you've got that whole strong, silent, butch thing going for you. Supremely attractive butch thing, I might add. I'm sorry if I crossed a line by looking at your drawings."

"It's okay. Did you finish your search?"

"Yeah. There are six groups I could join and hopefully get involved in." Blair picked up the laptop and clicked on the page that showed the summary of the six groups. She turned the laptop toward Maribel to show her.

"The Everytown for Gun Safety has a way for me to join the Gun Sense Action Network. I can make calls from anywhere."

"That sounds like a good group."

"It does. I could also join the Brady Network, but I couldn't find a local chapter. There's also the Coalition to Stop Gun Violence. I can sign up to help with twitter and email campaigns but not much more than that."

"You're not sounding enthused with those options."

"I'm not. I want to become intimately tangled with a grassroots organization. Maybe I can join them all and at least be involved to some degree. The one that seems most appealing is Giffords. That group has options such as testifying in a committee, meeting with legislature, telling my story, writing an op-ed, or organizing a town hall meeting or rally. I want to be more involved than making calls or sending tweets. Fundraising and grant writing are what I do best. Persuading people to let go of their hard-earned money and organizing events is a skill-set applicable to taking the lead on just about any cause."

Maribel smiled. "It sounds like you found the group to connect with."

"Yeah, I guess I did. It helped to talk it out. You know, say what I was thinking out loud to cement where I was leaning. I also started to look at the speeches and quotes from rallies that were the most impactful. I'm not going to steal the exact phrases, but it did give me an idea. I should write it down before I forget. Do you have pen and paper?" Blair asked. She was feeling a growing excitement. All her anger and the energy coursing through her body could be funneled into meaningful action, versus spewing hate and discontent.

"Sure, I'll get that now. Be right back." Maribel left the room, and Blair laughed as she heard her sprint down the stairs. The faint sounds of rustling could be heard right before Blair registered loud footsteps as she made her way back to the library.

Maribel presented Blair with a notepad and pen as if the gift was made of solid gold. Her effervescent smile created a cozy feeling in Blair. She got the sense that Maribel would always do everything in her power to give Blair whatever she needed.

"Thanks," she said as she accepted the items from Maribel. She knew in her heart she was thanking Maribel for so much more than the notepad and pen. So far Maribel was doing all the giving, and at some point, Blair would need to balance the scales.

†

Lost in thought, Maribel missed the turn onto the street she needed to go. Blair cleared her throat, and Maribel was jolted from her lack of concentration. She'd been thinking of all the times she redirected the conversation whenever Blair touched upon a topic that was uncomfortable to Maribel. She'd certainly been embarrassed when Blair had found her drawing. She hadn't been able to get Blair's pain-filled face out of her head, so she'd drawn it. Even through her tear-stained face, Maribel saw the exquisite beauty. She'd captured that on paper.

"Um..."

"Oh, shit, shit, sorry. I know where to go. I'll make a U-ey."

"If it doesn't reveal too much of what's behind that irresistible half-brood, what were you so focused on that you forgot to turn."

Maribel breathed in deeply and let the air out slowly. It was decision time. Should she be honest and tell Blair what she was thinking. Yes, she thought it was worth the risk to let her in a little more. She wasn't prepared to share how she made her money just yet, but admitting to her need to change the subject all the time was a small consolation.

"I was thinking about how I always change the subject when I'm uncomfortable," she admitted. "And how I had this compulsion to capture your face and the raw vulnerability, before it drove me crazy," she added.

"Drove you crazy? I'm sorry my grief was an irritant." Blair's tone left nothing to misinterpretation. She was hurt.

Maribel glanced over to see the pain reappear, and it nearly broke her heart. She refocused her eyes on the road, not wanting to see the sorrow anymore. "No, no, that's not what I meant. See, every time I try to express myself, it gets all twisted. That's why I hold my cards close to my vest. Because when I share them, all people see is crap cards. What I was trying to say is that your beauty haunted me."

"Better. Don't ever stop revealing yourself. Communication between two people is ripe for misunderstanding. That's the way it works. Best to continue to talk it through until both people understand the true meaning behind the words. Even skilled communicators screw up sometimes, especially when life-altering events occur. I should remember that for myself."

Maribel was approaching the turn again, and this time she didn't miss it. She'd had her doubts about whether the media would still be camped out in front of the house, but apparently there wasn't any other news in the sleepy little town to take advantage of. "You sure you're ready for this?" she asked.

Blair nodded. Her face was pale, but when the truck stopped, Maribel saw her resolve as she opened the door and stepped into the sunshine. Maribel emerged and joined Blair as she took several purposeful steps in the direction of the reporters.

The same blonde who had cornered Maribel earlier had a predatory grin on her face as she approached the two women.

"I'd like to make a statement," Blair announced. Maribel saw her hands shake as she held the paper and prepared to talk.

The blonde stuck the microphone in her face, and Blair's voice quivered at first as she began her statement. "I would honestly like to know whether a person's right to bear arms, trumped my sister's right to life, liberty, and the pursuit of happiness? You can't pick and choose the parts of what the Founding Fathers created and discard the rest. When will enough innocent lives lost be the final straw? Do you think the narrative would change for the Second Amendment enthusiasts if their son or daughter, sister or brother, was one of the casualties of the regressive politics? I don't want answers now. I'd rather people think on those questions. Really think on them. I don't believe I can live with myself if I don't take a stance and join the fight for common-sense gun control. Thank you, that's all I have to say."

The reporter's eyes narrowed, and Maribel was reminded of a predator ready to pounce. "Do you think your fight or words will hold any water as you stand next to the poster child for Second Amendment rights?"

"What?"

"Maribel Sanders. Surely you know who she is. Frankly, I'm surprised you've chosen to align—"

"Blair, you don't have to talk to the reporters. My staff is already working on a press release," Blair's father interrupted.

Maribel hadn't seen the distinguished man rush from the house until he was upon them. He pulled a very resistant Blair away from the horde of media, including the rabid blonde who was hell-bent on getting the story, especially now that she'd seen the two of them together. It was only a matter of time before Blair knew what Maribel was hiding. She would have to come clean. Soon. Maribel vowed to do that at dinner. She was relieved when the man interrupted the reporter, even if his rough intervention struck an angry chord with Maribel.

Blair was shepherded into the house before she heatedly replied, “Get your fucking hands off of me. I don’t need your protection. I made my own statement so keep your publicity entourage far away from me. I am confident we won’t have the same things to say.”

“Suit yourself, Blair.” The man let go. “I was only trying to help.” He turned his attention to Maribel. “Who are you? Her new girlfriend?” he asked with disgust.

“None of your fucking business. We’re here to collect a few things and then I’ll be out of your hair, and you can use your spin-doctors to create whatever narrative suits you with the reporters. Stay here, Maribel. I’ll only be a few minutes.” Blair made a beeline for the staircase, leaving Maribel awkwardly standing in the foyer. She remained quiet, not knowing what to say or do.

Maribel recognized Blair’s mother as she silently emerged from the large living room to the right of the foyer. “I remember you from the funeral. You were with Sandy.”

“Yes, ma’am,” Maribel answered.

“Did you attend college with Blair? I don’t remember ever meeting you before.”

“No, ma’am.”

“How do you know Blair?”

“I met her a few days ago, uh, in front of the funeral home. We went for coffee. Sandy is a mutual friend.”

“Oh. So, how come you’re here instead of Sandy?”

Blair bounded down the stairs carrying a duffel bag and another small sling bag over her shoulders. "Don't answer that. Mom, stop. I don't need you giving Maribel the third degree. Just leave it be. Change of plans. I'm not taking my car. Can I ride back with you?"

"Of course," Maribel answered.

"Blair? What are you doing? I'm worried about you."

"Don't be. I'm fine. You take care of yourself. If you need me, I can be reached by phone. Come on, Maribel, let's go."

Blair looked like she was on a mission that not even the devil himself could stop as she burst out the door and made a beeline to Maribel's truck.

"Blair, how do you honestly feel about—" the blonde reporter began.

"I've made my statement," Blair cut her off while tossing her bag into the truck, and then she pulled herself inside while removing the sling pack and placing it on her lap. She slammed the door shut, effectively shutting out the reporters.

Maribel resisted the urge to sigh in relief. Her time was running out. If she didn't confess to Blair tonight, things might get more than uncomfortable. They had the real possibility of turning ugly. She didn't want that. She also did not want Blair to look at her with disgust, like she'd done with the man that Maribel assumed was her father. Unsure of why Blair had chosen not to take her car, Maribel decided to keep quiet. Getting far away from the media was more important than understanding the change in plans.

†

The fact that Maribel kept her eyes glued to the road and had not ventured a glance in her direction for an entire ten minutes was not lost on Blair. If her grip was any tighter on the wheel, Blair thought it might be possible for her fingers to leave imprints. She decided enough was enough, she was going to break the eerie silence and tension in the car. Maribel wasn't the chattiest person in the world, but Blair didn't think she'd be able to cut the tension with the sharpest Dao. The Chinese saber would have zero impact.

"All right. I want to know what the hell is going on. Clearly that reporter has information on you that she believes is important for me to know. You aren't a convicted murderer, are you?"

"Can we please talk about this later? I'd rather look you in the eye. I promise I'll tell you everything and show you the room you are so curious about. If you want to leave after dinner, I'm sure Sandy would be happy to provide a place to stay. Honestly, I'm surprised you didn't ask her first."

"I'd rather spend more time with you," Blair answered with unvarnished candor. "You fascinate me, Maribel Sanders. Yes, I caught your last name. You must be famous. But famous for what is the question?"

"Later, please." Maribel turned and connected briefly with Blair. The look was so gut-wrenching, Blair couldn't bring herself to deny the plea.

"Okay. After dinner. I will hold you to your promise. In the meantime, relax. I'd prefer that we continue to slough off what just occurred, not only the weird thing with the reporter, but I'd like to forget running into the Sperm Donor as well. Sorry, I had to get out of there. I hope it's okay you're my chauffeur again?"

Blair knew she was causing whiplash and not giving Maribel a chance to respond, but moving to a new topic seemed safer than continuing to think about her absentee father.

"I'm looking forward to a scrumptious dinner. Not only are you my savior right now, but you're going to feed me like I'm some kind of royalty. I don't deserve this, but I'll take it." She relaxed back into her seat and was grateful when the waves of tension seemed to abate.

"I'll be your chauffeur anytime you want. I'm going to prepare the best chicken you've ever tasted. No worries there. I've got a secret marinade that folks have been trying to get their hands on for years. Even the CIA hasn't been able to break me for the recipe," Maribel joked.

"Oh, I believe that. You seem exceptional at keeping secrets."

Chapter Ten

Blair had decided to give herself and Maribel a break from pressure of the big reveal that would come after dinner. Trying to avoid the elephant in the room for the entire afternoon would have been excruciatingly unpleasant for both women. She'd told Maribel that she couldn't easily keep her super-secret recipe safe if Blair was hovering over her. Grabbing her laptop, Blair spent several hours in the library mapping out her plan to organize a rally. She'd contacted Giffords and floated her idea of planning a rally in Seattle. They seemed excited about the prospect, and she'd barreled on like she always did.

She needed to spark some interest using the various social media vehicles. Maybe one of the celebrities living in the state would pick up the thread and help jump-start her efforts. It was worth a shot. She had a few connections and so did Sandy. Activism often attracted musicians, actors, and actresses. All she needed was one person to respond to her plea for help. She wasn't looking for money, she needed a draw. An enticement to bring the crowds that would tempt the press. The local press was interested, but Blair wanted to aim higher than that. She wanted CNN or MSNBC to respond.

Intending to cast a wide net, she was so engrossed with her tweets and posts that she hadn't heard Maribel climb the stairs. Something made her look up from the laptop, and she saw Maribel leaning on the door.

"Hey, I didn't mean to interrupt you. You've been at it for two hours. I thought you might like a break. I noticed the kittens were out in the field playing. It's pretty adorable."

Blair smiled. "Skeeter isn't chasing them?"

"Nope, he's been inside with me, hoping I'll drop a few morsels on the floor. Whenever I'm preparing food, nothing else will distract him from his primary mission."

"Primary mission?"

"Begging for food. I'm a softie and can't ever resist his puppy dog eyes." Maribel cupped her mouth and whispered, "Don't ever tell him this, but I usually buy extra so I can feed him a few treats."

"You are a softie. I would like to take a break. I'd love to see the kittens frolicking in the back yard. I need to let my posts marinate. Hopefully someone will want to come for a taste. As much as I hate the idea of travel, I don't think a rally in Ellensburg will have enough of an impact. I know it's a college town and better than most places on the east side, but Seattle is known for its social consciousness."

"I can help. If you want." Maribel looked profoundly uncomfortable.

Blair appraised her new friend. "Don't take this the wrong way, but you don't seem like the activist sort. Sweet, kind, humble, yes. Wanting to be out in the limelight, nope."

"On occasion it came with the territory," Maribel mumbled almost too low for Blair to hear.

"What territory?"

"Later."

"Oh right, that mysterious revelation that you promised to tell me about after dinner. I shouldn't look a gift horse in the mouth. I'd be delighted for any assistance you have to offer. I hope you don't mind grunt work. I'm sure I'll have plenty of that." Blair lifted herself off the comfortable recliner. Taking a few steps until she was directly in front of Maribel, she gently placed her lips on the shy woman. "You're precious. Thank you for all your support. I sense that coming out of that comfort zone and getting political is going to be a real stretch for you."

"More than you realize. Pa was a simple man, with simple ideas. He wasn't a rabid right-winger or anything, but I suspect, had he been healthier when the whole MAGA movement started, he would have jumped on board. He was far too sick in the end to bother with politics. But he loved being American and was so proud of me. He watched every single Olympics, reveling in a US win. Talking smack about our country would have riled him up."

Blair's blood pressure began to rise. "Is that what you think the congresswomen are doing?"

Maribel shrugged. "I don't know. I try to stay away from politics. I don't even vote in every election. Pa had a hard time at first with my, uh…me being attracted to women. But when the church we went to started harassing me, he came around real quick. We found another place of worship and some of his views on certain things were beginning to soften."

"Hate is a dangerous thing. I don't think it's ever un-American to call out hypocrisy, hate, racism, sexism, or homophobia. That isn't tearing down America, that's challenging what we have come to stand for." Blair's voice began to rise.

"People have stopped listening to each other," Maribel added softly. "Too much yelling and not enough listening."

"Sorry."

"No, don't be. I like your passion. I'll listen but I kinda like a softer tone when someone's trying to educate me. My pa never raised his voice, and I always listened to him. Sometimes the quietest voice in the room and the person who doesn't speak the most is the one we all ought to listen to."

"Good point. I have a bad habit of raising my voice when I feel strongly about something. I'll try not to yell. I know you believe in God. I need to respect that. It's not that

I'm an atheist, I just don't subscribe to organized religion. There aren't too many organized religions that embrace the LGBTQ community. Sure, there are pockets, here and there. Churches you can find that are more accepting. It appalls me when we praise those churches for their acceptance as if accepting people is such a huge sacrifice." Blair chuckled. "Rant over, take me to the adorable furballs." Following Maribel down the stairs to the back patio, Blair looked forward to a relaxing evening with her enigmatic host.

The light breeze frolicked across Blair's skin as she watched the kittens playing in the field. They seemed to chase nothing and everything at the same time. Mama's tail swished while she kept a watchful eye. Blair was enjoying her time in the sun as she relaxed to the music piped to the outside patio through surprisingly clear speakers. This was another astounding feature to an already spectacular home. Blair noticed how many of the artists were women with sultry voices. Maribel definitely had a preferred style of music. Blair approved.

†

Maribel took a moment to study Blair after she'd settled outside. She watched as the breeze caused her hair to flutter in the wind. Blair absently brushed back the errant strand, tucking it neatly behind her ear before turning her attention back to the acrobatics of the kittens.

When Maribel opened the sliding glass door with one hand, pushing it farther to the left to create a large enough opening, Skeeter rushed outside. She knew he might make a beeline for the kittens. He only wanted to play, but Maribel knew a large dog barreling in their direction would scare the kittens away.

"Skeeter, stop," she commanded.

He turned his head back toward her voice, tongue lolling to the side and gave her a pleading look.

"No, you stay on the patio."

With his tail between his legs, he ambled to Blair who laughed when he laid himself heavily on the stones. An exasperated cross between a groan and a whine escaped his lips.

Blair patted him on the top of his head. "You're such a good boy. I know how you feel. If I didn't think I would have chased them away, I'd be right there with you in the field with those adorable kittens. No play time for us, huh?"

Maribel set the plate of marinated meat on the deluxe, gleaming stainless-steel grill. Turning the dial until the electric ignition sparked to create the even blue flame, she reduced the heat to medium. Before joining Blair on the patio, Maribel closed the glass door to her home. She hated to let the flies or worse, hornets, infiltrate her house. Skeeter had been stung on more than one occasion when she'd been too lax to keep them out.

"Hey, mind if I join you while I let the grill heat up?"

"You are so silly. It's your house. Are you always this polite?"

"Pa insisted on manners."

“Skeeter is well trained. That’s amazing that he didn’t keep going.” Blair turned in Maribel’s direction, shielding her eyes from the sun.

“He’s not that well trained. I tell him not to roll in whatever stinky pile of crap he seems to always find, but he never listens.”

“Why do dogs do that? I understand why pigs do it. They don’t have sweat glands and rolling in mud cools them off.”

“True. I read somewhere that it’s instinctual. Dogs are hunters, predators. They do it to mask their smell so they can sneak up on prey.” Maribel laughed. “Skeeter doesn’t need to sneak up on his food. The meat I give him has been dead for a long time.”

“Cats don’t roll in shit,” Blair noted.

“That’s because cats are fastidious and like pigs, they need to regulate their temperature. They do this by grooming because rolling in mud with all that fur wouldn’t work the same as it does with pigs.”

“How do you know all this?”

“I wanted to be a vet when I was younger. I read a lot. My life took a different direction. I never went to college. I made my living another way.”

“So you alluded to. I can’t wait to get the whole story.”

Earlier, Maribel had blurted her offer of assistance and she’d meant it. She did want to help. Sponsorship by the NRA, and until recently being a vocal supporter of their mission, had never registered with her before. She’d not had to face the fallout of a school shooting. Coming face to face with the grim reality was challenging everything she ever believed or had been taught by her papa. The real question would be whether Blair would accept the sincerity of her offer after she learned everything. Was there a happy middle ground? Maribel knew she could never give up her guns or her vocation. God had bestowed on her this talent for a reason. Could she help Blair understand and accept that? Maybe if Maribel helped Blair, she could be the very best spokesperson for reasonable gun control. She'd have to give up some of her sponsorships, but the tragedy had profoundly affected her as well. This was an easy sacrifice to make.

"I better check to see if the grill is up to temp. Strike while the coals are hot."

"I don't think gas grills work that way. You're uncomfortable and that's your go-to stress reliever. A redirect," Blair stated with mirth. Maribel was happy to see her lips curl in a smile to take any edge off the observation.

"And you call me on it every time. That's your go-to moniker." Maribel lifted the lid and carefully placed the steaks and chicken onto the grill. "I hope you're hungry."

"I sure am. I can smell garlic. My mouth is watering."

†

Blair watched as Maribel's nervous energy reached a fever pitch. Maribel wasn't exactly flitting around, that didn't quite fit. However, she kept grabbing the dirty dishes and fastidiously wiping every available spot on the counters, the grill, and the stone patio table where Blair had devoured a meal fit for a queen.

Blair had offered to help, almost demanded to, if she were honest, but Maribel won the battle with her quiet insistence.

"Please continue to sit and relax. I'd rather you take time to digest the meal. Doing the dishes and cleaning up is soothing to me. There's something comforting about the ritual. That's what it is to me, a ritual, a tradition. Pa used to grill until the very end when he handed over the tongs to me. I always cleaned." She held her hand up. "I know you think that's terribly sexist, but it wasn't like that. I've always enjoyed cleaning. He let me because he understood that."

When Maribel came back out, wiping her hands on her shorts and sucking in a large breath, Blair stood and grasped her hand to lead her to the empty chair next to where she'd been sitting.

"Please, sit down. I don't want you to tell me what you're so afraid to share. Talk to me about what it was like for you growing up. How you got Skeeter. What you were like as a little girl. Your friendship with Sandy. Blabber on about anything but the tiny nugget of information that put that look of terror on your face. We'll get to that later. For now, I want to know the real you, not an insignificant fact you believe will change what I think about you."

Maribel let go of Blair's hand and settled into the chair. She closed her eyes and then turned her head to look at Blair. "Okay, but do I also get to learn about little Blair?"

Blair brought her own chair closer and the scrape of the legs of the chair over the stone combined with the buzz of the hummingbird. The tiny bird was feasting on the bright red flowers lining the perimeter of the patio. She grabbed Maribel's hand again and started stroking her palm. That was something that had always relaxed Blair when her previous lover held her hand during a long flight. It was the thing she remembered most about that relationship and the one thing that had kept them together for far longer than she knew was prudent. They weren't right for each other, but at least Andie had always been sensitive to her moods and fears. She was a keeper for someone but not Blair.

"Little Blair was an angry child and not worth knowing."

"I doubt that very much. Sometimes hurt leads to anger, and we should pray for understanding. Animals lash out when they're hurt or afraid. That doesn't make them evil."

"Stop procrastinating. What was your favorite thing to do as a child?"

"Skeet shooting." Maribel cringed and Blair thought she was waiting for Blair to flare and chastise her. Blair held her expression in check. She hadn't been raised around guns, but obviously Maribel had. She'd already insinuated that, due to necessity, hunting wasn't a luxury sport for her and her father.

"Okay. Not what I expected, and I have to admit, I know absolutely nothing about skeet shooting." Blair smiled.

"Is it like in those cheesy carnivals? You shoot a bunch of little ducks on a conveyer belt with a rifle."

Maribel's eyes held her amusement. "Not even close."

"So, are you going to tell me what it is or not?"

Maribel got a faraway look in her eyes as she began to talk about what was clearly a passion. "I used to toddle around, following my pa everywhere. He didn't have anyone to care for me, so as far back as I can remember, he let me come with him when he went hunting for our food. I must have bugged him incessantly, because he finally let me hold a shotgun."

"How old were you?"

"Maybe five or six." Maribel crinkled her nose. "I was six, I think. Because I remember I thought I was a big girl now that I was in first grade."

Blair hadn't managed to hide her surprise or disapproval. "Your father gave you a loaded gun at six?"

"Nah, it wasn't loaded. He made me wait until I was maybe eight to shoot it."

Blair shook her head but smiled to lessen what might be perceived as judgment. "Well then, that's comforting."

Maribel laughed. "He gave me a quick run-down on how to shoot, and I don't think he expected I would hit anything. I was determined to be like my pa, and I wanted to shoot my own dinner. I'd been catching fish as young as five, so I thought I should be able to help my pa with fresh meat. I ended up on my ass, with a huge bruise on my shoulder from the kickback. But I was eating the duck I'd shot that same evening when we sat down to eat. Pa said I was a natural."

"I can't pretend to understand the need to hunt for my own food, but I don't think I could look an animal in the eye and shoot one. I'd see Bambi's mother if I ever tried."

"It was the obvious pride my papa had for me that made me love skeet shooting."

"Still haven't quite told me what skeet shooting is. The only thing I got from that is shotgun not rifle," Blair prompted. "Oh, and it all started with your need to hunt like your papa."

"Papa decided to nurture my talent. He made a deal with a guy he knew that had an expensive skeet thrower. If the guy would let me practice with the thrower, he would give him fresh elk. We barely had enough money to feed ourselves, so buying a thrower was out of the realm of possibility for us."

"What's a skeet thrower?"

"It's a mechanical device that sends clay targets into the air. The better the machine, the faster they fly. Being able to shoot the clay targets that come from different directions at blazing speeds was something I took to like a duck to water."

"Did you still continue to hunt with your dad?"

Maribel shook her head. "Not too often, no. I was happy to see the pride in my papa's eyes when he would watch me practice. And the bonus was not having to kill something in the process. It wasn't long before my stomach couldn't take seeing a dead animal that I'd shot. The one exception was elk. It's the best tasting steak you'll ever eat. I don't elk hunt anymore. I gave that up not too long ago. I'm more likely to nurse a critter back to health. Pa stopped hunting so much when I began making money for us. Shooting competitions can pay well. Especially when they underestimate who has signed up. Pa made a few side bets that doubled the winnings."

Blair began to laugh. "I can imagine there were hefty egos involved. I would have liked to see that. A little girl kicking their chauvinistic asses."

"It wasn't always very pretty. Pa got into a few nasty scraps. Bruised egos are a dangerous business sometimes. I had to patch him up on more than one occasion. I begged him not to antagonize the competition, but he said it was worth it to wipe the arrogant smirks off their faces."

Blair gestured to the house and the land. "So, all this is from shooting competitions?"

Maribel bit her lip. "Yeah, I know. It doesn't seem very fair. I think about professions like nursing or social work, teaching, too, and they get paid peanuts compared to what I've made in shooting competitions."

Blair let go of Maribel's hand only long enough to move her chair so she was facing Maribel and grabbed both hands. She squeezed. "You're like a sports heroine. A role model to little girls. Don't ever underestimate how powerful that can be. A modern-day Annie Oakley. That's wicked cool. Hey, I just thought of something."

"What?"

"Is skeet shooting an Olympic sport? I'll bet you could totally compete. I mean, if your house is anything to go by, you're good. Like Olympics good, right?"

Maribel looked down and wouldn't meet Blair's eyes. "Yeah, it's an Olympic sport. Although women didn't compete for a short time, they brought the sport back for women in 2000."

Blair was filled with excitement for her new friend. "You should totally go for it. Try out for the team or whatever a person does to compete in the Olympics."

Slowly raising her eyes, Maribel looked intently at Blair with a puzzled expression. "You're not disappointed or disgusted with me?"

"Why would I be disgusted with you? I don't understand. Is this the big secret?"

"Not exactly. I thought with you planning a rally against gun violence, you'd have a problem with, you know…"

"I don't think shooting clay pigeons is the same as threatening someone with an AK-47. It's ridiculous, this whole notion of a constitutional right to form a militia. Do those yahoos really think they would have any chance against the US military? It's the NRA and the rabid White Nationalists I have issues with. Just because I'd never have a gun in my home doesn't mean I have an issue with something like skeet shooting." Blair began shaking her head. "That's exactly the stupid shit those opposed to reasonable gun laws keep saying, trying to scare the masses by telling lies. No one is saying we want to take away all guns, but when it's as easy to buy a gun as a roll of toilet paper, innocent people die." The damn tears filled Blair's eyes again. Until she could convert her emotions into doing something to change things, she suspected she'd continue to be an emotional wreck.

Blair couldn't understand why Maribel still looked pale and guilty as she once again redirected the conversation. "Your turn. What was your favorite thing as a child?"

"Okay. Fair is fair. Then after, I want to know what else is causing that unattractive shade of white with a bit of green around the edges. You look like you're about to hurl any minute."

†

Maribel was glad to have the focus somewhere else as Blair took a few seconds to compose herself. She thought Blair looked like her competition when they were psyching themselves up right before they had to shoot. Ritualistic preparations weren't uncommon.

"The Sperm Donor met Mom when he was in his final year of law school. He was supposed to marry a high society girl but ended up getting my mother pregnant. I don't think he expected his parents to cut him off, so when the money stopped flowing, shit got way too real for him."

"I'm sorry."

"Don't be. He left when I was about five. See, his grandmother died, and she was the one who slipped him money for a few years. His trust fund didn't kick in until he turned thirty, but he couldn't hang on. Not all attorneys make a shitload of money. You have to be connected and his parents made sure those connections dried up until he 'came to his senses.' His abrupt departure festered and matured as I grew. Surly does not begin to describe my teenage years."

"All teenagers are surly. I had my moments where I'm sure my pa wanted to give me to anyone willing to take me."

"I was the kid without a father. What do kids who have no friends do? Solo activities. I read a lot. I found my voice in high school. Political activism was perfect for an angry young woman who was well read. Honestly, you would have hated me. I was an insufferable know-it-all. Only my opinions counted."

"You're still like that," Maribel teased.

"Hey now. I've only slightly railed against your Bible-thumping tendencies. And, I've given you a pass on skeet shooting. That should count for something. Trust me, I listen a lot more than I used to. At least I try to understand other perspectives now. Of course, that's only because I want to get inside the enemies' heads so I can find their weakness." Blair erupted in a version of an evil laugh.

"What else was little Blair like?"

"I think we have something else in common. I've saved my fair share of wounded animals. Bunnies, baby birds, kittens, you name it. When I was little, I also thought I might grow up to be a vet, but then I got bit by a dog and that scared me. Some dogs still scare me. Skeeter is a real treat because he's not very territorial or aggressive."

Not wanting to open wounds, Maribel didn't want to ask how Blair's father ended up back in her mother's life long enough to father Trina. She stayed on neutral ground. "Yeah, Skeeter's been a wonderful companion. Saved me from turning to drink when Pa died." And then the question simply popped out of her mouth because she was too curious. "How'd it happen…that Trina…"

"The Sperm Donor doesn't have a roving eye. He has a roving dick. I have two half-sisters and one half-brother. That I know of. Of course, I don't know them, not really. We don't run in the same circles. His wife was sick and tired of his shit and kicked him out for a while. He came running back to Mom."

"I'm guessing that added to your bitterness. You were what, seventeen when he came back?"

Blair nodded. "But then, the Republican Party came calling, and they needed him to reunite with his very connected wife. His political star was rising, and she decided she wanted to go along for the ride and took him back. She gave him the same deal as before. He had to sever all ties with Mom. I don't believe he had ever seen a picture of Trina, much less held or comforted her."

"I wish your father had been more like mine. I'm glad your mother was there for you. We have that in common. Being raised by one parent. I remember those times I wished so hard for a mother. I asked Pa once why I didn't have a mother. He said, I did, but she was called back to the Lord. Pa was quick to add that it didn't mean she wasn't there watching over us. He told me he couldn't go out and get a new one because she'd always be there in both our hearts and it wouldn't be right. I didn't like thinking I might be the cause of Pa doing the wrong thing, so I never asked him to get me a new mother that would be around to see me shoot."

"That's where you and I differ. The Sperm Donor left such a bad taste in my mouth, I never asked Mom to go out and get me another father. He had a quick temper and an even faster back hand. At least Mom nipped that in the bud. Once was enough, though."

Maribel's sorrowful eyes met Blair's. "I am so sorry. No matter what kind of trouble I got into and I got into plenty, Pa never once hit me. I'm sure I deserved it because I was a very active child."

"I don't believe any child should be hit, especially in the face. You're lucky. On occasion he used sweet treats to keep me in line, but that wasn't his go-to parental tactic. Yelling is an understatement. After the one time he hit me and Mom put her foot down, he turned to berating me at every turn. A crying child was an irritant. I'm glad he left. Okay, enough of these depressing topics. Even though it's painful to remember, Trina was the one who had the biggest impact on me. I couldn't continue to be that surly teen because she was such a happy baby. I loved being a big sister."

"I'll bet you were the best. I never got to be anyone's big sister. That would have been nice. A lot less lonely, too."

Blair turned her face to the sky. "Wow. It's late, isn't it?" Yawning, she continued, "I'm more tired than I thought I would be. I haven't done a damn thing all day except search the internet, but I'm exhausted. Your big confession will have to wait until tomorrow. Are you sure you don't mind helping out with the rally? I'm not keeping you from anything, am I?"

"Nope. My morning chores are easy. After I collect the eggs, make a few deliveries, and clean things up, I'm all yours. Put me to work. It will do me good to concentrate on something new."

Blair stood and stretched. "Are you coming? I think you deserve a goodnight kiss after this wonderful evening." Blair winked and Maribel turned a deep shade of red.

"Yeah. I want to make sure you have everything you need." Maribel patted her thigh. "Come on, Skeeter, time to go to bed." Skeeter lifted his body from the patio and stretched his paws out. A tiny sound came out of his mouth as he yawned in an exaggerated fashion. "Guess you're tired too, boy. All that begging earlier must have exhausted you."

Chapter Eleven

Maribel was deep into reminiscing about the previous evening as she lay in her bed. True to her word, Blair had taken the initiative and pulled her close for a searing kiss before she retreated to the guest bedroom for the evening.

Although she wasn't shocked by the kiss, she was surprised and had a lot of unanswered questions. Questions she should have asked last night before allowing the kiss to continue. Blair had announced she was going to give Maribel a goodnight kiss, but Maribel didn't know what it meant. Were they dating? Could this be a precursor to a real relationship? She didn't know anything, and she wasn't sure how to ask. Should she come right out and pepper Blair with the questions rolling around in her head about what the kiss meant to her? Skeeter interrupted her with a doggy version of a grumble as he resettled his body on the end of the bed. Apparently in her restless cogitations, she had inadvertently kicked him. It was more of a nudge, but Skeeter was a big baby.

The sound of a slamming door caused Maribel to abruptly sit up and throw the covers aside. She didn't have time to get dressed and rushed into the hall in her boi shorts and tank top. Skeeter jumped from the bed and trotted along.

An angry Blair met her in the hallway. Her bag was slung over her shoulder. Maribel wondered what the hell was going on. "Wh…what's the matter?"

"How could you?" Blair spit out. "The fucking spokeswoman for the NRA?"

Maribel grabbed Blair's arm. "Wait. Please. Let me explain."

Blair glared at Maribel's hand and shook it off. "Keep your hands off of me." She began to descend the stairs.

"I was ten years old. Ten. Three years older than Trina. What ten-year-old do you know that decides on sponsors?"

Blair turned to face Maribel and her eyes softened before she seemed to crumple on the stairs. "Quick to anger. You should stay clear of me."

Maribel cautiously approached and sat next to Blair on the step. She noticed Skeeter had slinked back to the bedroom. He always hated when anyone raised their voice, especially Maribel who so rarely showed anger or frustration.

"Pa made all the decisions. To him, what they were offering was a future. Guaranteed food on the table and our own high-quality skeet thrower. Pa was always afraid that those liberals would take away his guns, which in turn would take away his ability to hunt and provide for his little girl. That might be foreign to you, but that's what he'd been taught. He believed that with all his heart and soul, and I was the center of his universe."

A cold look returned to Blair's eyes. "That doesn't explain the statement you made to the press right after the shooting. 'Don't bother to follow me or this gun-toting Olympian might exercise her rights to shoot anyone who has the balls to trespass, and my nine gold medals prove that I don't miss whatever I set my sights on.' I believe those were your exact words," Blair ground out.

"Haven't you ever responded in anger? That reporter was using the tragedy to sell a story. I was mad. I didn't want to be in the spotlight. Especially not for this. It made me sick to my stomach and guilty. She said I wasn't a good role model for little girls, and I began to think she might be right. I'm not. You are."

Blair put her head in her hands. "We should be enemies. I suppose the NRA is still your sponsor."

Maribel hung her head before slowly rising. "Will you come with me, and I'll show you the secret room?"

Blair put her hands on her thighs and sighed before standing. She trudged down the stairs to follow. Maribel wondered if it was curiosity or had Maribel managed to reach a small part of Blair that had developed a bigger capacity to listen to another's perspective as she'd confessed. Maribel didn't care why Blair was softening, she was simply glad she had a chance to explain. Albeit a small one.

Opening the door, she wondered what Blair saw as she looked around the room filled with framed photos of Maribel, and handcrafted glass and wood cabinets that displayed all her medals, including the nine from the three Olympics she'd competed in. One wall had an entire rack of single-and double-barrel shotguns. Skeeter had followed but was keeping his distance. Maribel thought he was smart because she wasn't sure if Blair's anger would flare again. The picture that made her cringe most, was the one with the NRA logo prominently displayed behind a young gap-toothed girl.

Maribel broke the silence. "My pa had this room built. I never liked it, but he was so proud of it that I never had the heart to dismantle the room after he died." Maribel saw Blair's eyes looking intently at the promotional material in which the NRA had featured her prominently. They had rolled the dice, betting on Maribel gaining fame, and it had paid off.

"They used you. Don't you understand that? My God, you were just a little girl."

"I know that now. I did research on the NRA after the shooting and decided to begin distancing myself from them. There's a reason the NRA severed its ties with the Olympic Shooting Team in '94. There were valid arguments over how the NRA was using athletes for promotional purposes. A panel revoked their sponsorship, so they found other ways to capitalize. I was one of those ways, and we were easy pickings because we were so poor and desperate. They banked on me becoming a phenomenon before I participated in the Olympics. Pa was loyal to them because they helped in the beginning, and I went along because I loved my pa."

"That photo is disgusting. I can't even look at it," Blair cried out in agony.

Maribel marched to the picture and yanked the framed promotion from the wall, smashing it on her knee. The glass sprinkled the carpet.

Blair's eyes widened. "Don't move. You're going to cut your foot. Let me get something to clean up the glass."

A whine from Skeeter interrupted the tense moment.

"Skeeter, stay," Maribel commanded.

"Come on, Skeeter. Come with me and we'll search for something to clean up the glass before your mama cuts herself."

After Blair left, Maribel pushed her hand through her hair and sighed. She knew she wasn't off the hook yet, but she thought maybe she'd made progress.

†

The warring emotions inside of Blair were making it hard for her to separate Maribel the woman, from Maribel the literal poster child for the NRA. But the pleading look in Maribel's eyes was too hard to ignore. Blair was trying to understand. It was nearly impossible to think that Maribel had ever chosen to be in bed with the NRA. But then again, this was Maribel. The sweet compassionate woman she had come to know over the past few days. The one who built a mansion for feral kittens. The person who had a unique ability to soothe her grieving soul. She'd offered her home to someone she barely knew. Didn't she deserve a chance? Blair nodded. She did.

Opening closets and cupboards, Blair found a broom, dustpan, and vacuum. She decided she would need all three items. Noting how the dustpan could be secured to the broom, she pushed the pan in place and then grabbed the vacuum with her free hand. "All right, here we go. All set to rescue your mom."

Maribel was standing awkwardly in the same spot. Blair couldn't help but notice her vulnerability, especially clad in a skimpy tank top and underwear. God, she was sexy with her nipples peeking through the flimsy material. Long, well-muscled legs emerged from the sexiest boi shorts Blair had ever seen. Royal-blue material wrapped around her body, and Blair had an overwhelming desire for Maribel to turn around. She was sure the shorts would show off a finely shaped ass. *Stop it*, she chastised herself.

Blair approached the mess and began sweeping the large pieces into the dustpan. She looked around the room. Damn, she'd forgotten a garbage can. "Um, be right back. I don't imagine you'd have a garbage can in a trophy room."

"No, sorry. I rarely go in this room. No need for one."

After returning with the can she'd found under the sink, Blair finished the clean up. She smiled at Maribel who was looking at her sleepwear and blushing.

"I need to get dressed and gather the eggs. Do you mind if we finish this conversation over breakfast? I promise, there's nothing like fresh eggs to start your day right."

"Sure. Can I help? I've never gathered eggs before."

"It isn't a life altering experience, but sure. Although, I don't recommend you taking eggs from Henrietta. I'll gather hers. She still doesn't like me, even though I hand-raised her. Chickens are like people. They all have their own unique personalities, and Henrietta is a bit prickly. Always has been."

"What do you do with all those eggs? Surely, you can't eat that many in a day."

Maribel laughed and it was genuine, not the nervous laughter that might have filled the air as a result of their earlier tense exchange. "I like fresh eggs, but no, I can't eat that many in one day. Besides, I've heard it's bad for your cholesterol or something like that. Of course, tomorrow they'll say it's good for you. I can't seem to keep up."

"Do you sell them at the farmers' market?"

"Goodness, no. That would mean having to interact with hordes of people. I'm not very good at that, besides I don't need the money." Maribel looked away. "There's some folks in dire straits down the road. Sometimes I bring them to Sandy. She uses them in her baking, but most go to the families that remind me of Pa and me before…"

Maribel was making it impossible for Blair to stay angry with her. God damn it. Why'd she have to be a fucking saint in every way possible but her support of the NRA?

†

The sound of clucking chickens filled the coop. A few of the nests had eggs sitting on top, ready to add to the cartons Maribel had retrieved from the closet.

"You'd better start with those." Maribel pointed to the eggs sitting on top of the mixture of straw and hay.

Even though Maribel was sure that Henrietta would peck at her, she didn't want to grab the aluminum spade that would distract the irritable chicken. She was quick this morning, and Henrietta only managed a few pecks before Maribel had successfully gathered two eggs.

The whites of Blair's eyes grew. "Do they all attack like that?"

"Nah, only Henrietta. I don't blame them. What would you do if a doctor reached in and plucked out your eggs without your permission?"

"Not sure if that's the same thing. You didn't stick your hand or other device up Henrietta's hoohaw."

A deep belly laugh emerged from Maribel. "Graphic description, but true. Still, on some level, they know someone is stealing their babies. Sometimes I think about that and feel bad, but then my love of fresh eggs and those families in need trumps my momentary bout of guilt." Maribel hoped that explanation went further and created an analogy for why her pa accepted a deal with the devil.

Blair tilted her head. "Ethical dilemmas are challenging, aren't they?"

Maribel pointed to a spotted chicken whose head moved while her tiny eyes blinked. She was watching Blair, maybe studying her, Maribel thought. "Prudence is usually mellow. If you want to try to get her eggs, I don't believe she'll peck you. She's never pecked at me."

Blair grinned. "Okay." Hesitantly approaching Prudence, Blair cautiously moved her hand under the chicken and triumphantly held out the egg she'd gathered. "I did it, and she didn't even move."

"Yup, that's Prudence. She's like a Zen Goddess. I'll be sad when she stops laying."

"I'm almost afraid to ask what you do with your hens after they stop laying eggs."

"I don't kill them, if that's what you think. I've been tempted to give them to those families, but I couldn't do it. Probably for the same reasons I stopped hunting. Even worse."

"Because it would be like killing a member of your family, right?"

"Exactly! Even the crotchety old aunt, like Henrietta. I would have welcomed one of those growing up. It was always just me and Pa after my grandma died. I don't know what happened to the rest of my family. I think there was a falling out when my mother married Pa. And my grandma was the only one left in my pa's family."

"I'm sorry."

"Don't be. I had a good childhood. I was loved, and that's what counts."

"I suppose so. I need to find a way to forgive my mother. Even though Trina was the light of my life, she also represents my mother's weakness with respect to the Sperm Donor. Trina was too good to hate. Too innocent. She was pure joy, so all my anger went toward my mother. I don't think I've ever come to terms with that. And now that she's letting him stay, my rage is hard to control. I let it spill over. I'm sorry."

"You don't have a thing to be sorry for. I know I'm the last person you want helping with the rally, but I'd like to be part of it. I promise, I'm going to sever all ties to the NRA. I'd already decided to do that. I want nothing to do with them anymore. My papa wasn't an unreasonable man. He would understand my decision."

"You want to join the movement? Will you speak at the rally? Your voice might be more powerful than any other."

"I'm not so great with words. When they interviewed me before, I said some things. Stuff that will come back to haunt me and won't be helpful."

"Will you let me worry about that? You could speak from the heart and tell your story in a way that will penetrate the wall that has divided our country on this issue."

"I'll do anything to replace the look in your eyes that I saw this morning. I was so afraid."

"I know," Blair answered softly. "I know."

"Our views might not align all the time…"

"I better get used to that, huh? That might work to my advantage. I'd already know the competing arguments and be able to respond intelligently on the issues. Right now, I'll admit I don't know a lot about gun regulations currently in place, or ones that are being proposed by the groups I intend to join. I only know that I want the gun violence to stop."

Maribel tried not to become defensive. "Do you honestly believe that the rabid Second Amendment supporters don't want the same things? I don't think anyone is cheering after a mass shooting."

"No, I don't believe that most people who are opposed to stricter gun laws want people to die. But that doesn't mean I don't hold judgment about their resistance. Now, don't get mad. I saw the whole interview where you lamented about the inconvenience of background checks because of your need to buy large amounts of ammunition. Don't you think that people's lives matter more than convenience? And that law doesn't apply in the state of Washington, so you were spouting crap fed to you by someone with an agenda."

"Yeah, what do I know. I'm just a dumb hick." Maribel stalked off not caring if the eggs in her cartons broke before she reached the kitchen. Skeeter dutifully followed and Maribel caught him looking back at Blair. She imagined he was trying to figure out why his new friend wasn't coming with them. She knew she shouldn't have said that. She'd made progress with Blair. At least Blair wasn't angry with her anymore, but what she said hurt. Maribel needed time to lick her wounds.

CHAPTER TWELVE

Blair watched Maribel walk away and knew she had landed a mortal blow. Why did she have to take her argument so far? She always did that. Going straight for the jugular no matter who her opponent was. Prefacing the statement with, "now don't get mad" was like telling a person ready to jump in a pool "now don't get wet." The horrible thing was that Blair could handle anger, but the hurt in Maribel's eyes was nearly her undoing.

Blair didn't know what to do. Should she go after Maribel or let her cool down? Shuffling to the back patio, she set down her cartons of eggs and sat in the chair. Although it was a little chilly, she deserved to shiver without proper clothing for the morning temperatures. Maybe she was the one who needed to cool off. Perhaps her anger had not dissipated, and she'd resorted to an unattractive passive-aggressive jab at Maribel. She should apologize.

Remaining immobile with her arms wrapped around her body to fend off the chill, Blair let indecision keep her rooted to the chair. The sound of the sliding glass door opening caught her attention, and she turned around to see Skeeter bounding in her direction. She opened her mouth to say something to Maribel, but the door quickly closed, effectively shutting off any conversation. *Crap*. Blair was definitely going to have to make the first move.

Skeeter wagged his tail, and she began to pet him while she pondered what she would say to Maribel to make things right again. Various thoughts ran through her mind, and she rejected every one of them. Should she say something like she didn't mean to suggest Maribel was uneducated? No, that would likely call attention to the one thing that seemed to hurt her the most. What about simply saying, I'm sorry? Blair had discarded that as well. The words were inadequate. What was she sorry for? She continued to run different scenarios through her head and hadn't realized how much time had passed when she heard the door open again.

Maribel had two plates loaded with food in her hands. She set them on the table and announced, "Breakfast is ready. Better eat up before the omelets cool. Nothing worse than cold eggs."

Blair stood slowly and made her way to the table. She felt like she was walking to her own execution. She didn't know if the words she'd settled on would work, but she tried them out, anyway. "I'm an ass. The last thing I ever wanted to do was hurt you. We all drink the Kool-Aid, Maribel. It's just that my Kool-Aid and your Kool-Aid are different flavors."

Maribel smiled. "I hate Kool-Aid. Too much sugar." She pointed to the plate. "Eat."

"Looks scrumptious. Thank you."

Maribel nodded. "Welcome."

Blair picked up her fork and took a bite. "Mm. Oh holy hell, this is fantastic. Where did you learn to cook? You're like the perfect woman." Blair was desperately trying to get them to that place where they were at ease with one another and the conversation flowed freely.

"Pa taught me."

Okay, short sentences. Not great, but at least Maribel was talking.

Blair set down her fork. "I'm not eating another bite of this delicious omelet until we clear the air. No matter how good it is, I'll have indigestion if we don't get back to our normal."

Maribel sighed. "I'm overly sensitive about education. I dropped out of school at an early age. I think that was one of the reasons Sandy and I never worked. I always felt inferior to her because she has a college degree."

"I can work with that. Maribel," Blair grinned and began, "you have an entire room that is your library. I've checked it out, remember? Although I did notice a healthy number of romance and erotica books, you had an amazing variety. Your books on philosophy and science are a lot more sophisticated than anything I ever read in college."

"I doubt that very much."

"One thing you will learn about me is that I never lie. Since we both like to read, we can do a little independent research and then come together for a respectful conversation. I vow to keep my assholery to a minimum."

Maribel laughed. "Assholery? Is that a word?"

"It is. At least it's in the urban dictionary. I'm not sure about Webster's. Although asshat made it into Webster's."

"You're pulling my leg," Maribel insisted.

"Nope. I looked it up once. Do you want to know the origins of the word? I looked that up, too."

"Of course. I am on the edge of my seat," Maribel joked.

"Apparently it goes back as far as to the movie *Raising Arizona* in 1987. Then in 1991 there was a reference in the movie, *City Slickers*. Although *That 70's Show* had Red saying 'dumbass' all the time, he also said 'asshat.' Contrary to popular belief, this is not a word invented by the millennial generation."

"What kind of job did you have again? Clearly you've had way too much time on your hands."

"Clearly. I love the internet." Blair was so relieved that she'd managed to break through the ice, she picked up her fork and took another bite of food. "Still delicious even though it's no longer piping hot."

†

Maribel knew she should be practicing. The 2020 Olympics were practically around the corner. She hadn't planned on meeting someone who would shift her focus. Winning gold did not come without a lot of dedication to the sport. But Maribel didn't have the motivation, and she didn't want to scare Blair away. Surely it was only a small sacrifice to spend whatever time Blair needed while her father remained with her mother.

Maribel pushed away the panic that found its way to the surface when she thought about Blair returning to her job. A long-distance relationship was doable, especially one where plane rides weren't required, but she was enjoying the intense amount of time she was spending with Blair. Despite the argument this morning, Maribel was becoming more and more enthralled with Blair. In between her shifts of emotion, Blair was funny and passionate about issues. She cared about causes and was willing to put a great deal of effort into supporting her ardent views. Life with Blair would never be dull. Maribel was getting used to Blair turning on a dime.

They were back to their easy flow and that in itself was a minor miracle. Maribel hadn't made that happen, Blair had.

"So, besides collecting eggs, what's on your agenda for today?" Blair asked.

"I don't have anything planned. I should probably deliver the eggs. That's one thing I try to do every day. Um, you could come with me if you want."

"I'd love to." Blair picked up the breakfast plates and began to clear the table.

"You don't have to do that. Remember, I like cleaning."

"Confession time. I feel uncomfortable sitting here while you basically wait on me hand and foot. Please, I need to contribute."

"All right. You can load the dishwasher while I pull together the items to take with us."

"Items? I thought it was only the eggs." Blair's brow crinkled in confusion.

Maribel's face flushed. "I kinda keep various items in the freezer, like cookies and stuff that I bake, to give to the kids. I also grill up extras most nights and tell them I've made too much for myself again. There's a few steaks and chicken breasts in the fridge I need to pack up, along with those grilled veggies. Plus, I have extras from the garden to give away. When the fruit ripens, I gather that as well. There's way too much for me, and rather than letting it rot, I collect it for the families. There's three that are in dire need."

"How do you possibly decide who to deliver to? I suspect there's more families who could use the assistance."

Maribel tried not to view Blair's questions as judgment. She believed they weren't intended that way.

"That's the hardest part. I do the best I can, and I know it isn't enough," she answered honestly.

Blair nodded once and made her way to the door with the plates and utensils in her hand. Maribel gathered the juice glasses and ketchup bottle and followed Blair inside.

The women made quick work of the dishes and packing up the food. The large cooler was filled to the brim by the time they were ready to leave.

Maribel carried the large cooler, and Blair had the three dozen eggs stacked on top of each other in her hands as they made their way to the truck.

"Hmm, a master griller, cook, and now I see you're a baker, too. Was I ever going to get a taste of your cookies?" Blair shot Maribel a wolfish grin.

"I need to bake more later. I could use an apprentice, and your payment will be one fresh from the oven. Sandy taught me a few tricks."

"I'll just bet she did. How long were you two seeing each other?" Blair's clipped voice had an edge to it that surprised Maribel. Could Blair possibly be jealous?

"Not long. We discovered we were much better as friends."

"You were together long enough for her to show you her baking skills."

Maribel laughed. "That's all she showed me. We barely made it to the sleeping together stage."

"But you did sleep with her, right?"

Maribel sighed. "I was lonely. She's a beautiful woman."

Blair rested her head on the stack of eggs. "Shit, I sound like a jealous lover grilling her new girlfriend about past loves. It's none of my business."

Maribel halted. "Am I your new girlfriend?"

"Fuck." Blair slapped her hand to her mouth and almost dropped the eggs before grabbing the stack and securing them against her body. "I… I… didn't mean that. Of course you wouldn't want to claim me…"

"Sure I would. Well, not the claim part. I don't think claiming is quite the right word. I'd be proud to introduce you as my girlfriend, but I doubt, given our differences, that would be prudent for you. I'm guessing that reporter had a lot to say about us after we left. That's what set you off this morning, right?"

"Haven't we settled that already?"

"I suppose," Maribel hesitantly replied.

"Look, I don't give two shits what that little blonde shark says about you and me. How about we don't define things and see what happens?"

Maribel smiled. "Works for me. Although, it might be good to begin defining the boundaries of, um, the physical part."

Blair chuckled. "I am not having sex with you just yet. I'll let you know when we've spent enough time together to take that step."

"But I have cookies to offer?"

Blair smacked Maribel playfully on the arm. "No fair. You've discovered my sugar addiction quite by accident, and I'll do almost anything for a freshly baked snickerdoodle."

"Good to know."

CHAPTER THIRTEEN

As Maribel's truck traveled down the dusty dirt road, Blair's heart sank. The dilapidated trailers dotting the landscape became increasingly run down before Maribel stopped her truck and took a deep breath, then exited the vehicle.

A small dark-haired girl rushed from a trailer that Blair thought might have been held together with duct tape. The door banged against the side, startling Blair. The girl couldn't have been more than eight. She was wearing ragged clothes, frayed at the edges, with tiny holes in the material. Her feet were bare, but that didn't stop her short legs from propelling her in Maribel's direction. She flung her little body against Maribel who put her arms around the young child and hugged her.

"Mari," she squealed. "You're here. Ma said you probably weren't coming today 'cause it was getting late in the day."

"Got held up. Sorry, Squirt. You been practicing with the tin cans?"

"Yes'm. Ma don't like the noise, but I told her I gotta get good like you and then I can win us some money."

"That's right, Squirt. Now let me get the stuff from the truck to give your mama. I can't stay long. I got a friend with me today. You wanna meet her?"

Soft brown eyes looked up, and the girl turned shy when she nodded.

"Blair, meet Squirt."

The girl giggled. "That's not my name."

"It isn't? Well, dang. I guess I forgot again."

"It's Lucritia."

"Oh, right, right."

Blair held out her hand. "It's very nice to meet you, Lucritia."

Lucritia looked back toward the trailer as a young woman who, Blair guessed, was in her twenties walked toward the truck. She had the same shiny dark hair as Lucritia. "Go ahead, you can shake her hand."

"Sorry I'm late. You have breakfast yet?"

The woman smiled. "Yes, Mother. We still had eggs left."

"Did you run out of bacon or ham?"

"No. I was saving that for dinner."

"I made too much food again for Blair and me, so I brought chicken for you. Cook up the meat tomorrow for breakfast. It's the most important meal of the day."

"Yeah, yeah." The woman gestured with her head at Blair. "Did ya get yourself a girlfriend?"

"Hi, I'm Blair."

"I heard. Danella." The woman took her offered hand. "Mari's an angel. I hope you plan on treating her right."

Blair coughed. "Uh, we met a few days ago."

"Don't care how long ago you met. Still need to treat her right."

"I couldn't agree more. I'm working on it."

Danella squinted at Blair. "All right. You two want to sit a spell? I put water in the fridge to cool."

"Nah, thanks, Danella. I have a few more deliveries to make and then we've got work to do later. Did you find someone to watch Squirt so you can take that job?"

"Nah."

"My offer is still good. I could watch her."

"You can't do all your practicing if you got a kid hanging round. Nope, gotta win those gold medals again. Make us proud. I'll figure something out. It's minimum wage and part-time. Not sure that'll help us any more than what we get from the state right now. It's tempting to go back to…"

Maribel pulled her out of earshot from Lucritia who'd run to Skeeter after he'd jumped from the truck. "Don't you do that. Think of Squirt, if they take you away again."

"I know, I know. But then we wouldn't have to depend on nobody."

"Hang on a little while longer. Please? For me?"

"Sweet talker. Too bad I don't like pussy."

Maribel laughed. "Yeah, and stay away from Hank. I mean it, Danella. He's bad news. I don't want to have to come down here again and threaten to blow off his male bits, regardless of how much you like 'em."

"He's still pissed about that. You need to watch your back, Mari. I'm serious. He's out of jail now. You can't go around threatening every low life that smacks their lady around a little bit."

"He hit Squirt too."

Danella shook her head sadly. "I know and I'm grateful for you stepping in, but I worry about you. At least Lucritia can handle a shotgun. I'm sure he's afraid of her taking a shot at him. Kids ain't gotta worry about going to jail. I taught her that and he knows it. He also knows how good a shot she is. Thanks to you."

"Nothing like a loaded shotgun to even the odds," Maribel answered before going to the truck to retrieve the packages from the cooler and handing them to Danella.

"He come 'round the other day trying to convince me he'd changed. Said he needed someone he trusted to move product. Promised me quick dough for barely any work. I gotta admit I was tempted, but I told him no. That's when he got mean again. Said you was the reason he'd lost his family and his freedom. He swore he was gonna settle the score. Lucritia didn't hesitate. Ran and got that old shotgun you gave her and pointed it right at his crotch. He left, but I saw that look in his eyes."

"Don't worry. My place is secure and wired for contingencies. He isn't the first person to threaten me."

"Your fancy place ain't gonna protect you whilst you're delivering stuff to us."

"I can take care of myself. Promise me you won't go back to that life."

"I promise. I know I gotta think of Lucritia first. Our luck is bound to change soon, huh?"

"Absolutely. I believe in the Lord, and he'll provide the answers."

Danella scoffed. "Yeah, right, like he's been doing all along. You know I don't believe in all that crap. Is that lady of yours a Bible-thumper too?"

Maribel laughed. "Hardly." She turned toward Blair and asked, "Blair, will you give Squirt a dozen eggs, please?"

Blair reached into the truck and plucked the carton from the seat, handing them to Lucritia. While she was startled with the conversation, she tucked it away to ask about later. The nonchalant way Danella talked about the possibility that her young daughter might shoot someone was disconcerting at a minimum. This was a world completely out of the realm of her sheltered life.

"Say thank you to Blair and Mari," Danella commanded.

Before scrambling to the trailer, the small voice said, "Thanks."

"Go put them inside. You're a godsend, Mari. Thank you." Danella accepted the packages and turned toward her trailer. Before going inside, she waved to Maribel.

†

A hand-rolled cigarette dangled from the mouth of a heavily lined face. The old man was stooped over with a prominent curvature of his spine as he sat on a wood crate two feet from the open door of the trailer. If it were possible, this trailer was shabbier than Danella's. Blair didn't know how people survived the paucity.

As soon as the truck came to a stop, the man pulled the cigarette from his mouth and grinned, revealing an appalling lack of teeth. Blair counted two, she wasn't sure if others were hidden, and she wondered how he was able to chew properly.

As if Maribel read her thoughts, she answered, "Eggs are easy on him. I blend other ingredients. He likes my protein shakes."

Blair took another look at Maribel who didn't have an ounce of pity in her eyes. Not like Blair.

"He makes surprisingly good wooden bowls. I trade for them. I don't quite have a set of twelve yet, considering they take a long time to make." Maribel chuckled.

"That big wooden bowl you used the other day for our salad, he made?" Blair had admired the bowl with the interesting patterns running through the grain. She wasn't sure what kind of wood the bowl was made from, but it was beautiful. "Where does he get his raw materials?"

The snick of the truck door signaled that Maribel was ready to make her second delivery. "I find them for him. It gives him something to do. Something he's proud of." Maribel's boots hit the dirt, and before she walked to the man, she retrieved several other containers from her cooler. Blair scrambled to join her with a carton of eggs in her hands.

"Hey, Mr. Simpson. How you doing this morning? Sorry I'm late."

It looked like something was moving inside his mouth, and then he spit on the ground. "Piece of tobacco. I ain't fond of chewin‘ the stuff. Rather smoke it. Who's your lady friend? She's a looker."

"Hey now. Don't go charming her away from me. This is Blair. She wanted to help with the deliveries today."

The old man nodded at Blair. "That's kind of her. Could be a keeper, eh?"

"Early days, Mr. Simpson, so don't be chasing her away."

"Hank's been skunkin‘ around. Keep them sharp eyes open. If I was a younger man, I'd take care of him for ya, but I ain't."

"Don't worry about me. Is your fridge still working? This needs to be kept cold until you're ready to eat it." Maribel walked toward the trailer. "Don't get up. I'll put them away. Blair, can you follow me with the eggs?"

Squalor would have been a kind word to describe the insides. The threadbare couch had several large holes where the foam was peeking out. Maribel opened the old refrigerator and stuck her hand inside. "Damn. This piece of shit is on the fritz again. I wish he would let me buy him a new one."

"He lets you bring food, why doesn't he allow you to get him a new fridge?"

"Says the bowls aren't worth that much."

"So what are you going to do? He'll get sick."

Maribel ran her hand through her hair. "I know. I gotta think."

"What if I told him I liked his bowl so much when you showed it to me that I want to order one and, in exchange, I noticed he needed a new refrigerator?"

"That might work. He's not stupid. He knows that a new fridge is definitely a lot more than a handcrafted wood bowl, but it's the game we play. Thanks, Blair." Maribel took the eggs Blair held out and put them in the heavily chipped white refrigerator.

When Blair reached the bottom step, she turned toward Mr. Simpson. "You're a very talented artist, Mr. Simpson. I couldn't help noticing that refrigerator is on its last legs. Do you think you would be willing to trade one of those large salad bowls like you made for Maribel?"

The old man grinned showing his two teeth. "She's wily too, Mari. Sure, I could do that. Gonna take me a little time, though. You hanging out for a while?"

Blair smiled. “I am. I’d be willing to wait however long it takes. Spending time with Maribel isn’t a punishment,” she joked.

He cackled until a coughing fit overcame him. “Funny, too. You be sure to take good care of each other, and you got yourself a deal.”

†

The man snarled as he watched the truck roll down the road. He was sure neither of the women paid any attention to the ramshackle cabin set a small distance from the dirt path, partially hidden behind the trees. The police knew about the meth houses littering the rural areas in Washington, but they simply could not keep up. At least that was the pat answer given to the public. The greasy haired dealer suspected a bigger reason was their distaste for the area. No one wanted to travel to this part and see the despair and poverty. They would avoid that like the plague. Besides, busting up meth houses was a dangerous business.

That dyke do-gooder was gonna get what was coming to her. He would bide his time and take a shot when she came back ’round again. The times were always different. Today she was later than usual which hadn’t given him enough time to set up, but he knew another opportunity would present itself. He’d be ready.

She’d turned his own flesh and blood against him. Lucritia had pointed the shotgun at his balls, and he knew his girl had the skills. He’d been watching her, too. There was a small part of him that took pride in her for that, but that pride was overshadowed by his anger that she'd had the nerve to point a shotgun at him. He'd need to teach both her and her mama a few lessons on who was in charge.

He let the curtain fall back in place. He needed to cook up more product. He didn't have time for this shit. He'd already wasted the morning waiting for her, and just when he'd given up, she'd rolled down the lane, and he was caught off guard. Fucking bitch was lucky.

He wondered if he should pay his lady and kid another visit later on. Nah, plenty of time for that after the bitch was long gone. There was another woman in the vehicle with her today. He wondered who she was and if she'd provide leverage.

He sniffed, bringing the snot back up his nose and then cleared his throat spitting a large glob of phlegm into the dirty sink. Grabbing a beer from the fridge, he considered his options. He wasn't stupid. He hadn't ever used meth, but a beer and a joint would relax him enough to come up with a plan. Maybe he'd snort a line of coke instead. He'd developed a taste for cocaine while in the joint. It wasn't relaxing, but it sure gave him energy and the feeling of invincibility. Marijuana had been his drug of choice before he ended up in prison for the third time.

Making marijuana legal in the state was a good thing, but it didn't help with his primary business. The legal entities were making a killing, and that had negatively impacted his flow of clients. He still had the meth heads, but the potheads had all dried up. They preferred dealing with the legitimate stores versus what they considered poor white trash. This enraged him even more. They thought they were better than him. He'd show them. Maybe after he took care of the bitch, he'd shoot up every one of those dispensaries that had popped up like weeds all over his town. She wasn't the only one good with a shotgun. His Kel-Tec KSG-25 was a high-capacity shotgun with twenty-five rounds, twenty-four in a magazine and an additional round in the chamber. Plenty of ammo to do the kind of damage he wanted. His dick got hard just thinking about it.

†

After returning from what Blair suspected was Maribel's daily ritual, Blair had a renewed respect for the serious woman. She also had a greater understanding of the challenges for individuals with different experiences. Danella's world couldn't have been further from her own.

Blair broke the silence when Maribel hit the power button in her truck and started to exit the vehicle. She followed her into the house and asked the question on her mind since they'd left Danella's trailer.

"How do you know Danella and the rest of those families?"

Maribel motioned to the back patio. "We should enjoy the weather and sit a spell for this conversation." She made her way to the chairs and sat with Skeeter and Blair following. "Pa and I lived next to Old Man Simpson. He used to come by when I was little. Even though I moved to

California for a few years, my heart has always been in Washington. When I came back to the area, I went to see him. He was watching Squirt while Danella was…"

"Doing a drug deal?" Blair shaded her eyes as she looked at Maribel.

"Yeah. Danella's not evil. She's just had a hard life. When the police came to arrest her and social services took Squirt away, I applied to be a foster mother. Danella was only going to be away a short time, and I wanted to take care of Lucritia so she wouldn't be put into a foster home with strangers. They denied my application."

"Why the hell would they do that?"

"Single, a lesbian, and a shit-ton of guns. That was the trifecta for the snooty social worker who did a home visit. I was not foster material."

"So, a shit ton, huh? I heard that was the equivalent of several metric ass loads and a fraction of a fuck ton." Blair laughed.

"Funny."

"Well, snooty social worker? You know that's my vocation. I'm surprised you didn't go screaming and running in the other direction when you learned more about me."

"The thought crossed my mind." Maribel grinned.

"So why didn't you?"

Maribel shrugged. "Don't know. You seemed fragile. Broken. Not like that woman who had perpetual pursed lips when I took her on a tour of my place. Your judgments seemed a little kinder. Honestly, my first instinct was to wrap my arms around you and never let go."

Blair groaned. "Not always, apparently. Case in point, this morning."

"Yeah, well, at least you didn't start lecturing me right off the bat when I told you about my love of skeet shooting when I was a kid. You listened without judgment and that mattered to me."

"I have my moments."

"Broke my heart when Squirt ended up in the foster system. I vowed to do whatever I could so that would not happen again. Danella is a good mother as long as she stays away from Hank. I figure if I can keep her away from the drugs and she gets a good job, she'll stay clean."

"So who is this Hank dude?"

"Danella's common-law husband and Squirt's sperm donor. Learned that one from you." Maribel chuckled. "When they arrested him for beating on Squirt, Danella led the police to his drugs and testified against him. She got a reduced sentence for her cooperation, but he pled down and got his sentence reduced as well. Personally, I think they should lock people up for a good long time for hurting a child, but our system doesn't work that way. They also let rapists off too easy for my comfort."

The crease in the middle of Blair's forehead deepened. "Danella said that Hank is out now and none too happy with you. I'm not sure how smart it was for you to piss off a meth head. They are notoriously unpredictable."

"Hank doesn't do meth. He cooks and sells it."

"A very minor distinction. Will you please be careful? I can't believe I am going to say this." Blair blew out a breath. "You should grab one of those fancy guns I saw hanging on the wall in that shrine of yours."

"Shrine?"

"Yeah, I know you don't have that room for your own entertainment. Bragging is not in your DNA. It's a shrine for your papa."

"Behind the seat."

"What?"

"If you had reached behind the seat of the truck, you would have found my favorite shotgun. Don't leave home without one. That's my motto."

Blair chuckled. "I'm oddly calmed by that. I hate having to go inside and miss communing with nature, but I need to check my email, social media, and the other bait I tossed out, hoping to catch a big fish."

"Ooh, look at you getting all country."

"When in Rome. I'm betting on Emma Bronson responding. I don't know if all those rag magazines are correct, but she seems like this might be right up her alley. She and her wife have three kids, and I know she's passionate about the issue. Even though it's been a few years since *Off Screen*, I believe she would pull in a crowd."

Maribel smiled. "I liked that show. Not too many television shows feature lesbians. I was sad when it ended. Now those two are true role models."

"Don't sell yourself short. Even though I must admit to being more than a little uncomfortable with you showing Lucritia how to shoot, I sort of understand. The way she looked at you; it was clear you are a heroine to her. I need a bit of time to readjust my thinking. I won't ever agree with the NRA, though. They are evil personified in my book. And every politician, including the Sperm Donor, who takes their money is a disgusting piece of shit. Money over innocent lives."

Maribel blanched and Blair immediately recognized the power of her words. "Damn, I'm sorry. I don't mean to suggest you're a piece of shit."

"But I did accept money from the NRA. Maybe you could offer some of them, including your father, a different flavor of Kool-Aid. Don't open their mouths and pour it down without their consent. I don't think that ever works."

"I'll keep that in mind. First order of business, the biggest rally Seattle has ever seen."

"My Wi-Fi signal works on the patio, and I have an outlet you can plug into. I have my own research to do. If you don't mind, we can both do a little work and soak in the fresh air and sunshine."

"That sounds like the perfect plan. How does pizza sound? My treat. I heard there's a place not too far from here that has outstanding pizza and they deliver. I'll feel better if I can contribute a bit more."

"I could eat pizza."

"Perfect, then it's settled. Anchovies okay with you?" Blair asked.

Maribel choked on her words. "Uh, c…could we make half anchovies and the other half—"

Blair was slapping her leg and guffawing loudly. “I gotcha. You should have seen your face. I was kidding. You probably want a meat lover’s special, right?”

Maribel nodded. “The chicken and artichoke pizza is good, too. I could eat that.”

“Sold.”

Chapter Fourteen

Not only did the sun reflecting off the screen distract Maribel, but she also kept glancing at Blair. She didn't seem to have issues rotating her laptop away from the light as she plunked the keys and concentrated on whatever she was bringing up on the screen to review. Maribel thought Blair looked so sexy as she absently tucked her hair behind her ear. The sunshine caught the reddish highlights, and Maribel didn't think she'd ever seen someone with hair as shiny as Blair's.

"I can feel your eyes on me." Blair looked up from her laptop. "Have you even clicked on one site yet? I could tell you all about how despicable the NRA is, but I want you to discover that all on your own. You have to want to drink that different flavor."

"The sun makes it hard to read the screen." Maribel offered the weak excuse knowing full well that Blair would scoff at her and tell her to shift the computer to avoid the glare.

"Angle it a little bit." Blair reached across and moved the screen until the angle made it easier to see the words. "You might want to type in NRA propaganda. I think that will be quite eye opening for you. When you get bored with that, I could use your help with facts and figures on countries with strict gun laws and how that's affected mass shootings and other gun-related deaths. I've heard there is a correlation, but I need data." Before returning to her own computer, she smiled at Maribel, showing off her lopsided dimples. One side was more prominent than the other, giving Blair's face a bit more character. Maribel never knew that dark brown eyes could sparkle, but Blair's definitely did.

She continued to stare like a lovesick puppy and was startled by Blair's loud declaration.

"Hot damn. She answered me!"

Maribel didn't think Blair was seeing anyone, but a small part of her panicked as the question flew from her mouth. "Who answered you?"

"Emma Bronson. She said, depending on when we plan to do the rally, she's in. I should find out when she can do it and plan the event around her schedule. What do you think?" Blair was vibrating with excitement.

"She's a woman who puts her pants on one leg at a time just like you and me. You don't need to fawn all over her. She's married, too."

Blair burst out laughing. "Not that she isn't crush worthy, but I'm not fawning over her because she's hot. I know she's married. She has the star quality and social media contacts to make the rally successful. No one's going to pay any attention to my tweets, but they will hers. Hey, you could put out the word. You're famous. Sorry, I didn't realize I have a star sitting right in front of me."

Maribel scoffed. "Hardly. No one knows I exist."

"What are you talking about? You are an Olympic gold medalist with nine frickin' medals. That's gotta be a record."

"You had no idea who I was. What makes you think Josephine Public does?"

Blair laughed. "Josephine Public? I think the saying is Joe Public."

Maribel half-smiled. "Sexist much? You ever seen a skeet shooter on a box of Wheaties?" she challenged.

Blair crinkled her nose and looked as though she was wracking her brain for an answer. Maribel powered on. "Nope, didn't think so. That's because the shooting sports aren't sexy. Nike, Wheaties, and any other popular media brand does not sponsor a sport nobody watches. Remington, Winchester, and Beretta, sure they jump on the opportunity to sponsor us. But Coca Cola, Procter and Gamble, the big names who coincidentally back the other Olympians stay far away. The only sponsors I ever got were from the firearm industry. When I was younger it was more important. I don't think it is anymore."

"I'm not trying to start an argument here, but isn't it possible the mass shootings make the sport something companies don't want their name attached to? I'm not saying it's right, just offering an explanation…"

"Bingo, which is why you don't need me sticking my nose into this and being front and center. Besides, I don't have any social media accounts. Never went in for that crap."

"The conversation is not over. You could be a huge impact at the rally. I need to compose an email right now. Oh my God, this is happening. This is really happening." Blair returned to her laptop, her fingers flying over the keyboard.

Maribel tried not to feel jealous. She wanted to be the one to create that excitement in Blair. She didn't think she ever would, and that saddened her. This was worse than two people who grew up on different sides of the railroad tracks. Their fundamental belief systems might be too far apart to bridge the gap.

After Blair finished typing, she looked at Maribel, her brows knit in worry. "What's going on? You look like someone stole your puppy."

Maribel shook her head. "Nah, I've got more research to do. That's where I can help. Maybe you shouldn't put all your eggs in one basket. There has to be other well-known actors or actresses who are willing to speak. Or prominent people who live in this state, instead of dragging someone from California. Besides, you need more than one person to speak. Don't rallies parade a bunch of people in front of the crowd?"

Blair frowned. "Yeah, they do. Thanks. I got all excited because Emma Bronson responded. And, she lives in Kansas now. I should check my other emails. I did toss out a line to Lara Beck and her wife, Dillon Sanders. They're a big deal in Seattle. Oh, and I also thought of Gail Forrester, the famous architect and her partner, Mandie Carter. They would be great choices. Mandie used to live here on the east side. She's an amazing photographer. I was hoping she could create something eye-catching for us to send out to people."

As Blair's excitement returned, Maribel pushed aside her dark thoughts about how different she was from Blair. She didn't want to consider how they would never make it as a couple.

†

The afternoon passed quickly. Maribel suggested they take a break to collect eggs again and see if the kittens were napping in the extension she'd built for them. Blair was eager to stretch and move a bit. Blair hadn't worked out that morning as usual, and the sedentary activities were causing a fair amount of restlessness.

"I'm interrupting your routines, aren't I?" Blair asked.

"Not really." Maribel wouldn't meet her eyes.

"Don't lie. I know that you do more than collect eggs twice a day and play with the kittens. Don't you practice shooting or something? You must. I would imagine Olympians are always in training."

"It's okay. Maybe I've decided I need a vacation."

"Some vacation. I'm sure searching the internet beats sipping Mai Tai's on a beach," Blair replied sarcastically.

"It does as long as I'm doing it with you. A beach wouldn't be a lot of fun on my own. Not that I've ever been to one."

"What? You've never been to a beach? What about on your travels? I mean, you went to the Olympics! Rio had to have amazing beaches."

"I kept mostly to myself. I wasn't a fish out of water. More like one of them hillbillies in Beverly." Maribel stood with her computer tucked under her arm.

"We should put these inside. It isn't good for them to remain in the sun. Mine's pretty hot. I'm surprised I didn't get an overheat message like I sometimes see on my tablet."

Maribel held out her hand. "I'll set them in the kitchen for now."

Blair handed Maribel her computer. "Okay. But we haven't finished our conversation. I'm feeling guilty for totally hijacking you. And I also feel a bit like a slug. I'm going to need to run off some excess energy later on. I don't suppose you'd want to take a run with me, would you? Probably aren't a lot of cars to worry about out here, huh?"

"Nope. The roads are even better for cycling. Running seems boring to me, so I usually hop on my bike if I feel the need to exercise." Maribel stacked the two laptops together and headed for the sliding-glass door.

"I didn't bring my bike with me. Too bad. Going on a ride with you might be nice."

"I have an extra you can use."

Blair placed her hand against her heart. "Now you're just being perfect. Anyone who has more than one bike gets my vote as the ideal woman. I developed a passion for cycling a few years back, but it isn't as much fun riding by myself. I used to ride with a group on the weekends."

"Be right back and then we can head to the coop. I'll grab the cartons."

When Maribel returned, she caught Blair with her arms out and her head tipped back, a contented look on her face. Slowly she brought her arms down and glanced at Maribel. "How come we didn't collect eggs yesterday afternoon?"

"I wanted it to be more like a date. Interrupting our time with a chore seemed all wrong. Besides, you had to take care of stuff."

"And you gallantly chauffeured me back to my mom's place. You are too good to be true."

"No, I'm not. I kept an important piece of info from you."

"Ancient history. Already forgotten, for now, until our next big row." Blair winked.

"Come on." Maribel gestured for Blair to start walking. "We have adorable kittens to visit. This time of day they are barely waking from their naps and likely to let you pet them before they realize a big hairless being is touching them."

"Hey, I've got hair."

"Not on your hands you don't, or at least not enough for their liking. You're an alien monster to a tiny kitten."

"Good point. I will follow your lead and lay on a dirty floor if they let me touch them."

"It's not dirty, I sweep it out."

"Aha, caught ya. That's another chore I've been keeping you from. I should do more than help you collect eggs and make deliveries. I need to earn my keep."

"No, you don't. Having a chance to look at you all day long is payment enough for me."

"How is it you're single again?"

Maribel didn't want to say out loud that she hoped she wasn't, and that Blair was the reason for the change in her status, but she didn't want to jinx anything.

Instead she called for Skeeter who came bounding toward them from around the corner. "Skeeter, come." Maribel groaned when she saw his golden fur splattered with mud, and who knew what else he'd gotten into. "Dammit, Skeeter." She shook her head. "My crystal ball indicates you have a bath in your very near future."

Blair's melodious laugh filled the air.

Chapter Fifteen

Ten miles down the road, Hank snorted his third line of coke. He wanted to march to that meddling cunt's fancy house, but he knew better than to attack her in her own territory. He needed to bide his time, but he could take a trip to see Danella while the dyke was busy with whoever she had in her truck. He could control his temper long enough to sweet-talk his way back into Danella's bed.

Hiking up his baggy pants, Hank swaggered outside and slammed the old door to the cabin. His rusty junk car sat forlorn in the grass waiting for him. He'd hid it in the back to keep the nosy cops from tracking him down. They didn't know he was squatting in the abandoned cabin. The creak of the door reminded him of an old man. He thought of Old

Man Simpson and how he always silently watched from his crate. Hank wasn't stupid. He knew the old man was judging him, but he was old and couldn't do a damn thing.

The car sputtered to life, and he put it in gear, spitting dirt and weeds into the air as he peeled off, heading in the direction of Danella's trailer. He needed a few weeks to get back on his feet, and then they could move somewhere better. Maybe to a trailer that wasn't falling apart. He could take her somewhere that bitch wouldn't find them. There were plenty of out of the way places in the woods close to his meth lab.

When he pulled up to the trailer, he saw his kid playing in the dirt. It was time to teach her some discipline. He'd tried to do that before, and things had gotten out of hand. But she needed to respect him. He was her father.

After slamming the car door, he looked at Lucritia and snarled, "Where's your momma?"

Lucritia's eyes went wide, and she scrambled away, running into the trailer and letting the door bang the aluminum frame behind her.

Good. He hoped she was getting Danella, and then he would tell her to scram while he satisfied his need. Danella was his woman and his dick needed her.

Danella appeared in the doorway, a grimace on her face. That was not the sort of welcome he was expecting. She stepped out of the trailer and yelled, "Get the fuck outta here, Hank. Thought I made myself clear last time. Don't want nothing to do with you."

"Look at this shithole you're living in. I need a few weeks, and then we can go somewhere real nice. You don't got to do much. Just a few deals here and there."

"I said no. I ain't going back and leavin' Lucritia again."

"It was only for thirty days, and I'll bet they took good care of her. Look, baby, I ain't mad at you or nothing. I know them cops twisted your head and got you to say stuff you didn't mean to. We can start all over again."

"I'm not tellin' you again, Hank. Leave us alone. We don't need you. I'm gonna get a real job."

Hank narrowed his eyes when the little brat appeared in the doorway of the trailer. She could barely hold the shotgun she had in her arms. Little shit had the nerve to point it at him. Again. But this time, he was invincible. There was no way she had the balls to shoot. He started to advance, and her little hands pulled back the pump.

"Mamma said to git." Her voice quavered, and he smirked at her.

"You ain't got the guts. When I get my hands on you, I'm gonna teach you a lesson you'll never forget. Don't you dare disrespect me."

A loud shot reverberated as his kid pointed the shotgun in the air.

Hank took another step, and he heard the pump again before the second shot landed between his feet clipping his big toe. He jumped and began hopping around on one foot.

"She shot me," he exclaimed. Not sure whether she had aimed for somewhere else and missed, he stared at her, reappraising his situation.

"She's been practicing. Don't miss too much of what she aims at. I'm guessing the next shot will be higher. I wish she'd enjoy being a kid, but you know what it's like. Kids grow up fast around here. She's a lot more mature for her age. Believe me when I say she won't hesitate to shoot you. I taught her that if she kills you, self-defense or not, they ain't gonna lock up an eight-year-old." The harsh edge to Danella's voice told Hank he wasn't going to win today. He'd need to come up with a new plan. A plan to get that kid taken away for good. She wasn't ever going to behave, and he didn't need that shit in his life. He never wanted a fucking kid, anyway.

"This ain't over," Hank called over his shoulder as he turned and limped away.

He heard Danella whisper, "You done good, Lucritia. Mari would be so proud of you."

†

Blair was happily sprawled out on the wood floor as she stretched her hand toward a small calico kitten that had the most unusual markings. A triangle of orange sat above the kitten's eyes surrounded by black. Green eyes watched Blair warily. A white muzzle, chest and tiny boots made the miniature furball unique. Blair flexed her index finger, and the kitten inched closer. Her curiosity causing her to be brave. Mama kitty was laying in the swath of late afternoon sunshine that filtered in through one of the windows. Three other babies were happily kneading her belly and sucking on her nipples.

"I can tell she wants you to pet her," Maribel said. "Be careful though. She thinks your finger is a play toy."

The kitten flopped down and batted at Blair's finger.

Blair laughed. "I think you're right. How do you know it's a she? I doubt you're able to get close enough to see her junk."

"Tri-colors are almost always female. I have baby food in the house. It's chicken flavor. That usually works to get them to come closer. Food is a powerful motivator."

"And you didn't think to grab that before we came out? No wonder you're the cat whisperer. You've been bribing them."

"Motivating, not bribing."

"I don't think there is any difference. It's not like there's the cat police making a distinction here. You don't have to worry about them coming to arrest you for bribery."

Maribel flopped on her back and began laughing, startling the kitten in the process. "God, you're funny. You sure have a different way of looking at the world."

"Maybe, but I don't think I've cornered that market. I've heard you say a few things that are quite distinctive."

"Hmm, we can be atypical together." Maribel lifted her hand and made a puppet. "Odd meet Quirky." Bringing her other hand in the air she mimicked the first gesture. "Why good to meet ya, Quirky. Does eccentricity run in your family, too? Ah, good, good, we'll make beautiful weirdness. Can't wait to start. Shall we get naked now or wait until we're in more sanitary conditions? Although, you have to admit, this floor is remarkably clean."

"It is." Blair jumped up and offered her hand. "I think it's egg duty time, but I'm going to let you deal with Henrietta. I might offer my hand for the little one over there"—Blair jerked her head in the direction of the calico—"to bite at, but a pecking hen is beyond my level of tolerance."

†

Hank was all wound up now that he hadn't gotten what he'd come for. In fact, he'd ended up with something he hadn't bargained for, a bloody fucking toe. Screeching to a halt in front of the cabin, he hobbled inside and grabbed his shotgun.

At first, he thought about heading back to Danella's place and filling the trailer with bullet holes, but he was sure the police might come looking for him. They weren't stupid, either. They'd figure he was pissed about Danella ratting him out. They'd be wrong about the reason, but that wouldn't matter. Instead, he'd work out his anger at one of those stores that took away the easier part of his business. Selling weed was a lot less dangerous than meth, and now the distribution line had dried up. That would teach them not to compete.

Hank had two choices, the small mom-and-pop store or the big, fancy, cannabis store right in the middle of town, looking downright reputable. They were making a killing from just the kind of people Hank had always wanted to sell to. People with money who wouldn't squabble over the cost of his shit. The damn store looked like an upscale coffee house.

"I'll teach them who's boss," he mumbled to himself.

This wouldn't take long. Hank pulled into the parking lot and left his old beater running. Who would want to steal that hunk of junk? Yanking on his baggy pants again, he reached inside the car with his other hand and grabbed the gun.

As he approached the heavy door to the store, he sniffed loudly and then spit a glob of mucus on their pristine sidewalk next to the blooming flowers.

"Keep your fucking noses out of the weed business," he shouted.

The clerk and two customers didn't have time to react as Hank unloaded his shotgun sending twenty-five rounds into the freshly painted walls, gleaming display cases and soft flesh of the only people in the store. Too bad there were only three recipients of his rage. He would have liked the death count to be higher. Next time.

Hank spit again, this time on the gleaming floor littered now with glass, debris, and three widening swaths of bright red blood. The puddles were growing exponentially, and Hank wondered if they would eventually come together in one large pool of destruction. With a final glance back at his message to anyone brave enough to fuck with one of his business lines, he pushed the door open, then climbed into his running car and sped away.

†

Blair was acting jittery after they had collected the eggs and set them in the refrigerator to hold until they would be able to deliver them in the morning. Maribel didn't think it had anything to do with being hungry. She had called in their order for the pizza, and they were waiting for the delivery. She decided to come out and ask, rather than speculating.

"Okay, spill. What's got you more skittish than those kittens?"

Blair made a face before glancing at her laptop lying on the kitchen table. "I feel bad about wanting to check my email. I know I spent all afternoon working on my project and completely ignoring you…"

Maribel laughed. "Is that all? God, I thought I'd done something wrong again, and you were working up the nerve to lecture me. Go for it. I'm sure your secret crush wrote back. The sooner you log in and check, the more settled you'll be."

"I promise, once I have a date locked in, then I can begin to plan."

"I know," Maribel answered. "We have the whole evening to enjoy pizza and watch the sunset. It's gonna be a dandy tonight."

"A dandy?" Blair chuckled. "You sound like you walked off the Mayberry RFD set."

Maribel's face screwed in confusion.

Blair waved her hand in the air. "Never mind. I like watching old television shows on MeTV. I'll make you watch one with me someday. They're quite entertaining when you want mindless fun back to a time when things were simpler. Sheriff Andy never carried a gun, and he wouldn't let his deputy, Barney, put bullets in the gun he carried in a holster attached to his belt. Wish that were true in today's world." Blair sighed.

"I don't think that's realistic, Blair." Her quiet voice was tentative with her answer. "If the only people who have guns are the bad guys, because you know they'll find a way to get them, not arming the police is honestly a recipe for disaster. Most of the small towns these days have the worst drug problems. With drugs, comes violence."

"We'll have to agree to disagree." Blair pivoted and grabbed the laptop, before sitting heavily on the couch and popping open the screen.

Maribel took the cue to keep quiet lest another argument ensue. She began to busy herself in the kitchen, preparing Old Man Simpson's blended meals and putting together food containers for Danella and Lucritia. The other families she delivered to received fresh eggs but were a lot more self-sufficient and, besides, Lucritia had captured her heart more than any other. She wanted to make sure she and her mother were well taken care of.

Above the noise of the blender, Maribel heard the gasp. When she looked up, Blair's face was a ghostly white. She pressed the button to stop the blender and asked, "What's wrong."

"There's been another shooting. Three people are dead. They have security footage and have identified the man as Hank Gooding. Please tell me that is not the same Hank who has it out for you?"

Maribel rushed to where Blair was sitting with the computer resting precariously on her lap. She slid in next to Blair, touching her hand in an effort to ground her.

"Can I see?"

Blair turned the laptop toward Maribel, who frowned when she looked at the screen. The shooting had made national news. Two shootings in a relatively rural area in such a short time were causing a news frenzy. It wouldn't be long before the major news networks high-tailed it to the area and began covering the latest shooting. Maribel wasn't sure how she felt about that.

"Do you know the shooter or not?"

Maribel nodded. "I know him."

"If the police know who it is, they'll catch him and put him behind bars, right?"

Maribel was shaking her head. "Depends. Hank's got a lot of places he can go to hide, especially if he catches wind that they know who he is. I don't think he banked on the store having security cameras. But my biggest worry is Danella and Squirt. Desperate people do stupid things. That's what I'm most worried about. Will you be okay here, waiting for the pizza while I go check on them?"

"No, no way. I'm not letting you go there on your own. You should call the police. Let them handle it."

"Danella doesn't trust the police. She taught Lucritia to have a healthy skepticism about local law enforcement. Even after she gave them Hank, some of them aren't the kindest sort. There are a few who believe once a drug dealer, always a drug dealer. She insists they consider her poor white trash and not worthy of protection. An eight-year-old might not have the best judgment when it comes to who she points her shotgun at."

"I don't like this. Not one bit. I don't suppose there is anything I can do to convince you not to put yourself at risk?"

"You don't need to worry about me. I can take care of myself. I promise I'll be quick. Keep the pizza warm for me, but eat if I'm not back by the time it gets here." Maribel stood and headed for the back door.

"Please be careful."

Maribel saluted. "Always am."

†

Before turning off the engine to her truck, Maribel reached into the back and grabbed her shotgun. Scanning the area, she didn't sense anything out of place, but neither Danella nor Lucritia were outside. She saw the threadbare curtain in the trailer move and a tiny face peeked out. The immediate smile warmed Maribel's heart. She shook her head indicating she was coming to them and made her way to the trailer door as rapidly as she could.

Danella opened the door. The crease in her brow deepened. "What ya doing here, and why do you have your shotgun?"

"Has Hank been by to see you today?"

"He has. Lucritia shot his toe. He was pissed, but I told him next time Lucritia would shoot him in the balls. Warned him that she wasn't afraid to take him out, and they'd never put a kid in jail for it."

"He shot up the fancy marijuana store. Killed three people. Why don't you and Squirt come stay with me until this all blows over?"

Lucritia peeked her head around the corner. "I was aiming for his foot, like ya taught me, but I missed. Caught his toe, though."

"I'm real proud of you, Squirt. How'd you like to come stay with me for a few days?"

Lucritia looked at her mother.

Danella leaned against the frame, and a determined look crossed her face. "That's nice of you to offer, but I'm not letting him chase us away from our home. I know this isn't much, but it's mine. We can take care of ourselves. We both have good instincts. I promise if he comes 'round again, Lucritia won't give him a warning shot. I'll tell her to aim higher. Will that make you feel better?"

"Not really, but I have to respect your decision. I'd rather not put that onto a child even if I'm the one who has given her the tools to protect herself. Has Squirt taught you how to shoot yet?"

Danella chuckled. "Yeah, she's been bugging me to try it out. I'm not as good as her, but I can shoot, and if the target is big enough, I catch a piece of it."

"Good. I've got another shotgun in my truck. I want you to take that. If he forces you to use it, don't hesitate, okay? You let me worry about getting you a lawyer if it comes down to that."

"Don't worry, Mari. If he comes after my kid again, the last thing I'll be worried about is going to jail for shooting that prick."

"Good, good. I'll be back as usual tomorrow morning. Hopefully, Hank heard how the police know about his shooting spree and he's lying low. He isn't stupid. He knows that coming here is not the smartest choice, but then again, shooting up the marijuana store is the very definition of a dumb-ass move. I wonder if he started using when he landed in prison?"

"Probably, he looked hopped up when he came by before."

Maribel retrieved the extra shotgun and handed it to Danella. "Please be careful. Bye, Squirt. Take care of your mom."

"I will." The determination in the little girl's face both saddened Maribel and made her proud. An eight-year-old kid should not have that kind of responsibility.

†

Hank entered the run-down cabin and sneered. "I'll be living the good life soon enough. Respect, that's the name of the game. They're all gonna respect me now."

He walked in pain to the white refrigerator and yanked open the door. Cheap beer was the only item sitting on the middle shelf. He grabbed a can and popped the top before picking up the remote and then slumping onto the dirty brown recliner. Greasy stains covered the fabric, but Hank didn't seem bothered by the condition of the chair. As he cycled through the channels, he stopped on one of the news stations when his mug shot flashed on the screen.

"What the fuck?"

Turning up the volume, he listened to the newscaster with his perfect hair and teeth. The solemn expression was all for show. Hank knew that. He didn't give a shit about the people Hank had chosen to earn a lesson in respect.

"Police have identified the gunman in the latest mass shooting that occurred less than two weeks from the tragedy at Cedarbrook Elementary where twenty children, most under the age of nine, lost their lives. Hank Gooding is described as armed and dangerous. The police are looking for any information on the gunman's whereabouts…"

Hank jumped from his chair, spilling beer on his ratty T-shirt. "How the fuck do they know it was me?" he shouted into the empty cabin.

As he paced the dirty floor, he began mumbling. He didn't have anything to lose now. Maybe he'd go out in a blaze of glory. That dyke bitch was at the top of his list.

She'd be by again in the morning. He was sure of that. She was like clockwork, thinking she was an angel protector, giving food and stuff to his woman and kid. That was his job, not hers. Danella better not be fucking her in return. He'd blast a hole in her pussy for that.

Gulping down the rest of the beer in his hand, he grabbed another and thought about his situation while pacing the floor. She usually came early. He would have to make sure he was up, and then he'd blast her truck when it passed his cabin. With twenty-five rounds of ammo, she didn't stand a chance against his assault. After he took care of her, he'd head to Danella's place. She had proved she wasn't worth handling with finesse anymore.

Chapter Sixteen

The pizza deliveryman had come and gone. Blair placed the piping hot pizza in the oven to keep warm while she waited. Her nervous energy took her to her laptop, where she kept clicking on the various apps to see if there were any updates. She knew it was unrealistic to expect the police to have captured Hank in the short time since she'd seen the breaking story. Maribel hadn't been gone that long, but that didn't stop Blair from entering the panic zone.

The mudroom door opened, and Maribel walked in with her hands deep in her pockets. Blair sighed in relief.

"The pizza is in the oven. How are Danella and Lucritia?"

"They're good, but I'm worried. Hank is hopped up on something, and that makes him dangerous. I turned on the radio and heard more about the shooting. He's got a high-capacity shotgun."

"A what?"

"A shotgun that holds up to twenty-five rounds, counting the one in the chamber. A person can do a lot of damage with one of those. They're almost as bad as automatic weapons."

"Of course he has a gun like that. Nobody gives a shit who they sell their guns to. Convicted felons. No problem. Private dealers don't even have to do background checks at gun shows."

"That's not true. Washington State requires checks on all purchases."

"Whatever. So we're an enlightened state. That doesn't mean they can't get someone without a record to purchase for them. I read that in a lot of instances, the clerks don't care. A person will come in, point out a gun, and then someone else will buy it. Or he bought it from a corrupt person at a home-based commercial gun dealer. There are no shortages of those assholes. People ignore the laws. You did when you gave Lucritia a shotgun. How is that any worse than any of the other dishonest gun dealers?"

"I'm going to ignore that dig because I know you're upset right now. Can we eat the pizza and have a nice evening, please?"

"Shit. I keep having to apologize. I know you aren't the problem. I'm just so frustrated and scared. I don't know what I would do if…" Blair walked to Maribel and brushed her hand across her cheek. Her words were choked as she finished. "…if something happened to you." A half-hearted chuckle slid out. "I've only just started getting you to see the truth about gun control. We can't have my powers of persuasion interrupted, now can we?" She kissed Maribel on the mouth and offered, "Truce?"

"Just so you know, I gave Danella a shotgun for protection. If it weren't for the fact that she was tagged a drug dealer, I wouldn't be breaking the law. State law allows for the temporary transfer of a gun to a person to prevent harm. One thing you are right about. Hank is dangerous, and I wanted to make sure they were armed."

"I am tempted to make one more remark, but I won't because I'm starved and don't want you to kick my ass to the curb." Blair kissed Maribel again, grinned, and then danced away.

"No matter how exasperating you can be, I would never kick you to the curb. I need someone to challenge me now and again. More importantly, you need someone to challenge you, too."

"You may be right. I never thought I'd end up dating a modern-day Annie Oakley. You are perfect in every other way. How in the world am I going to reconcile my complete aversion to guns? I've always imagined settling down with another pacifist, having a few kids, and strictly prohibiting them from hanging out with kids whose parents owned guns. It goes without saying that I never would have envisioned allowing a firearm in my home."

"Compromise. Isn't any decent relationship based on that premise?"

"Relationship?" Blair tested out the word. Yes, she supposed it fit.

"I was hoping what we're doing isn't casual dating. It's not, is it?"

"No, it's not. Relationship is the right word." Blair smiled.

†

Maribel was getting used to how Blair dealt with stress and fear. That didn't mean her digs didn't hurt, but at least she understood they were not coming from a place of anger toward her. She supposed if she tried to look at things from Blair's perspective, she wouldn't be very comfortable with guns, either.

Regardless of how diametrically opposed they were on this one issue, Blair was an addiction she had a hard time resisting. Not only did they need to cross the wide divide on gun control, but it seemed like politics in general was a particularly dangerous area of discussion. Ironically it was Maribel's lukewarm views that were the issue.

As Maribel and Blair sat outside enjoying a second beer, Blair had started down the perilous road. Tossing out the bait, Maribel had innocently answered, not realizing where it would lead.

"I can't understand the Log Cabin Republicans. Frankly, I can't understand how anyone in the LGBTQ community would think it was a good idea to support this president. Please tell me you didn't vote for him."

"No, I didn't. Pa might have. I never asked."

"Whew. I don't think that whatever we've started would survive if you'd voted for that appalling excuse for a leader. I can honestly say I hate the man."

"I didn't vote. I wasn't enamored with either choice, so I stayed home that year." Maribel shrugged as if it were no big deal.

The look of disbelief with a hint of disappointment on Blair's face was puzzling to Maribel. "Why are you looking at me like that? A lot of people I know didn't vote."

"You know that by not voting, you helped to elect that asswipe? I blame those of you who stayed home more than the lifelong Republicans. I can almost understand that sort of loyalty. Almost."

"So, I was supposed to vote for someone I didn't support because I hated the other choice?"

"Yes. Are you at least sorry you didn't now? Knowing what's happened."

"I don't agree with how he's running the country, but I can't say a lot has changed for me personally."

"Yet. How can you care so much about people like Danella, Lucritia, Mr. Simpson, yet not care how we're treating immigrants? The hate seems to exponentially grow each day with his rhetoric. This is not the world you want. I know that about you. It doesn't compute."

Maribel shook her head. "I'm one vote. Insignificant, really. Especially since Washington State never votes red, so what does it matter?"

"It matters because millions of people had those same thoughts and look what happened. You better vote in 2020."

"Okay, I will. If it means that much to you."

"Don't do it for me. Do it because it's important."

Maribel pinned Blair with a look of adoration. "I admire your passion. You're like a beautiful fire, burning so bright. The yellow, orange, and red flames reaching to the sky as the wood pops and crackles. Your words are always punctuated by the pops and crackles. It gives them an extra punch. That's why you're going to be so good at the rally. People will listen to you. I'm not like that."

"But you could be. You have passions. They just aren't the same as mine. I know you love Lucritia. Now envision her one day realizing she's in the wrong body. She wants to go in the military, but they say no because she's transgender. Or maybe she identifies as a lesbian. Then, she goes to high school and a couple of boys beat the snot out of her. They're wearing MAGA hats and calling her a dyke. Screaming she's unnatural. Not worthy of living. Doesn't that make you want to fight for her?"

"Of course."

Blair took Maribel's hand and pinned her with a pain-filled gaze. "That's the world we live in now, because that's the hate that he's not only brought to the surface but fed and stoked. Don't believe me? Do your own research on hate crimes. Mass shootings. White Nationalism. It's all there. And, don't even get me started on climate change. Lucritia might not have a world to live in by the time she's old and gray."

"Isn't it possible that's the other side of the coin, the liberal side doing a different kind of fear mongering and stoking of the fires?"

"Do the research, that's all I ask."

"Can we get back to getting to know each other without venturing into politics?"

Blair laughed. "Okay, tell me more about your father. He sounds interesting."

†

Talking with Maribel about her father gave Blair a whole different perspective on people who embraced a set of beliefs so foreign to her own. Maribel had forced her to put her own views under a microscope, and the picture wasn't free from another kind of virus. Hating every single person who had voted for the president was no longer possible. Maribel's father was a kind man who had clearly loved his daughter and tried to do the best he could to make sure she had a good life. That was apparent with the stories she told.

Maribel had a special smile when she talked about her father. "Pa was with me for every single competition I ever entered. All the way until the end when he was no longer physically able to get out of bed. He was good at supporting my shooting, but he floundered when I hit puberty. I got my period early, and it was a disaster."

"No parent excels at those discussions because they always accompany the sex talk."

"Oh, we never had the sex talk. He figured since I was a lesbian, he didn't have to worry about me getting pregnant."

"He knew you were a lesbian at…how old were you when you got your period?"

"I was ten and yeah, it was obvious even before I declared I didn't want to marry a boy."

"So, what happened?"

"I never cried as a little girl. Even when I would skin my knee or fall out of a tree. But when I went to the bathroom one day and saw the blood in my underwear I went running to my pa. I thought I had a terrible disease and I was going to die."

"I can see how that would have been terrifying."

"Pa grabbed a clean rag and a new pair of underwear. He told me to stuff the rag inside the panties. He assured me I wasn't dying, and he was gonna get something for me. I'm standing there with tears streaming down my face, and I just nod and do what he says. He's my pa, and if he's says I'm not dying, well that's the gospel. I believe him and begin to calm down."

"Why do I think there's more to this story?"

"Oh, there is." Maribel chuckled. "I'm washing out my blood-soaked panties, and he comes back about fifteen minutes later. He'd gone to one of the neighbors, and she gave him a half-filled box of tampons. It was a variety pack."

"Oh shit, no. I wasn't allowed to use tampons until I was at least fifteen."

"Oh, yes. He hands me the box and says I gotta plug the hole. Now, remember, I'm ten so I blink at him and ask, 'what hole, Pa?' He shuffles and points to his private parts and says, 'ya got a hole somewhere in there,' and he points again to his crotch. 'My butthole?' I ask."

Blair began to laugh so hard she snorted. "No way."

"Yes way. He says, 'no, the other one.' So, I ask, 'how am I gonna pee out that hole, Pa, if I plug it up?'"

Holding her stomach, Blair shook with laughter. "Did he give instructions on how to use the tampons?"

"I still hadn't quite figured out which hole to plug. Innocently, I asked, 'I got three holes, Pa? Do you have three holes, too?' He said, 'yeah, you have three holes and if you put your finger down there, you'll find the other hole.' He told me girls are special 'cause they have one more hole than boys."

"You know this conversation is priceless."

"I know. But wait, it gets better. So, I'm smart enough to figure out that I need to remove the outer paper on one of the tampons. I'm even smart enough to figure out that I need to find the smallest tampon to plug the little hole I discover. Oh, and as a side note, that discovery leads to other joys." Maribel grinned. "But what I don't figure out until later is that I needed to remove the cardboard on the tampon."

"How in the world did you ever figure out you were supposed to remove the cardboard?" Blair asked.

"I must have been walking strangely afterward, and then I told my pa I'd plugged the hole, but something didn't feel right. Finally, he got the neighbor to come by. By this time, he figured he needed to bring in the cavalry. He found a way to get me sanitary napkins after that."

"Thanks for telling me that story."

"Your turn. Tell me something funny from your childhood," Maribel implored.

"I don't think I can beat your story, but I can tell you something embarrassing from high school."

"Deal."

†

With each hour Maribel spent with Blair, her affection grew. They'd sat on the back porch, telling story after story, and laughing until their sides hurt. As Maribel stood outside of the guest bedroom, readying herself to say goodnight to Blair, she experienced a different sort of ache than the one in her side from so much laughter.

All of Maribel's awkwardness came rushing forward. She had no idea what to do. Should she kiss her goodnight and let nature take its course? A course she very much wanted to lead to them sharing a bed. Fortunately, Blair did not let the pause ruin their evening. Her boldness was one more thing that Maribel admired about her.

"Do you want me to retire to the guest bedroom?"

Maribel gulped air. "No."

Blair took Maribel's hand and tugged her toward the master suite. "I think it's time you showed me that third hole of yours."

The joke broke the tension enough for Maribel to laugh and allow herself to be led to her own bedroom.

"I sleep in the nude sometimes," Maribel blurted.

Blair chuckled. "Good to know."

"Are you sure?" Maribel asked.

"Oh, yes. I want to know what joys you discovered after you found your hole."

"I'm never going to live down that story, am I?"

Blair looked at Maribel, and the arousal was so evident in her eyes. "Seriously, I want to make love to you, and I want your hands all over my body. Your mouth, too. It's all I can think of right now." She proceeded to pull the T-shirt over her head and Maribel followed suit.

With their clothes co-mingling in a small pile on the carpet at the foot of Maribel's king-sized bed, Maribel reached for Blair. Naked, the two women came together, and Maribel began exploring Blair's mouth. She sucked gently on Blair's bottom lip, taking her time before asking for entrance with her tongue.

Maribel's moan merged with Blair's, and Maribel experienced a rush of awakening so powerful her body vibrated with excitement. The kiss turned almost frantic as Blair indicated her need to find the bed, subtly moving Maribel closer to the edge.

Maribel broke the kiss and yanked the covers down while adeptly pushing Blair onto the bed and then climbing on top. She immediately rolled Blair so that the entire length of her naked body rested on top of Maribel, and then she began to caress her ass while reaching behind and brushing her fingers against the entrance to Blair's vagina.

Feeling the wetness, Maribel continued her stroking as Blair's body began to move in sync with the rhythm of Maribel's caresses. She could almost feel how close Blair was to a climax as she whispered in her ear, "Tell me what you need. What you want."

Blair's breathless response was almost instantaneous. "Keep doing what you're doing."

Maribel let her fingers travel farther, barely brushing against Blair's clit, teasing her with the fleeting connection. Maribel maneuvered Blair's body until she had easier access to stroke Blair from behind and reach her clit as her fingers slid easily along her pussy lips. When she thought Blair was about to tumble over the cliff, Maribel pushed her middle finger inside and luxuriated in the contractions as they pulsed around her finger. It was such a glorious sensation, and Maribel reached a new height when she heard Blair cry out in ecstasy.

"Oooooh, fuck, so good, so good," Blair exclaimed before her body stilled on top of Maribel.

Maribel carefully removed her finger and wrapped her arms around Blair, holding her tenderly while kissing her with reverence.

Blair shifted to Maribel's neck and began to kiss her pulse point. As she moved down Maribel's body, stopping at various spots, Maribel began to squirm.

Blair took one of Maribel's nipples in her mouth and started to lick and suck. Maribel's breasts had always been an especially sensitive part of her body. Sandy had joked once about there being an invisible thread between Maribel's breasts and clit. Pull on one and the other spasmed. That had embarrassed Maribel, but it was true. Maribel was so close to a climax that she was lost in the flurry of feelings and almost did not register Blair moving lower. As soon as Blair's tongue hit Maribel's clit, Maribel bucked upward. Unfortunately, the movement was so forceful her pussy hit the edge of Blair's mouth.

"Oops, better watch out before I lose a tooth," Blair quipped. "How about I give you forewarning? I'm about ready to suck you until you scream my name. Ready?"

Maribel nodded and Blair proceeded to do as she warned. She responded exactly as Blair had predicted and came so hard, she did in fact call out Blair's name.

As Blair lay in Maribel's arms, she lifted her head and grinned, then declared, "I still haven't found that hole yet. I guess round two is necessary."

Maribel began to laugh and had a hard time stopping.

Chapter Seventeen

Blair became aware of the tips of Maribel's fingers moving lightly across her back after slowly coming awake. Her arm was draped over Maribel's stomach, and her head rested on a pillow propped on Maribel's shoulder. Blair did not ever remember feeling so safe and loved. Yes, loved. Maribel's affection flowed from her fingers. Shifting slightly, she felt Maribel's fingers stall.

"Good morning," Maribel said.

"Hey, you don't need to stop. That is hands down the nicest way I've ever been roused from sleep. What time is it?"

"Around seven. We've got time. It didn't hurt when we delivered the supplies late yesterday, so I'm not too worried if there is a delay today. The only thing I worry about is what Hank's next move might be."

"We got off on a tangent yesterday, and you didn't say much about your visit with Danella and Lucritia. I know you gave them another shotgun, but what has you so worried besides the obvious?"

"Squirt shot his toe."

Blair popped up, and the sheet fell off her body as she sat there naked from the waist up. "What?"

"Yesterday, he came 'round before the shooting, and Squirt did what I taught her. She only grazed his toe, but I imagine he was pretty pissed about that. I wanted them to come back and stay here for a bit because I have good security, but Danella refused. I had to respect her decision to stay, although I completely disagree with it. At least they're on notice and will be ready if he decides to make another visit. There aren't any trees or other barriers around the trailer for him to hide, so they'll see him coming well before he tries anything. Squirt's a good shot and apparently, isn't afraid to take a shot when she needs to."

"She's a kid, for fuck's sake."

"When you grow up like Squirt, you don't have the luxury of being a kid."

"That's not right."

"Didn't say it was. Just stating the facts." Maribel sat up and stroked Blair's arm. "Blair, you and I come from two very different worlds. I don't think you quite understand what a kid experiences when they come from poverty.

Maturity comes fast in some ways and in others, like the story I told about my period, innocence prevails."

"I'm coming with you this morning," Blair stated. "You respected Danella's decision to stay put, now you have to respect mine."

"Stubborn woman. How about we head to the chicken coop, have breakfast, and then we'll do the deliveries?"

"Can I check my email before we start?"

"Sure, I wouldn't want to keep you from your crush." Maribel winked.

"The sooner I have a date nailed down, the better. Then I can do a full-court press on the other pseudo-famous folk. I might need funding, and Lara Beck is known for her philanthropy. Plus, she is positively loaded."

"I can donate to the cause. I have plenty of money. That is, if you don't mind that some of it may be considered blood money."

"Actually, I like the idea of funding from the gun manufacturers and NRA going to rallies on gun control. Poetic justice? Irony? I'm not sure what applies in this situation. But I don't care. I hope the media tracks that down and it causes a big old burr in their sides. Oh!" Blair smacked her hand against her mouth. "Shit, that might affect your sponsorships."

Maribel shrugged. "Don't care. I can always win money in competitions."

"You are truly an anomaly. A woman with too many contradictions for me to unravel in one night. Speaking of nights. Last night was glorious, and I hope we will have many more."

"Me too."

†

A feeling of impending doom crept into Maribel's thoughts like an unwelcome guest. She didn't want to invite them inside, but she didn't possess the skills to keep them at bay. Traveling down the rural route with her heightened senses, Maribel saw a flash of something and reacted without thought.

"Get down," she ordered.

The loud blast echoed in Maribel's ears, and then she heard the telltale *chuchak* sound of racking a round before another blast rang in the silence of the morning. Maribel slammed on the gas and fishtailed down the road but not before one of the slugs blew through both windows and tiny shards of glass made their way inside the cab. She heard several more blasts before she knew she was far enough out of range for any of the shots to hit their target. That didn't mean he wouldn't come after them in his own vehicle.

Afraid to glance at Blair before they were safely out of danger, Maribel kept her eyes glued to the road. The whimper she heard forced her to look.

Blair had her arms crossed over her head. There was a decent sized hole in the window, and a few small shards of glass glittered in her hair. Panic set in when Maribel noticed the blood. She wanted to pull to the side of the road to find the source, but she couldn't chance Hank following and causing more harm. It was vital to put more distance between them and the very real possibility that one of his shots would hit their mark. Maybe one had already done that.

After they screeched to a stop in front of Danella's trailer, Maribel surveyed the damage. She gently brushed along Blair's arm coaxing her to look her way. There was far too much blood for the culprit to be a small piece of glass. She needed to find the source. A smear of blood was on her arm, and Maribel wondered if there were multiple injuries and something sharp had somehow managed to pierce her arm.

Maribel was so worried about Blair she hadn't heard Danella and Lucritia emerge from the trailer. The loud blasts still echoed in her head.

"Blair, are you hurt?"

Blair removed her hands and sat up. Her body shook when she answered, "I don't know."

"Mari," a scared tiny voice called out.

Maribel looked to her left and found the frightened eyes of Lucritia. Danella stood several feet away with a shotgun resting in her arms.

Torn between reassuring the frightened young girl and attending to Blair, Maribel climbed out of the truck, then squatted down to meet Lucritia's eyes. "Everything's fine. I need you to go inside the trailer. If any other car or truck comes on the property, you know what to do, right?"

"Yeah, wait 'til I'm sure it's a bad man, then shoot to kill if they got a gun in their hands. Even my daddy."

"Especially your daddy. You already gave him a warning shot. I have to help Blair. I'll be right in after. Okay?"

"Okay."

Maribel stood, glanced in the direction of the young woman still holding a shotgun and aimed her next directive at Danella. "Don't hesitate."

Danella's grim expression settled Maribel. She knew that Danella wasn't prepared to let Hank have the upper hand. No matter what.

Maribel ran around to the passenger side of the truck and pulled on the door. The multiple holes had done something to the door causing it to stick. She pulled hard until the frame gave way and creaked open.

Blair's face was pale as she stared at her right leg. A glance at the large hole in the inside of the door was the only evidence that Maribel needed to know Blair had been shot. Quickly unclipping Blair's seatbelt, Maribel gathered Blair in her arms and carried her to the trailer. Danella opened the door, and Maribel gently set her on the couch. "I'll be right back. I need to call for an ambulance."

Running back to the truck, she plucked her cell phone from the cup holder and then grabbed the shotgun from behind the seat. While walking back to the trailer, she pressed 911 and frantically started to talk before the woman on the other end finished saying, "911, what's your emerg—"

"I'm on rural route three about five miles in. A woman's been shot. Pretty sure the shooter was Hank

Gooding. He is armed and dangerous and shot at the truck about two miles away in that ratty cabin on the north side as you travel down the road. Hurry please."

"Okay, ma'am, hang on, we've got vehicles rolling."

"I gotta go and tend to her leg."

"Please stay on the phone with me."

"I can't. She needs me, but I'll put someone else on the phone. You can talk with her."

Danella banged open the door, and Maribel handed her the cell phone. "Talk to the dispatcher, please."

Danella frowned but took the phone from Maribel. Lucritia was holding Blair's hand and tears were streaming down Blair's face.

"Help's on the way." Maribel pulled off her T-shirt and pressed it against the gaping wound. A shotgun slug could do a lot of damage. "You're going to be fine. I promise and I never break my promises."

A few tiny pieces of glass clung to Blair's hair, and Lucritia started to pick them out.

"You be careful, Squirt. I don't want you cutting yourself on a piece that might be a bit too sharp. Besides, I need you to be on the lookout. If you see anything roll up besides a car with flashing red lights, I want you to shoot. Don't wait, okay? I doubt anyone else will be coming in hot besides the police or the ambulance. So, if you see a fast-moving car, you go ahead and take the shot."

"Okay, Mari. I won't shoot the police even if Mama says they're a bunch of assholes who like to rough up people for fun."

"That's right. Today, they'll be here to help us. And we need their help. Blair needs their help."

"Yeah, that's the place. We're almost to the end of the road. I don't know. Do I sound like I got medical training?" Danella asked in exasperation. "She's looking pale. Got a hole in her leg and Mari just pressed her T-shirt against the wound."

The faint sound of sirens wailed in the distance. "Thank fuck. I think they're almost here. I guess I don't need to talk to you anymore."

Maribel shook her head. "Danella, she was just doing her job, trying to give the paramedics more information."

"She was asking me questions that I couldn't answer. You shoulda stayed on the phone. I'll hold your shirt on her wound. You go out and meet the cops. They're more likely to help you."

Maribel was once again stymied by what to do. Finally, she nodded and headed out. Fortunately, she had the wherewithal not to take her shotgun. She was depending on an eight-year-old to make sure she didn't get her ass shot off by a hyped-up Hank looking for revenge. Figuring he wasn't crazy enough to come anywhere near where the sirens were heading gave her a small measure of confidence.

Maribel waved her hands in the air, and the ambulance pulled next to the battered truck. Two uniformed medics jumped out of the rig, and Maribel pointed to the trailer. "She's inside."

"Is the shooter still around?"

"We were shot about two miles from here. I'm not sure where he's at."

Two police cars rolled in after the medics went inside to attend to Blair. Maribel was glad she recognized one of the officers. "Hey, Sam. Danella's got nothing to do with this. She ran Hank off yesterday and that's why he's gone nutso."

Sam jerked his head at the truck. "That your truck?"

"Yeah."

The other man emerged from the second vehicle and grabbed his belt after he swaggered to join his colleague.

"What were you doing out here, anyway? Don't you live out by Cedar Ridge?" Sam asked.

"Close enough. I was making egg deliveries."

Sam squinted at Maribel. "Lot of drug deals out here. You should keep your distance."

"Danella's clean."

The other police officer scoffed.

"This isn't about a drug deal. It's about Danella sending Hank on his way and him not liking her version of divorce papers."

"How come you're involved?"

"I don't like assholes who beat on little kids. I might have taught Danella's kid how to defend herself."

"Aw, Maribel. Don't tell me you gave that kid a gun."

"Okay, I won't tell you that. Look, Sam, I've got more important things to attend to right now. My friend's been shot, and I'm gonna ride in the back of that ambulance with her."

"I need a statement," Sam clarified.

"Fine, come to the hospital and I'll give you my statement. You better go check out that cabin about two miles up the road. Be careful, he's got a high-capacity gun. Took about six shots before we were out of range."

"I doubt he's still hanging around. Sirens undoubtedly chased him away, but we'll check it out." Sam tipped his hat, and then his eyes traveled to the left of Maribel. "They're about to load your friend."

The rolling gurney was bumping on the ground on its way to the trailer. Maribel waited patiently while the paramedic secured Blair and rolled her to the back of the ambulance.

"I'm coming with," Maribel declared, leaving no room for argument. Looking over her shoulder, she noticed the two officers walking toward the trailer.

"I would think you have better things to do right now than hassling Danella and her kid. Like chasing after a maniac before he starts shooting up the town. I mighta left three of my shotguns in her trailer, so don't start hassling her for having unregistered guns. They're mine. Seriously, Sam, he's out there and he's hopped up. Serve and protect, not hassle and annoy. If another innocent person gets shot, that's on you."

Sam stopped and jerked his head at his colleague. "Come on, let's check out that cabin."

As the ambulance doors closed, Maribel sighed in relief when she saw the two police cars turn around and lead the way down rural route three.

Maribel turned her attention to Blair and stroked her arm. She caught the attention of the female medic hanging the IV bag and asked, "How bad?"

"She'll be fine. Vitals are good, considering she has a slug in her leg. She's young and strong. It could have been a lot worse. A little higher and the shot might have hit a vital organ."

"I'm Maribel and this is Blair. You should know our names. Makes things more personal. Medical folks are more diligent if they know who they're working on."

"Most people around these parts know who you are, Maribel. We'll take good care of your friend. Don't worry."

†

From a hiding place in the dense foliage, Hank ground his teeth as he watched the police pull next to the cabin. The forest was uncharacteristically quiet. It was as if nature recognized pure evil and was holding its breath in a sort of stasis until the negative energy vacated their home.

"Fucking cops," he muttered.

Discarding the fleeting thought to empty his shotgun in their direction, he melted farther into the heavy cover of the trees. They wouldn't find a lot in the cabin. A few beers, a tiny amount of coke, and the extra ammo he hadn't thought to grab.

Hank still had eighteen or nineteen rounds left in his shotgun, and he thought he might need every one to seek his revenge. At least he knew one of those slugs had found its mark when the ambulance went rushing by earlier.

Slinking down farther into the brush, he watched as one of the cops pushed the mic on his shoulder. The other pig had opened the door to the cabin and disappeared inside. Although he strained to hear what the asshole was saying, the words were too muffled to hear. Whatever. As soon as they left, he wasn't about to stick around. He had a few loose ends to take care of, and then he would leave this shithole town.

Patience. He could exercise patience. That was something he'd lacked earlier, and that had earned him a consolation prize. If he'd managed to kill that bitch, they never would have rushed away in the ambulance. No, his shots had not done their job like in the weed store. No one had walked away from that.

After he took care of his final loose ends, he might turn on Danella's shitty TV and find out how much damage he had managed to do earlier. Hank continued to watch as he crouched down in the ferns and moss. The cop who spoke in the mic was leaning against the open door of the car. Hank wondered what he was waiting for, when he got his answer. This time he could just make out what the other man was saying to the other asshole who had emerged from the cabin.

"They're sending out a team to comb the cabin. Let's head to the hospital and get that statement."

The other cop nodded and folded himself into the car. The lights were still flashing as he pulled away. Hank spit onto the ground. “Assholes don’t need those lights. They’re just flaunting their power.”

Carrying the shotgun in one hand, he yanked at his pants again and made the slow trek to Danella’s trailer. A plan was forming in his head about how to approach that run-down piece of shit without getting his ass shot off. That fucking kid of his would likely blow his dick off if he came at them without cover.

†

Maribel heard the swoosh of the doors and looked up in time to see Sandy rush inside. She looked frantic until her eyes settled on Maribel.

“What the fuck happened? Is Blair okay?”

“They said she was going to be fine, but they’re still working on her. I didn’t know if I should call her mom or not.”

“Tough call. Her mom came in this morning with Senator Chadwick. So, I’m going to take a wild guess that perhaps she isn’t too excited to have them visit her here or know what happened. I advise you to wait until you can ask her about it.”

“Thanks for coming, Sandy. I didn’t know who else to call.” Maribel ran her hands nervously through her hair.

“Of course, I love Blair like a sister. You too, you goof. Here’s a shirt. It should fit fine. I don’t have your muscles, but I have plenty of flab to warrant buying tees with extra room in them." Sandy held out the plain blue T-shirt, and Maribel slipped it over her head.

"This is all my fault," Maribel moaned.

"I seriously doubt that. So, what happened?"

"Have you been listening to the news?" Maribel asked.

"A little."

"That shooting in the marijuana store…"

"Yeah, what's that got to do with anything? Blair doesn't smoke weed."

"No, the shooter is someone I know."

"How the hell do you know a crazed drug dealer?"

"He's Danella's ex."

"Danella? You mean the one with the kid?"

"Uh huh. I gave Squirt one of my old shotguns for protection. I've been showing her how to shoot. She shot Hank's toe and he's pissed."

Sandy slumped back into the waiting room chair. "How'd he slip through your security?"

"We were making a delivery to Danella, Mr. Simpson, and the rest of the folks I usually give eggs and things to. When we drove by this shitty little cabin, he started shooting. I slammed on the gas, but I wasn't quick enough, and Blair caught a slug in her leg."

"I thought bullets bounce off of cars or trucks."

Maribel shook her head. "This isn't Hollywood, Sandy, bullets and especially single slugs from a shotgun do not bounce off of fiberglass or metal."

"Oh. I know the woman at the admitting desk. Do you want me to see what I can find out about Blair?"

"I tried already. I'm not family, so they wouldn't tell me anything."

Sandy narrowed her gaze at Maribel. "You care for her, don't you?"

Maribel lifted her watery gaze to Sandy. "I think I might be falling in love. Sometimes, she's so exasperating, but she makes me think. She challenges me to consider stuff I've never thought about before."

Sandy chuckled. "The liberal and the conservative. This should be interesting to watch."

A nurse with blue scrubs called out, "Is there a Maribel here?"

Maribel stood. "That's me."

"Come with me. She's been asking where you are and telling us she has to pee. The drugs have impaired her and distorted a few facts. She thinks you're the one who was shot. Coming out of anesthesia tends to wreak havoc on a person's understanding of what's going on, but don't worry, the surgery went well. The ortho who was on call is the best one we've got. You've got five minutes. Then we're transferring her to a room on the unit."

"Can I come too?" Sandy asked.

"Who are you?"

"A friend."

"No, only the girlfriend. Who I assume is Maribel? You can wait until she is settled into room 102. Give us another hour. Okay?"

"Thanks." Maribel followed the woman in scrubs through the automatic doors and hoped like hell that Blair was as stable as the paramedic said.

†

"I have to pee," Blair slurred.

Maribel looked helplessly at the woman in scrubs who was shaking her head.

"She has a catheter in her. It only feels like she has to pee. We'll have to keep telling her that because the drugs make her forget." The woman chuckled.

"Okay." Maribel stroked Blair's sweaty forehead. "Honey, go ahead and pee, you're on the toilet. Sort of," Maribel added.

"Maribel, I have to pee. Tell them I have to pee. Blood. Oh, God, you're shot. I can't lose you, too."

"It's okay, babe. I wasn't shot. You were. You had me so scared."

"Don't leave me, Maribel."

"Never."

Blair's eyes closed. "I have to pee. I don't want to pee the bed."

The nurse pushed a button and Blair's face seemed to relax. A tiny bit of drool escaped the corner of her mouth. "She'll be out for a while. If you want to come back later, that would be better." The nurse patted Maribel's arm. "For her, and for you."

"Can I stay for a bit?"

"Not right now. We have to make the arrangements to settle her in her room. I can come get you when we're done. Are you her health care proxy?"

The rush of panic returned to Maribel. "Why, is something wrong?"

"No, no, nothing like that. She should make a full recovery. I just need to know if you are authorized to make any decisions. I also can't give you much information about her condition unless you're approved and until the drugs wear off. I don't think there is documentation on her wishes. I thought maybe you had that."

"No, uh. Her mother might. She lives here. Blair is only here for a bit of time. She, uh took a leave of absence or something from her job to be with her mother after the shooting..."

"The school shooting?"

"Yeah, her sister died in the..." Maribel choked up and couldn't finish. The reality hit Maribel that Blair didn't live here, and she was going to go back, sooner rather than later. Especially after this latest incident. There wasn't a damn thing she could do about it, either.

"Maybe you should call her mother, then."

"I don't know. They, uh, had a bit of a falling out."

"Oh, well, I hate to kick you out, but we need to get her settled in her room. I'll come get you, I promise."

Maribel had a decision to make. Should she take these few minutes while they were settling Blair to check on Danella and Lucritia, or remain at the hospital ready to stick like glue to Blair's bed after they situated her in a room on the unit? When Sam and the other officer entered the emergency department and made a beeline for Maribel, who was waiting patiently with Sandy, her decision was made. They hadn't found Hank. He was still on the loose. Maribel had a bad feeling, and she was rarely wrong.

After finishing her statement and signing the report, she set the pen on the clipboard she'd borrowed and pulled Sandy to a far corner in the waiting room. She hoped the low tones in her voice would not be overheard by Sam and his buddy.

"I'm going to get one of those Uber drivers to take me out to Danella's place and check on her and Lucritia. This time, I'm not giving them an option. I'll drop them off at my place and then come back. Hopefully Blair won't wake up before I return. If I'm not back in a couple of hours, max, send Sam out to her place." Maribel jerked her head in the direction of Sam and the officer who seemed to have a perpetual scowl on his face. "Hopefully only Sam will check on us. The other guy seems like a total tool."

"For the record, I don't like your plan." Sandy held up her hand. "But I know better than to convince you otherwise. Besides, you are the most stubborn woman I know. You two deserve each other. You know that?" Sandy scoffed.

"Thanks, Sandy."

†

At first the driver was hesitant to take Maribel to the end of the road. The area had a reputation for rampant drugs and crime. Maribel offered him a hundred dollars for his inconvenience and told him he could drop her off a half mile away. He didn't have to take her all the way to the end.

"This is good," Maribel directed.

"You got a way back, lady? Talk about shithole places. I don't think you can get more shithole than out here. How do people live like this?"

Maribel ignored his commentary and handed him the money. "My truck's here."

"I don't see no truck."

"It's up the road a bit, but I'd rather get a little exercise and walk the rest of the way."

"Suit yourself, lady. This area of town gives me the creeps."

Maribel pulled open the door and stepped into the sunshine. Closing the door carefully, she waved away the Uber. Her senses were on high alert as she kept scanning the area. There was a better than fifty percent chance that Hank was waiting in the wings, ready to ambush her as soon as she approached the trailer.

Maybe she should have thought to have the driver swing by her place so she could grab another gun, but that would have freaked him out too much. She was heading to the danger zone unarmed but not completely unaware or unprepared. Although she was approaching a section of the road where there was nowhere to take cover, and she'd be completely open and exposed around the trailer, so would he, and Lucritia was a very good shot. She had to bank on him either having to shoot from too far away or exposing himself to someone who wouldn't hesitate to protect her mother or Maribel if it came to that.

As she cautiously proceeded down the road, doing her best to walk silently on the cracked pavement that was in desperate need of repair, a rustle in the brush caught her attention. Turning her head in the direction of the scarcely audible noise, she once again heard the sound she knew so well. She was still a fair distance from the cabin but took off in a sprint in a desperate struggle to find shelter against what she knew would be Hank's attempt to fill her with several slugs. She understood the damage one slug could do to her body. It wasn't pretty. She'd seen Blair's leg. Even after several hours of surgery, Maribel realized there was a good chance Blair would never recover enough to avoid a reminder of this terrible day. It was a toss-up which day in her life would be worse. The day her younger sister died or the day she was shot—both events a result of gun violence.

Maribel knew the truck wouldn't be a sufficient barrier, but it was all she had. She might have a chance if she crouched in front of the engine block. There was a lot of metal to get through. It was better than nothing. He'd have to come close and put himself at risk.

Zig-zagging her way down the road, she could see her truck. Counting in her head, she heard six shots ring out and none had hit her so far. He was undoubtedly too far away for accuracy. At least there was that.

"You fucking bitch. I'm gonna kill you and then gut you like a pig."

Maribel slid in front of her truck and gulped air. Three more shots rang out and one managed to hit metal. She took a chance and peered out, catching a glimpse of her attacker. He was brazenly walking in her direction. A barely audible squeak momentarily distracted Maribel, and she turned in the direction of the noise in time to see the barrel of a shotgun poking out from one of the rusty windows on the trailer.

That's my girl. If she'd heard the noise, it was possible Hank had as well, and there was no way she was going to let him shoot at the trailer. The flimsy material was no match for a shotgun slug. She prayed for good fortune, and when she heard the *chuchak*, she jumped from behind the truck and waved her arms.

"Right here, asshole, I'm right here."

Hank swung the shotgun away from the trailer and aimed at Maribel. As if in slow motion, she saw his finger on the trigger and heard the snick as the gun jammed.

His frustrated voice yelled out, "Fuck, fucking piece of shit."

The *chuchak* filled the air again as he repeated the pump action, putting the slug in the chamber this time for real. The loud shot was deafening. Maribel closed her eyes.

Oh Blair, I'm sorry I couldn't keep my promise, but I couldn't stand by and let him hurt more people.

Chapter Eighteen

Sandy sipped her third cup of coffee. Her leg bounced in agitation. Earlier she'd paced the room like a caged animal. Standing, she approached the desk and smiled politely at the woman.

"Hey, Lise. Any chance you have updated information on Blair Chadwick? They were getting ready to set her up in a room. Is she there yet? If so, can I visit her now?"

Lise looked up and returned Sandy's smile. "I'm not sure. Let me check for you? Even if she is in her room now, she won't be too alert. My guess is they pushed a bunch of pain meds after she woke from surgery."

One of the police officers was standing a few feet away and took a step closer. “Hey, where did Maribel go? I thought she was with the shooting victim. Didn’t she go to the room earlier?”

Sandy turned her wrist and glanced at the time. It had only been forty-five minutes. Maribel said to wait two hours. Her hesitation earned her a glare. “Um, no, I don’t think Maribel is in the room with Blair.”

“You need to tell me if she went back to that cabin.”

“Cabin? No, she wasn’t going to any cabin.”

“You look awfully guilty. Where did Maribel go? Look, she could be in real trouble. Hank is armed and dangerous. She needs to let the police handle this.”

“I told her that,” Sandy said.

“Shit. Come on Joe, let’s go. Maribel is playing hero again.”

“Maribel is going to kill me,” Sandy murmured. Not much she could do about that now. She could, however, ensure Blair was doing okay and help her understand that Maribel’s absence in no way indicated her lack of interest. In fact, Sandy was going to spill the beans about how Maribel felt, because the stubborn oaf would never tell Blair the truth. A little nudge would not hurt. Blair deserved to be loved by someone like Maribel, and Maribel deserved to have someone special in her life.

Sandy was knocked from her internal reverie when Lise put her phone handset down and announced, “She’s settled in her room now. Room 102.”

“Thanks, Lise.”

Sandy made her way down the long hallway. When she entered the room, she took in a deep breath. Blair did not look like herself. Sandy had never seen her look so vulnerable or pale. It hit Sandy that Blair could have died. Being shot was a major trauma. The beeping of the monitors distracted her, and she looked at the lights on the machines. She wasn't sure what the numbers meant, but the nurse fiddling with the machine did not seem concerned. Her kind brown eyes met Sandy's.

"She'll be fine. It was a pretty big hole to repair. Shotgun slugs will do that, but she'll recover, and that pasty white look on her face will change as she gets stronger. You've probably never seen anyone recover from major surgery. They all look like this."

Sandy nodded. "Thanks." She felt better knowing what she was seeing was normal. Normal. That was a loaded word. Nothing about the events over the last few weeks was normal. She didn't want to normalize gun violence. Too many people were doing that, and it wasn't making things better. Placid acceptance of status quo was not going to work. As soon as Blair recovered, she'd jump on the bandwagon and help with whatever plans were already in the works. Because she knew Blair had plans. In that respect, her friend was predictable.

Sandy sat in the chair next to the bed and waited until her friend opened her eyes. Maybe with the police getting involved, she wouldn't have to worry so much. She could wait and give Blair an update when she opened her eyes.

†

Sam flipped on the lights and headed to the part of town he hated going to. Besides the area being dangerous and unpredictable, it was depressing as hell. He'd asked Joe to follow in his own cruiser. Joe didn't seem too happy about that but had grudgingly gotten into his vehicle, and then Sam made the call to let dispatch know where they were heading in case they ran into trouble and needed more back up.

They'd stopped at the cabin and made a cursory search of the dilapidated shack before proceeding along the rural route toward the end of the road where Danella's trailer sat, looking forlorn in the middle of a patch of weeds and dirt. When Sam heard the unmistakable sounds of a shotgun, he pushed his foot on the gas.

By the time he reached the open area and could clearly see the scene before him, the shots had subsided. Maribel crouched next to a prone form with her finger pressed to his neck. She looked up and immediately stood, holding her hands in the air. As Sam was emerging from his vehicle, quickly taking in the scene before him, he noticed her look back at the trailer.

"It was self-defense, Sam. Check his gun, it's been discharged, and I'm sure if you get people out here to search the area, you'll find the same slugs that were in my truck before matching up with the new ones. Could be a few in the dirt, too, where he missed."

Sam waited for Joe to join him and then narrowed his eyes. "Where's your gun?"

"Inside the trailer."

Joe's eyes swiveled to the trailer. "I don't see any holes in that trailer."

"Did you take the shot?" Sam asked.

"Am I under arrest?"

"Maribel, you know I need to determine what happened here. Why are you being so cagey?" Sam asked.

"I already told you. It was self-defense. That's all I'm saying until I have a lawyer."

"Suit yourself. But if you don't have anything to hide, you don't need a lawyer. Is Danella and her kid inside the trailer? Maybe I should be asking them the questions." Joe put his hands on his belt and glared at Maribel.

Sam watched Danella slam open the door and come barreling out. "I ain't answering no questions either without a lawyer present."

The kid crept outside. "Mari didn't do nothing wrong, I—"

"Squirt, you let me handle this," Maribel interrupted.

"Yeah, shush up, Lucritia."

"I'm gonna need to take the gun, Maribel."

"You do whatever you need to do, Sam. I'll get the gun. You know charging anyone here ain't right." Maribel turned toward the trailer and laid her hand on top of the kid's head before ducking inside. When she came back out, she handed the shotgun to Sam.

"Not for me to decide, Maribel. You know that," Sam answered.

"But you have some say. Do I have to come with you, or can I go back to the hospital? Blair might wake up, and I don't want her to think I don't care."

Sam sighed. He liked Maribel. He actually respected the hell out of her but suspected it was either Danella or the kid that shot Hank, and Maribel was likely protecting one of them. She was probably right to do that. They would never convict Maribel, but Danella could get into a lot of trouble for possession of a firearm, much less killing a man. And Maribel might not fare too well if they found out she was the one to give her the gun. Nope, the authorities wouldn't be pleased to hear she'd given either Danella or the kid a shotgun.

"Fine, we'll sort this out later, after they've had a chance to scour the scene and collect the evidence," Sam agreed. "Joe, get my digital camera. I need to photograph her truck before she leaves."

"What? You're going to just let them all go on their merry way?" Joe asked.

"Yup, I am. Maribel, you need to take Danella and the kid with you. We can't have them impeding our investigation in any way."

Joe grumbled as he walked to Sam's car and retrieved the camera.

Maribel smiled. "Thanks, Sam. I'll take them to my place, and I promise when you're ready to interview us, we'll be cooperative. With legal counsel, of course," she added.

Sam nodded and accepted the digital camera from his scowling colleague, who continued to glare at Maribel,

Danella, and the kid. She brought the kid close to her and waited while Sam took several pictures of the bullet holes in Maribel's truck from various angles, both inside and out.

When Sam was finished with what he thought might be acceptable, knowing he'd still get his ass reamed, he motioned to Maribel that he was done. Maribel patted the kid's shoulder and directed, "Danella, Squirt, get in my truck. You're both coming to my place until we can figure this out and give the police time to do their job. Hopefully my truck will still run with a bunch of holes in it. She may not look pretty anymore, but all she needs to do is fire up and I'll be happy. Sam, I'll bring the truck in later if someone else needs to take a closer look."

Sam waved her away and earned another glare from Joe.

†

When the truck immediately roared to life, Maribel sent a small prayer that she'd bought such a durable vehicle. At least none of the slugs had affected the engine block. Before leaving, she heard Sam say to the irritated officer, "I'll take accountability for the decision to let them leave, so stop your bellyaching. Hank got exactly what he deserved. People will likely want to pin a medal on whoever took the shot, and I don't give a fuck right now which one of them it was."

Maribel rolled down the road and didn't hear his response. Her heart broke when Lucritia's tiny voice asked,

"Did I do something wrong, Mari? I only done what you told me to."

"No, Squirt, you done good. I am so proud of you. You saved my life. I owe you a debt of gratitude that I'll never be able to repay."

"Aw, Mari. You done so much for Ma and me, you ain't got to repay me."

"We're going to tell the police what happened, but only after I make a few calls and we have someone who can help us. But don't you ever think you've done anything wrong. You haven't."

"Are you going to get in trouble for giving us the guns?" Danella asked.

Maribel shrugged. "That's what lawyers get paid the big bucks for. The public's going to side with us on this. No way they'll make an issue of it without a shit ton of bad press. Sam knows that. I'm sorry I can't give you a proper tour because I need to get to the hospital. You can snoop to your heart's content. There is plenty of food in the fridge. Don't let Squirt drink all my beer, no matter how much she begs," Maribel joked.

Lucritia giggled. "I don't drink beer."

"You don't? I thought you were a mini adult. All grown up. You mean you're not old enough to have a beer?"

"No. I'm only eight."

"Thanks, Mari. We'll get out of your hair as soon as this is resolved. I can't afford a lawyer, but maybe one of those public defenders can help us."

"Don't you worry about that. I'll be sending one to talk with you. Just answer the door when someone rings. Oh, and if you're interested, you might find a few kittens out back next to the chicken coop. I made them a little house."

Lucritia squealed in delight. "Mama, can we go see the kittens?"

Danella wrapped her arm around Lucritia and squeezed. "Sure, baby. Want us to gather the eggs?"

"Oh shit, I forgot. I'm not sure if the eggs I have in the back are intact or if the food is still good. I can't worry about that now. I really need to get to the hospital."

"You love this woman?" Danella asked.

"You're the second person to ask that question today. Yeah, I think I might."

"Good. I was hoping you would find someone special," Danella answered.

"Are you gonna teach her how to shoot, too?" Lucritia innocently asked.

"Nah, I don't think she wants to learn. Besides, I don't pass along my secrets to anyone. You're special."

"But Mama said she was special, too." Lucritia peered at Maribel.

Maribel smiled at the young girl. "She's special in a different way."

Lucritia scrunched her little face. "Oh. Like someone you wanna kiss, right?"

"Yeah, something like that." Maribel laughed.

She was glad to be off of the rural route and back onto the highway. She wasn't sure she would ever shake the memories of what had occurred. She would have to find a way to overcome her reaction because several families depended on her. Even more important, Maribel knew that Lucritia would need support and counseling. She'd make sure she got the best help that money could buy.

†

A blanket of fog seemed to engulf Blair as she opened her eyes. Slowly, like in the fall mornings when fog was a common occurrence, the haziness began to lift. She turned her head and found Sandy sitting in a chair, absently scrolling through her phone.

"Sandy?" Blair's voice came out in a gravely whisper.

"Hey there. How ya doing?"

"A dull ache in my leg, and it feels like someone stuffed cotton in my head, but other than that, if I were so inclined, ready to run a marathon."

"Glad to see that bullet or whatever is in a shotgun didn't blast out your sense of humor."

"Maribel?" An immediate sense of panic caused the beeping of the monitors to go crazy.

"Whoa, whoa. She's fine. Told me to tell you she would be back after she took care of something. She wanted you to know she's not abandoning you, but this was important."

"Please tell me she did not go to my mom's."

"No, no. She did wonder if she should contact her, but then we decided to let you make that decision."

Blair's muscles relaxed, and the monitor returned to a slower cadence. "Do you know what she had to do?"

Sandy avoided looking at Blair. "Um, yeah. I told her I didn't like her plan."

"She went back to Danella's place, didn't she? Never mind, you don't need to confirm that. Of course she did."

"Don't be mad at her. She's in love with you. Did you know that?"

Blair turned away. "I'm tired. Go home, Sandy. And, tell Maribel not to bother visiting me. I'm exhausted and wouldn't be able to give her a proper lecture right now."

Sandy patted the hand attached to the IV. "I'll tell her, but obviously she doesn't listen to me. Just for clarification, you don't want us to tell your mom?"

"Hell no." Blair closed her eyes.

She kept them tightly closed and several minutes passed, but sleep would not come. She had too many thoughts invading her brain. When she heard a rustle in the room and the sound of the chair scratching along the floor, she thought Sandy was heeding her request until a hand brushed along her forehead. She knew that touch.

"Maribel."

"Yeah, honey, I'm right here. Everything is going to be fine. I needed to see you before I go make my statement to the police."

"Really? And where were you before? Clearly not at the police station."

"No. I had to make sure Danella and Squirt were safe. And they are now."

"How can you or anyone make sure we're safe these days when the go-to response is to shoot first and ask questions later? The government should just issue an assault weapon to everyone. Isn't that what the Second Amendment says? We can all march around like this is the wild west," Blair spit out in disgust.

"Hank's dead," Maribel answered.

"Great, one asshole dead and a million others still out there. Live by the gun, die by the gun. I suppose you killed him."

"No, Squirt did. That's why I have to hire a lawyer and try to unravel this mess without anyone getting in trouble."

"Great. And you put the weapon in her hand. How is she ever going to live with herself? Fuck, Maribel, she's eight."

"She saved my life. He had me pinned behind my truck. Doesn't that mean anything to you? If it wasn't for Squirt, I'd be dead. Is that what you want?"

"I can't do this right now. Please leave. Don't come back. I'm going to ask Sandy if I can stay with her. If you could grab my bags and give them to Sandy, I would appreciate it. It's the last favor I'll ask of you, but I can't just walk out of here and do it myself right now."

"All right. If that's what you need..." Maribel reached for Blair's hand then pulled back to wipe the tears on her face.

Maribel's slumped shoulders and dejected posture as she left the room were almost enough to have Blair call her back. Almost.

Chapter Nineteen

"I'm not your personal secretary." Sandy held out her cell phone. "Answer the damn call."

Blair shook her head. The laptop was propped on her lap while her leg remained elevated on the couch. "Honestly, Sandy, I have too much left to do. The rally is in a month. Tell her I'll call after all of this is done."

"Tell her yourself." Sandy glared at Blair.

Blair shook her head again and whispered, "I can't, please not yet."

Sandy walked into the other room and Blair heard her say, "Give it a little more time, Maribel. I promise you she won't be immune to your persistence forever. How's the rest of the mess going? Good, good. That's a relief."

After Sandy walked back into the room and set her cell phone on the counter, Blair asked, "What's a relief?"

"Why should I tell you?"

"Aw, come on, Sandy. I still care about what happens to her. Are they going to charge her with anything, like the accessory to murder or something related to our firearms laws, pitiful as they are? It's still against the law to sell or give a gun to a convicted felon or someone who is not family."

"Not that you're deserving of this answer, but no, they aren't going to charge her or Lucritia. She has to pay a hefty fine or something, but that's all. Danella is completely in the clear, which is good because she was the one with the greatest risk. People make assumptions about those who have been in prison, even for a short time."

"You think I'm being too hard on her, don't you?"

"Honestly, yeah. You two have different perspectives on a lot of things, but Maribel is not the symbol of the evil right. No matter what she believes, you can't paint her into that corner. It isn't right. She isn't your father who, by the way, is introducing legislation for background checks and a ban on assault weapons. Maybe it's time for you to bury the hatchet. He could be a powerful speaker at your rally."

"No fucking way. His previous stance on gun control isn't the only reason I hate him."

"I'm just saying, there isn't always a clear right and wrong in every situation. There are shades of gray. It sounds like he's here to stay. Your mother is happy, or at least as happy as she can be at this moment in her life after dealing with tragedy. Like it or not, he's the source of that happiness. I believe he truly loves your mother, and it's clear she loves him back."

"He's still married to that snooty bitch. All I have to do is bide my time until he goes running back."

"I don't think so. I believe he was served divorce papers, and he didn't seem unhappy about it."

Blair raised her eyebrow. "You're shitting me."

"Nope. He was having coffee with your mom, and the server tracked him down at the shop. Of course, I had to slip from behind the counter to ask if they needed anything and managed to catch a glimpse of the papers. He had a smile on his face, so I don't think he was devastated by the news."

Blair shifted on the couch. "Wow. I'm still holding my judgment. He's a wishy-washy politician. He could go running back to her if it suits his interests."

"I also heard a rumor that he might be leaving the Republican Party."

"Okay, now I know hell has frozen over," Blair joked.

"No, apparently he's been profoundly affected by…"

"You can say it, by Trina's death." Blair swiped at her cheek. "God damn it. When will the pain subside?"

Sandy approached the couch and squatted next to Blair. "Oh, hon, eventually the pain might lesson, but your grief will never completely go away. Tragedy has that effect on people. Life is filled with pain for everyone and no one escapes that, but for some, tragedy hits harder. That sucks. I know that. You have a lot of people around who can provide love and support, some that you need to let back in."

"Right now, the distraction of planning this rally is what I need. The rest I will have to figure out later after the pressure is off. Can we leave it at that for now?"

"She's hurting right now, too. For different reasons, but still you should know that."

Blair frowned. She didn't like knowing she was responsible for Maribel's pain. "Please tell her I need more time, okay?"

"I'm a fucking baker, not a damn secretary," Sandy mumbled as she walked back into her kitchen.

†

Danella shuffled to the pot of coffee that had recently completed brewing and poured herself a cup. Maribel was leaning against the counter with her head down and the phone still held tightly in her hand. She'd been calling every single day since Blair was released from the hospital, but Blair refused to talk with her, giving every excuse imaginable.

"Still not taking your calls?" Danella asked.

"No, and I'm not sure why I'm hell-bent on making the effort. Maybe I should give up."

Danella took a sip. "Look, I don't mean to be abandoning you in your time of need, but Lucritia and I need to move back into our trailer. The grocery store offered me a full-time position, and I'm gonna take it. Thanks for sticking your neck out again for me. The cops finished tearing up my place, and that fancy lawyer you hired is taking care of everything else. It's time."

Maribel nodded. "Will you please let me help you buy something safer to live in? Manufactured homes are a lot nicer these days, and you can consider me a kind of bank. I'm not offering to give you the money, but a loan is something that'll make all of us happy."

"Fine. It sorta breaks my heart to take Lucritia away from what she considers a palace. If I get something a little nicer, it'll make the transition easier. You think you can catch that little calico she's been playing with?"

"Squirt could do that. The little fuzz ball lets Squirt pet her. They've bonded. I'll grab the dog carrier. It's bigger than we need, but it'll do the trick. Why don't you wait until we arrange for the new place before you leave? I could use the company for a few more weeks while I continue to lick my wounds and prepare myself for a life of loneliness again."

"She'll come 'round. You should show up at that big rally she's planning. Make a speech or something. Show her you've been thinking about things and listening to her. Women like it when they think someone is listening to them and what they gotta say about things."

"You tired of eggs yet?"

"Nah, I appreciate food, period. Can't afford to be picky. Can't afford a lot just yet, but maybe my fortune is changing. I never had a full-time job before. Not a legal one, anyway. Squirt is collecting the eggs right now. She likes having a job, too."

"I'm going to rename her the chicken whisperer. Even Henrietta doesn't peck her when she's grabbing her eggs."

"Yeah, my baby is multi-talented. You don't think she'll be scarred for life 'cause of what she done?"

"I don't honestly know. It haunts me sometimes to think I might be the cause of any future trauma. That's one thing Blair got right. I never should have given her that shotgun. Or at the very least, I never should have told her to shoot Hank if he stepped one foot on your property. What kind of monster am I to tell a kid to do that?"

"It's a slippery slope, I'll give you that. But she idolizes you. When she learned you started at almost the same age, she decided she wants to be exactly like you. You can't take her shotgun away now. But maybe we can emphasize the shotgun is for skeet competitions not blowing holes into loser drug dealers."

"Hank's buddies haven't been hassling you, have they?"

"Are you kidding? Not after hearing about Hank. Nope. One good thing to come out of this is no one from the old life would think about coming 'round now. Hank's death is a much better deterrent to leaving us alone than possible jail time."

"That should make me feel better but oddly it doesn't. I'm still working through the ethics of this whole mess and missing Blair in the process. I got used to her being around, even though it was only a few days."

Danella picked up the teapot and poured hot water into a mug with the dry chai-tea mixture, then pushed it toward Maribel. "Love will do that to ya. Maybe someday I'll find my own Blair. Someone who doesn't sell meth."

"Sam might be interested."

"A cop? No way."

"Stranger things have happened. If I can make it work with someone who is my polar opposite, an ex-con can at least consider a cop."

"You fix it with Ms. Gun Control Activist, and maybe I'll consider it."

"I'm trying, Danella. I really am. But at some point, even a dumb country bumpkin like me catches a clue. If she continues to refuse to talk to me, I'll have no choice but to give up."

"Maybe you should skip a few days or few weeks and then try again. Give her time to consider what she might be missing if you stop calling. Right now, she knows you'll keep calling. She'll take comfort in that. Shake it up a little. Make her wonder."

"Are you telling me to play hard to get? That's playing a stupid little game that isn't who I am."

"But being a stalker is?" Danella shook her head.

"I'm not a stalker. It's not like she's issued a restraining order against me."

"Exactly. She wants you to keep calling. She's the one playing the game."

"I don't know, Danella. It doesn't feel right."

Lucritia banged open the glass door holding two cartons full of eggs as she rushed into the room. "Cali jumped on me today and licked my face."

Maribel chuckled. "What'd you do, put cream on your face?"

"No, she likes me." Lucritia set the cartons on the counter.

"How do you know it's a she?"

"All calico kittens are female. Everyone knows that."

"Danella, did you know that?" Maribel asked.

Danella shook her head and smiled at her daughter. "I haven't spent every second of my free time on Mari's computer reading everything I can on how to care for kittens."

"Can I get my own computer now that you got a job?" Hope was written on Lucritia's face.

"We'll see. We got other priorities to take care of. The first one, paying back Mari who's gonna loan us the money to get a new place to live."

Lucritia frowned. "I don't wanna live out there anymore, a new trailer ain't gonna make it safe. Why can't we stay here with Mari?"

"Because this isn't our home."

"What if we put a new trailer on Mari's land? She's got plenty of land. I could help. I'd be real good at gathering the eggs every day. That could be my full-time job."

"Aw honey, we can't intrude on Mari. She's already done too much for us." Danella placed her hand on Lucritia's shoulder.

Lucritia turned her hopeful face in Maribel's direction. "We're not intruding, are we? You like having us here, right?"

"I do and that's a mighty fine idea. Why don't you let me talk to your mama?" Maribel ventured a look at Danella who was shaking her head but smiling at the same time.

"We'll see," Danella said.

Chapter Twenty

Blair was hobbling to the front door to answer the buzzer when Sandy entered the condo carrying a pizza.

"Hey, I was gonna pay for that." Blair leaned on her crutches.

"Go back to your spot on the couch and keep working on that indent. I want an excuse to buy a new one. Not that I don't love having you here because it's been like a three-week slumber party, but now that you're talking with your father, maybe you can do some additional bonding with him at your mom's place."

"Ouch, that hurts. Kicking out the wounded warrior. Seriously, am I cramping your style? I don't want to take advantage of you."

"No, it's not that. I just think it's been good to see things working out with at least one person who doesn't share every single opinion you have of the way the world should work. I thought if you could make total peace with him, then someone else might stand a chance. I know for a fact that if you didn't want to go back and live with your mom while you're on leave and planning your rally, someone else would jump at the chance to have you back at her place."

"Doubtful. She hasn't called in two weeks. Have you talked to her?" Using her crutches, Blair made her way back to the couch, pushing the throw pillow underneath her leg.

"No, no, no. I'm not letting either one of you make me the go-between. This isn't high school. The two of you need to grow the fuck up." Sandy tossed the pizza on the coffee table. "I'm grabbing myself a beer. Your stubbornness is driving me nuts, and I need to chill. You get water. I don't need those pain meds mixing with alcohol and me having to drag your ass to the ED."

Blair decided to steer Sandy in another direction. "Just for clarification, I'm not exactly at peace with the Sperm Donor, but I recognize how he could be helpful in my fight. He's agreed to speak at the rally, and I'm not stupid enough to let our past history screw up a golden opportunity for the press to cover this. I've been able to take him in small doses for the greater good."

Sandy pulled beer and water from the refrigerator, handing Blair the water before sitting on the chair. Popping the top of the beer, she took a large swig. "Someone else could also make a big impact at that rally. I don't understand why you don't call her and ask her to come. Jesus, Blair, if you can work with your dad, why not Maribel?"

"Because I hurt her too much. When I was still processing everything and wouldn't take her calls…" Blair lifted the lid to the pizza and avoided Sandy's penetrating gaze.

"I'm not gonna lie. You did hurt her. She's in love with you."

Blair's head jerked up. A piece of pizza hung loosely in her hand. "What?"

"You heard me. She's in love with you. Come on, Blair, you aren't stupid. You had to know that Maribel doesn't open up to anyone. She let you in her heart and her home. And you stomped all over her with barely a look back."

"I did not. I got shot for fuck's sake. Shot!"

"And that was her fault, how?"

"I don't know. She has guns all over her house. She gives them out like candy on Halloween. If it were in my power, I'd take away every single person's guns in the whole damn United States. Fuck the Second Amendment. What about the Declaration of Independence and everyone's right to life, liberty, and the pursuit of happiness? Shouldn't that inalienable right trump the Second Amendment?"

"You know the constitution was written by a bunch of men. Who, by the way, did not include women in that statement about being created equal? They also weren't referring to people of color, so all of it's a bunch of crap if you want my opinion. That was a different time. You know I agree with you to a certain extent. I'm not sure what the Second Amendment rights were intended to protect, but I know that Maribel's guns have kept her from the cycle of poverty. I shouldn't get to take that away from her. Nor would I want to. We all have our special talents. Nobody is trying to take away your right to hold a rally and rile people up about gun control. Why would you want to squash her passion?"

"Not the same thing. My passion doesn't lead to massive death."

Sandy shrugged. "I'm just saying that it doesn't have to be all or nothing. Even those most rabid about gun control aren't suggesting we take away every single gun in the whole United States. If you lead with that at the rally, I guarantee you won't get very far."

"Did she tell you she was in love with me?" Blair took a large bite of the pizza flopping in her hand.

"Sort of. She said something about you being so exasperating, but she thought she was falling in love. I told you this before at the hospital. I echo the exasperating part." Sandy grinned.

"I'm not the only person who is maddening. She's pretty irksome, too."

"Not disagreeing on that, but I would like the two of you to be infuriating together. You can start Irksome Island and live happily ever after annoying the hell out of each other." Sandy laughed.

"You think you are such a comedian. Maybe I'll call her. Just to see how she's doing." Blair chomped on the pizza and ventured a side glance at Sandy to determine her reaction.

Sandy grinned and took another large swallow of beer before grabbing her own piece of pizza and taking a huge bite.

†

Lucritia bounced on the balls of her feet while holding the small calico kitten against her neck. Maribel heard the tiny kitten purring from several feet away.

"You excited, Squirt?" Maribel asked.

Lucritia bobbed her head and grinned. "I get my own room."

Danella had her arm around Lucritia watching as the men made quick work of placing the new home in the space marked off. Maribel had suggested the spot that was finally agreed upon because it was convenient for the necessary water and utility hook-ups but far enough away that Danella and Lucritia would feel like they weren't living on Maribel's land. For whatever reason, that seemed important to Danella. She'd planned out a budget that would allow her to pay off the loan within ten years. Maribel thought the plan was a bit too aggressive but had agreed to it. She had even settled on the three percent interest rate that Danella insisted was only fair if this was going to be a business transaction. Danella didn't want this to be another gift that would make her feel like she hadn't established the kind of independence she desired to feel like a productive member of society.

"It's really happening," Danella said through a happy sigh.

"I'm very proud of you," Maribel said.

"What about me?" Lucritia asked.

"You too. I'm not sure I would have been able to get as much practice in if it weren't for you collecting the eggs for me. And that's a mighty nice garden you have started over there." Maribel pointed to the patch of dirt filled with plants that would endure the colder temperatures as they eased into fall.

"Heard anything from Blair yet?" Danella asked.

"Nah. I'm giving her space. Besides, I've been busy lately."

"Yeah, right," Danella scoffed.

"Hey, you're the one who told me to stop calling every day."

"Isn't that big rally of hers in a few weeks?"

"Yeah, so?"

"So, you've let her cool off. Maybe you should call and offer to help. Make a speech or something to show you support her, even if you don't agree with her on everything. I know you agree on some things."

The buzz from her phone vibrated in her back pocket. "Hang on a sec." She held up her finger and then pulled out her phone.

"Hello."

"Hey, Maribel, it's Blair. I was wondering if you might want to come to town sometime and join me for coffee."

"Really? You mean that? Sandy didn't put you up to this or something?"

"Sandy might have been yapping at me, but she didn't put me up to this. More like banged on my thick skull. In a good way. I miss you. I know that seems odd since we only spent a few days together, but it's the truth."

Maribel let out the air she was holding inside. Danella mouthed, *who is it*?

Maribel waved her hand, but the smile on her face must have revealed her exuberance.

Danella had an ear-splitting grin on her face as she made kissy noises.

"Are you making kissing sounds?" Blair asked.

Maribel laughed. "No, that was Danella, Sandy's counterpart. She's been advising me on what to do. Told me I needed to leave you be for a bit. Said I needed to stop being a creepy stalker and give ya space."

"Well, do you want to have coffee or not?"

Maribel thought she heard a bit of hesitation behind the clipped tone and hurried to answer as honestly as she could. "More than I can express over the phone. You tell me when and I'll be there. I assume the where is Sandy's place."

"How about tomorrow? Does nine sound okay? I know you have deliveries to make in the morning."

"That sounds perfect and thank you. I am looking forward to seeing you, Blair. I've missed you, too." Maribel pressed the end call symbol and couldn't stop the giddy smile from overtaking her face.

"Awwww, see I told you giving her space would work," Danella said.

"Okay, if you know all about how I can repair the damage, I'm all ears. Should I bring flowers like I did the first time we had coffee together?"

"Maybe, but can you come up with something less ordinary? Besides her social activism, was there anything that made her eyes light up? How'd she feel about this place? Did she like the whole country chic?"

"She liked my house, except for the trophy room. That wasn't a big hit. She loved the kittens."

"Perfect. Catch one of the little furballs for her. If nothing else, it would be a unique gesture."

"Yeah, Mari. A kitten is a great present. I love Cali. Mama says she can come in the new house with me," Lucritia offered her opinion.

"Sandy might tar and feather me if I gave her a kitten and she brought her back to Sandy's place."

Danella wiggled her eyebrows. "That's even more reason to catch one for her. Then you could invite her to crash at your place again since Sandy won't be too happy about another guest she hasn't planned on having."

"Devious. Maybe that works for you, but I'm more of a straight shooter."

"You might want to keep any mention of shooting from your conversation. Besides you ain't straight. Honest and forthright, sure, that's you to a T. Okay, how about if you come right out and say that you wanted to bring something for her, and it had to be extra special. Plus, you miss having her around. And you thought the gift would serve another purpose. You could admit you thought the kitten would entice her to stay with you 'cause Sandy might not appreciate a kitten clawing her furniture or having to deal with a litter box."

"The little gray one likes me. He eats out of my hand, and he's been letting me pick him up. I could try to catch him for ya, Mari. Since Mama won't let me have two, you should take him. He's awful sweet."

"If you think it's a good idea, then it must be." Maribel ruffled Lucritia's hair. "Tomorrow morning after you gather the eggs, could you see if you can catch him for me?"

"I sure will." Lucritia offered Maribel her gap-toothed grin, and the plan was settled.

CHAPTER TWENTY-ONE

After ordering her coffee, Blair rested on her crutches as she stood in front of the counter. She'd arrived half an hour early for her date. Was it a date? She didn't know. Maribel had considered it a date when they'd had coffee before, but that was prior to the game-changing day she was shot. The crutches were a stark reminder of the terrible events of the last month. Blair kept changing her focus to the door and jumped when Sandy called out to her. She imagined she looked like she had a nervous tic.

"What the hell is going on with you? Are you expecting someone? Oh my God, you are. You called her!"

"Sshh. I'm not sure I want the whole coffee shop in my business."

"I'm proud of you. I'll bet Maribel is over the moon about this. What time is she coming? I'll make her favorite drink and heat up the cinnamon rolls. Maybe that'll sweeten you a bit so you don't start something." Sandy swiped the counter where a few crumbs had fallen from the last customer's blueberry coffee-cake muffin.

"Funny, but go right ahead. This time, I'll have the tea and rolls waiting for her. If you don't mind, I'm going to go to the couch and sit. My leg is starting to throb. If I'm vertical for too long, I get nasty messages from my leg."

"Then sit your ass down, and I'll deliver the goodies. I know Maribel's drink of choice, so I'll make that along with yours."

"Um, can you wait to make hers? I might have gotten here a little early. She isn't supposed to arrive until nine. By that time, I'll be ready for a second coffee."

Sandy raised her eyebrow. "Okay, then I'm only adding one shot of espresso to the first drink."

"Good idea." Blair hobbled to the couch and sat heavily, setting her crutches to the side. She kept her focus on the door, even after her first coffee was delivered.

Taking a sip of the sweet beverage, she couldn't help the smile that expanded on her face when she saw Maribel push open the door with one hand, while holding something against her chest that apparently was hidden inside her light jacket. Blair wondered why Maribel would be hiding flowers beneath her clothes. She was fifteen minutes early, and that did not surprise Blair, because the last time they had a coffee date, Maribel had been nervously waiting for Blair. This time Blair wanted to turn the tables.

Maribel scanned the shop, and when her eyes landed on Blair, they widened in surprise. Blair waved her over and then motioned for Sandy to hurry up with the cinnamon rolls, coffee, and tea. Maribel was still holding her chest, and Blair saw movement underneath the jacket. A fuzzy gray head popped out of the opening, and then Blair heard the tiny meow.

Maribel looked at the squirming bundle of fur, and a shy smile appeared on her face.

"You caught one," Blair remarked.

"Not me. Squirt caught two, actually. Uh, I wanted to bring you something, but flowers seemed so conventional."

Blair laughed. "You brought me a kitten, instead of flowers?"

"Apparently, like with many other things I do, not my finest moment, huh? Damn, I don't seem to get much right, do I?"

"No, no, this is about the sweetest gesture anyone has ever tried on a date. I love it. Sandy might not agree, but it's flawless and perfectly you. Sometimes you amaze me. I've never quite met anyone like you, and that is a good thing, despite our many differences."

Maribel sat and pulled the irritated kitten from beneath her jacket. "He's still feral, but Squirt has done a lot to tame him."

Blair brought the kitten to her chest. He snuggled against her neck and began to purr. "Wow. He's already bonding to me. Thank you. I hope Sandy will let me keep him at her place."

Sandy approached the table and set down the hot drinks and rolls. "Oh my God, that is the cutest kitten. Look at that white around his little muzzle. It looks like he stuck his face in a bowl of milk." She leaned in and stroked his head. "But, no, I don't think my rental allows pets. You'll have to see if Maribel will let you stay with her again." Sandy's wry grin was clearly unapologetic.

"You can stay with me. The offer never expired. I could either set up a bedroom downstairs or carry you up each night if you want," Maribel added. She looked down and wouldn't meet Blair's eyes. Blair thought it was almost as if she were afraid of what Blair would say in response to the offer.

"I don't want to inconvenience you. Besides, I'm guessing without me in your hair, you've been able to resume your practice sessions." Blair hesitated before continuing to express her qualms, but she thought Maribel deserved her candor. "The truth is, I may be suffering from a bit of PTSD. The other day I heard a car backfire, and to say it sent me into a tizzy would be putting it mildly."

"I'm sorry." Maribel leaned forward and those kind, compassionate eyes caused Blair's tears to leak out.

"Don't be. You weren't the one who shot me. I've got to stop blaming everyone who owns a gun for my issues. I'm working through things. I just can't handle anything that might trigger a meltdown."

"I'll lock the guns away. I won't practice at the house." Maribel sounded almost desperate.

"I can't ask you to change everything in your life to accommodate me and my quirks. I'll figure something out. I might consider going back to Mom's place, but that isn't my preference right now, even if the Sperm Donor and I are in a temporary truce."

"I gotta get back to my customers. Let me know what y'all figure out. I still think Maribel's place is the right answer, and I'm rarely wrong about these things." Sandy sauntered off.

"That's great about you and your dad." Maribel took Blair's hand in hers. "Honestly, I miss you, Blair, and I miss what we were building on. I feel like I might only have this one chance, and if I can't somehow do something to make it work, I'll lose this window of opportunity forever. It will vanish into thin air, never to return again. Or at least not in my lifetime."

"Can I think about it?"

"Of course. I better take the little furball back with me until you have things figured out."

"Do you have to?"

"No. You could come back with me after coffee. Problem resolved."

"You don't play fair."

"All's fair in love and kitten saving," Maribel declared.

Maribel looked so hopeful that Blair almost agreed right on the spot, but for once in her life she needed to not react without thought. Passion always seemed to entice her to leap without looking first.

"Tell me what's been happening in your life since…" Blair couldn't finish the sentence and instead barreled into her confession. "I'll admit I've been pumping Sandy for whatever scrap of information she would offer me, but she's such a brat she didn't give up much."

"First, why don't you tell me how the rally planning is coming along. I'd like to help. I've been thinking about things. Nonstop if you want the God-honest truth. I could say a few things that might be interesting to hear from someone like me. I'll need help writing out what to say, though."

"I doubt it. When you speak from the heart, you're compelling to listen to."

†

Maribel was whistling when she entered her kitchen. As she put away her groceries, she began planning the meal she would prepare. Maybe a repeat of the first dinner they shared together would go over as well as an echo of their first coffee date with a minor deviation. The kitten had been a big hit. The gesture had been received better than she had thought possible. She would have to thank Danella and Lucritia for thinking of that. She wondered if having them there would put a damper on the evening or provide a reminder of the day Blair was shot. This was a conundrum she wasn't sure she'd be able to resolve. Danella would understand not having dinner together like they'd been doing for the past several weeks, but Lucritia would be hurt, and Maribel couldn't do that to her. They'd almost been like a small family, except Danella wasn't a lesbian, and Maribel didn't think about her like that. Instead, she wondered what it might be like to have a child with Blair. She didn't know if Blair wanted children. They hadn't gotten that far in their discussions about what the future looked like for either one of them. And they had not approached the other elephant in the room. Would Blair return to her previous life and move away? She was still writing grants on the side so maybe that meant she could do her work anywhere. It was making Maribel's head ache thinking of all the possible paths in life that each person could choose to take.

The back door slammed open, and Lucritia barreled inside, holding Cali firmly against her body. "Did she like Grayson? How come she didn't come back with you?"

"Whoa. One question at a time. Yeah, she liked the kitten. Thank you for catching him. She's coming for dinner tonight."

"Cool. I like how much you smile when she's around or right now after she called you, not like before when you were so sad. Are we still going to eat out back? I can set the table for four." Lucritia grabbed the calico kitten and gently pulled her down to stop her from clawing up her neck and chewing on her hair.

Maribel resigned herself to having a dinner party and hoping that the important people in her life would get along. Because Danella and Lucritia were her family, and she couldn't think about the possibility of making a choice between them and Blair.

"That would be great, Squirt. It's still nice out, so yeah, we can eat on the back patio. I got chicken and steak. You can be my apprentice tonight. I'll need to focus on grilling to make sure I don't overcook anything."

"I can do that." Lucritia grinned.

A short knock on the back door interrupted her conversation with Lucritia. Maribel waved Danella inside.

"Did you knock before coming in and bothering Mari?" Danella pursed her lips as she gently chastised Lucritia.

Lucritia looked at her feet and mumbled, "I forgot."

"We talked about this. We got our own place now. You can't go barreling into someone else's home before knocking. That ain't proper manners."

"I'm sorry, Mama."

"Don't say sorry to me, apologize to Mari. She's the one you been rude to."

"It's okay, you don't have to knock and neither does Squirt. You're family and family doesn't have to knock." Maribel placed her hand on Lucritia's head and smiled.

Danella shook her head. "That's nice of you to say, but I need to teach her proper manners and that means knocking. Where's Blair? I thought for sure she'd be coming back with you. It would have been perfect timing. Now that we got our own place, we'd be outta your hair so's you could entertain her without us getting in the way."

"Baby steps. She's coming for dinner tonight. I told Squirt here that I needed her to be my apprentice so I don't burn the meat."

"We should let the two of you have a meal together without us horning in on your evening. I got stuff in the fridge to cook up. You don't have to make dinner for us every evening. I got my first check last week, and with my discount I was able to fill my cupboards. It might be a little while before I have enough to start paying on my loan. I need to look for a used car soon with winter coming. I'd rather not bike to work in the cold and rain. Too bad the bus don't come all the way out here," Danella lamented. "Living out in the sticks has its advantages but getting around ain't one of 'em."

"You save that food for another time. I want us to all have dinner together." Maribel held up her hand to stop Danella's protest. "I have my reasons. We'll go car shopping. Before you raise a ruckus, we can simply add to that loan but still make it affordable. It wouldn't kill you to accept a reworked payment plan that is fifteen years instead of ten."

"I'm not stupid, I know they won't give me a loan for a car. We can cross that bridge when we come to it. Lucritia's been showing me things on that computer of hers, which I'm still a little pissed that you got for her. I want to pay you back for that, too. There's all these resources out there for doing a budget and figuring out loans and stuff. I know exactly how much I gotta pay each month for how much you loaned me. I can put new numbers in that X sheet she showed me and we'll see."

Maribel chuckled. "You mean Excel?"

"Yeah, that one."

"It took me a little while after high school to learn those fancy programs. Pa insisted that if I wasn't going to continue to go to school, I needed to start learning on my own. He was the one that told me to get my first computer. He planned for me to go to college, but that wasn't a path I chose to travel."

"I hope Lucritia decides to go to college. I'd prefer a different life for her. She's smart as a whip."

"I want to be like Mari, I'm gonna make money shooting things. I don't want to go to college," Lucritia argued.

"I thought you wanted to take care of animals. Be an animal doctor. You gotta go to college for that," Maribel answered.

"Oh." Lucritia scrunched her face in concentration. "I'll think about it."

Danella and Maribel laughed at the seriousness of her response.

"So what time is this big dinner?" Danella asked.

"She said she'd be by around 5:30. I've got to find a place to store all my guns. She doesn't need anything to trigger her. Maybe if I do that, she'll reconsider staying with me. At least until the big rally. After that, I'm not sure about her plans."

"Why can't you leave them in that room of yours? Most of them are stored there right now. Just keep the door closed," Danella suggested.

Maribel shook her head. "No, she's been in that room. I need to turn it into something else."

"How you gonna do that in the short time you have before dinner?" Danella asked.

"I don't know." Maribel crinkled her nose in consternation.

"How about you carry them to our place, and we can figure something out later," Danella offered.

"I can help. I'm careful with guns, like you taught me. You gotta respect your shotgun and make sure it ain't loaded until you're ready to practice with it," Lucritia said.

"Yup, that's right, Squirt. Okay, I guess I don't have a better option. Thanks, Danella."

"It's the least we can do. Lead the way, and we'll turn that room into something else. Something she'll like."

"I got an idea. It isn't only the guns that I want to clear outta that room, so I can't ask you to store all my crap at your place. I'm planning to go into town anyway to do a little shopping, so I might as well rent one of those storage units. Squirt, do you wanna go shopping with me? I might need your help to pick out stuff for what I want to turn this room into."

Lucritia swiveled her head to look at her mom. "Can I go with Mari?"

Danella nodded. "Sure. We better hurry up and box the trophies. As I recall, you had a shit ton in that room of yours. How come? Doesn't seem like you to be all braggy about stuff."

"My pa."

"Oh, right. Your pa was a good man. He used to come 'round when I was a kid. Always brought us fresh game. I guess you took up the mantle, huh? He taught you how to be a decent human being. I need to teach Lucritia that. And manners."

"Yeah, he was the best. I miss him every day. Don't you worry about Squirt. She's a good kid."

Lucritia beamed at the comment.

†

The door banged open so hard, Maribel heard the noise reverberate all the way back to the room she was putting the last touches on.

"She's here," Lucritia yelled.

"Lucritia Mary, what did I tell you about knocking first," Danella reprimanded.

Maribel walked out of the room chuckling. "It's okay. So, what do you think? Open or closed?"

"Closed. It'll be like a surprise. I like surprises, especially if they're good surprises." Lucritia vibrated with energy. "Can Cali come and play with Grayson?"

Skeeter stretched and stood. Wagging his tail, he made his way to Maribel.

"Sure, Squirt." Maribel ruffled Lucritia's hair. "Let's go out and meet our guest. We can be prim and proper and use our best manners. That'll make your mom happy."

Blair had emerged from her car and was undoing the seatbelt that held in place a cat carrier in the passenger seat. She seemed to be having a little trouble as she leaned on her crutches while reaching inside. Maribel couldn't help staring at her shapely rear end. A flash of when they'd made love rendered her speechless.

Maribel was disrupted from her thoughts when Lucritia touched her hand and whispered, "How come she's got Grayson in a cage?"

"It's not a cage, Squirt. It's a carrier," Maribel explained.

"I didn't know what to do. I couldn't leave him at Sandy's or my mom's. Is it okay that I brought him? I didn't want to let him run free in case we couldn't catch him again. I thought we could let him out while we're eating. That way he won't feel like he's in prison or something. I bought a litter box, just in case. He's smart. He already knows how to use it. It's in the back." Blair pointed to the open space in the back of her hatchback. Maribel grinned when she saw the large duffel bag and other items in the back besides kitten food, litter, and the litter box. The travel bags gave her hope that Blair might be considering staying with her. She prayed the transformation of the trophy room would seal the deal.

Maribel heard the click of the belt and Blair exclaimed, "Finally. Working around crutches is a bitch, but at least I've managed to adapt to driving as long as I'm careful. It's been an adventure, learning to use my left foot for the gas pedal and brake."

"Shit. I shoulda thought to come get you instead." Maribel shook her head.

"No, it's okay. I already feel like such a burden. I want to be as independent as I can manage."

Skeeter ran to the carrier and began sniffing. The kitten backed into the corner of the carrier and hissed.

"Skeeter, come. Sit," she ordered. "You didn't have to bring stuff for the kitten. Um, I might have that covered for you. Let me get the carrier and I'll show you." Maribel patted Skeeter on the head and commanded, "Stay." She made her way to the passenger side of the car and reached for the carrier.

"Thanks, that's one trick I haven't quite managed. I can pull him from the carrier, and he does well clinging to my shoulder while I crutch around, but that's been in an enclosed space. Grayson, huh? That's a good name. I think it's perfect." Blair glanced at Lucritia and smiled.

"Do you want me to grab them other bags, too?" Maribel hesitated to ask, not wanting to presume anything.

"We can wait on those. See how things go. I like to keep my options open." Blair readjusted herself on her crutches.

"I'm just glad that staying here is one of those options," Maribel said.

"It is," Blair answered.

Tiny meows emanated from the carrier when Maribel started toward the house. Skeeter was hot on her tail whining. “I want to show you something. Do you think you can be on those crutches for a few more steps? I got a lounger all set up outside for you, but what I want to show you is inside.”

“Yeah, the leg is getting stronger every day,” Blair answered.

“Lucritia, why don’t you let Blair and Mari have a little breathing room. We can set the table while Mari shows Blair the surprise. Probably would be good to distract Skeeter. I know he just wants to play, but Grayson hasn’t spent as much time around him as Cali.”

“But I wanna see if Blair likes her surprise,” Lucritia whined.

“A surprise, huh?” Blair smiled. “I hope it’s a good one.”

“It sure is,” Lucritia declared. “I helped.”

“Well, then, you better come with. Maybe I’ll be so overwhelmed with joy, I’ll need both of you to be there to keep me from keeling over with excitement.”

“All right. I guess I’m overruled on this. Best join in on the fun, then,” Danella conceded.

The group made their way inside, and before Maribel opened the door to the room, she glanced in Blair’s direction. It broke her heart to see Blair’s face erupt in perspiration as her face turned pale. Maribel set down the carrier and went to Blair’s side.

“Sorry, sorry, I…I…”

Before Maribel could say anything Lucritia had run to the door and flung it open. Blair's eyes widened. Inside the room was a playground fit for royalty. Kitten royalty.

"I thought that if you decided to stay, I would have a room ready for Grayson."

Tears formed in Blair's eyes. "You sacrificed the room where memories of your father are strongest—for me, for Grayson?"

Maribel nodded. "I'd do just about anything for you."

"Aren't you happy?" Lucritia's worried voice came out in a tiny whisper.

"Yeah, I'm happy, Squirt," Blair assured.

"Time to go set the table now. No more arguments. Get Skeeter to come with us." Danella's voice was firm as she gently led Lucritia away.

"Can we let Grayson out and spend a few minutes here?"

Maribel led Blair to the recliner in the room. "This is the mama chair. You get to hang out with your furbaby while he explores his new territory. He'll ignore these wonderful toys if I crumple a piece of paper and toss it into the room."

"Maribel."

"Yeah," Maribel shyly met Blair's teary eyes.

"Get my other bags."

"Really?"

"Yeah, really. We'll give this a trial and see how it goes. How could I possibly refuse to let Grayson have this wonderful playground? He is going to be a very spoiled kitten. Do you spoil Skeeter this much?"

"Maybe. It's easy to spoil the important people and animals in my life."

"I'm sorry I pushed you away. Recovery for me has been a lot more than physical therapy or changing bandages."

"I know."

"I'd be crazy not to figure out a way to make things work and see where this goes. You're too important to me. Something started between us that I'm not willing to let go of."

Blair took a step in Maribel's direction and was quickly enveloped in her strong arms. She let the crutches fall to the floor, balancing on one leg as she melted into the embrace. They stayed like that for a full minute not saying another word. When they broke apart, Blair lowered herself onto the recliner.

"Oooh, this is comfy. I feel like a queen on my throne."

Maribel laughed. "Good. That was what I was going for."

"I already understand that I've grown up far more privileged than you, and yet, I am the one continuing to be pampered. Something doesn't feel quite right about that."

"I'm in love with you, Blair," Maribel blurted. "Nothing would make me happier than to continue to pamper you."

"Oh, Maribel." Blair stretched her hand out to Maribel, and Maribel squatted next to the chair. "You better give me a proper hello kiss now that it's just the two of us."

Maribel leaned in and explored Blair's soft lips, earning a loud moan that was eventually blended with tiny meows. She didn't care that Blair hadn't said she loved Maribel. She'd agreed to stay. It was a start. Baby steps.

After breaking the kiss, Maribel clarified, "I don't think it's just the two of us. The prince has made his presence known. I think he wants out."

CHAPTER TWENTY-TWO

Grayson curled inside Skeeter as the two basked in the heat of the fireplace. The temperature had dropped, seemingly overnight, and the fall chill was definitely in the air. Blair was relaxing on the couch with her laptop precariously perched across her thigh. Her wound was still tender at times, and it was hard to position the computer on one leg while typing. Maribel had offered to buy a computer tray that was a lot like the old TV trays, but Blair wasn't used to that and complained that the angle for typing would be all "catawampus." Maribel had chuckled and remarked, "Like balancing the laptop on one leg is not?"

Maribel walked to the couch and set two chai teas on the table. She sat next to Blair and asked, "How's it going? Are you ready for tomorrow?"

The spices in the chai tea filled the air with that heavenly scent she'd come to appreciate. After her first taste, she was addicted. Gradually, she had replaced her heavily doctored coffee with chai tea.

"I would be lying if I didn't admit to being nervous. The press is saying this will be the largest crowd to hit Seattle since the protests right after he who shall not be named was elected. The women's march was huge. If we even get half the amount of that event, I'll be over the moon."

"Are you sure you don't want to drive there tonight and stay at a hotel? We can still do that," Maribel asked.

"Nah. Danella would never want you to pay for a hotel, and I want them to be there. I've written and rewritten my speech so many times that I decided to have two versions, in case I can't tell the whole story. Squirt has been working so hard on her speech and, honestly, her version might be a lot more powerful than mine. That kid has the strength of Wonder Woman."

"Maybe I don't need to do mine then," Maribel tossed out.

"No way. You promised."

Maribel picked up her tea, took a sip, and sighed. "I did. Stupidest thing I ever agreed to."

"Just speak from the heart. Pretend that I'm the only person in the crowd and talk to me. Will you read it to me now?"

"I'm still working on it. You aren't the only person who has cornered the market on obsessiveness." Maribel grinned.

A flash of gray streaked across the floor and catapulted onto the couch. Grayson pushed his nose against Blair's arm and began to crawl on top of the laptop. "Someone has determined I've fixated enough over the speech."

"How come he can so easily get you to stop working on it?"

"Not true, there is that thing you do before we end up in bed…" Blair giggled. "Of course, I had to get through that thick skull of yours that I wasn't going to break if you touched me. There are a lot of creative ways to make love without jostling the injury." She set the laptop on the coffee table and began petting Grayson.

"I can be inventive when I want to be."

"Oh yes, you sure can. Plus, I've grown quite fond of that third hole."

Maribel started to lean in and kiss Blair. The knock on the glass interrupted the two women. Grayson jumped down and made a beeline for Skeeter who was yawning and beginning to wake from his nap.

Lucritia was grinning at the back door with Cali in her arms. She'd lost both of her front teeth, and her smile was so adorable it got Blair thinking about what it might be like to have kids with Maribel. They'd both carefully avoided the subject of what Blair would do after the rally. Blair had seen how Maribel was with Lucritia, and she couldn't think of another person more suited for motherhood than Maribel. She was patient, loving, and full of tenderness toward the little girl. Blair imagined that with her own child she'd be just as wonderful. The counseling Maribel had paid for, despite Danella's protests, had done Lucritia a lot of good. That kid was a marvel in resiliency.

Emma Bronson would be bringing her wife, Addison, and their three kids, and Blair wanted to have a chance to talk with her about her experience in a lesbian couple with children. They'd developed an online friendship that had surprised Blair. None of her friends had taken the plunge yet, and she worried about how the world had evolved and if hatred was beginning to infect society again. She wasn't sure she wanted to subject her kids to hateful taunts by mean-spirited kids who learned that behavior from their God-fearing parents. Emma and her family were not subject to the same challenges because of their fame, but Blair still wanted to gain a bit more perspective on the issue.

Blair was jolted from her thoughts when Maribel called out, "Come on in, Squirt. We're having tea. Do you want a mug of hot chocolate?"

Lucritia nodded and plopped down on the floor. Cali scrambled out of her arms and joined Skeeter and Grayson who were starting to play together. "I'm scared."

Maribel was already in the kitchen making the cocoa, so Blair jumped in before Maribel could ask. "You're scared? That doesn't sound like you. You're the bravest little girl I know."

"I'm the only little girl you know."

"Not true, but you are my favorite. What's got you so worried?"

"I was watching the TV, and they were saying there's going to be thousands of people there tomorrow. What if I flub my speech?"

Blair patted the spot next to her on the couch. "Why don't you run through your speech right now. If you practice it enough, like when you and Maribel go to the shooting range, you get so good at it, you don't have to think about it. It just comes natural to you."

"How come you've never given me that advice before?" Maribel asked.

"Shush, this isn't about you." Blair wagged her finger.

"You think so, Blair? Can I practice so much I'll be really good at it?"

"Absolutely. I'm positive," Blair answered.

"I'm gonna get what Mama helped me write out." Lucritia scrambled off the couch and slammed open the door before running out.

"One of these days, she's going to bang that door so hard, the glass is going to break. I should see about replacing it with an indestructible material."

"Yeah, something that would stop a bullet." Blair gasped. "I can't believe I just said that. God, when will my fear go away, and I won't think about things like that?"

Maribel joined Blair on the couch and stroked her back. “I don’t know, honey. But I would replace every single piece of glass if that’ll settle your nerves.”

“No, it’s an irrational thought. Shit, you have the best security system money can buy. And, you’re not fooling me one bit. I know you’ve got at least one shotgun hidden somewhere. I appreciate the fact that you found a place so well hidden that you’ll forget where it is when you get old and gray. Out of sight, out of mind. That has worked as a compromise, so don’t get all nutso on me and decide to change everything to suit my neurosis.”

“It isn’t neurosis.” Maribel kissed Blair on the cheek. “I love you so much. I’ve said it before, I’d do anything to make you feel safe.”

“Let’s leave it as is. You keep it out of my line of sight and we’re all good. As much as I would like to rid the world of their one billion guns, I know that is not realistic. I’d settle for a reduction. It makes zero sense that the US has nearly half of those one billion guns. Even you have to agree that is way too many.”

“Save your arguments for tomorrow. I know the stats. Remember, you keep spitting them out to me. I’ve been your sounding board for the last three weeks. I’m starting to dream about the facts swirling all around me. The other night the words started to form a sort of rope and began choking me.”

“Really?”

"No, but I have dreamed about the speeches. Mostly me standing in front of a large crowd in my birthday suit. It was not pretty."

"Doubtful. I'll bet you making a speech without a stitch of clothing would bring in a lot more people," Blair joked.

Lucritia banged open the door again, and Blair saw the papers in her hand with the large block script.

"You ready?" Lucritia asked.

Blair and Maribel nodded. "Show us your brilliance," Blair said.

"My name is Lucritia, and I want to tell you a story…"

CHAPTER TWENTY-THREE

Maribel looked out at the enormous crowd of people who had gathered despite the light drizzle Seattle was known for. The public address system and stage were covered, but the blocks of wall-to-wall people remained in the elements.

"God, I sure hope the press does not focus on crowd size and instead places the emphasis on the messages we intend to share today," Blair announced to no one in particular who happened to be standing on the stage with her.

"Do you know how proud Lucritia is to be the first speaker? You constantly amaze me." Maribel placed her hand on Blair's shoulder. She'd had to argue vociferously to have a chair on stage that Blair could sit on while everyone made their speeches. She wanted to stand with the rest of them, but Maribel had been adamant that she wouldn't go unless Blair was smarter about her health. Blair had finally acceded.

"I guess it's time." Blair grabbed her cane and walked to the microphone. "Hello everyone. My name is Blair Chadwick. I have a story to tell a little later, but I couldn't be prouder to introduce our first speaker. Lucritia is a special little girl in my life, and she has been profoundly affected by guns. They are a part of her world, and she has a unique perspective to share with everyone. But rather than tell her story, I'll let her tell you herself."

Lucritia patted her pocket, the one that held her neatly folded speech. Maribel knew she'd memorized it but needed the paper as a crutch in case she was too nervous. Maribel brought the crate for Lucritia to stand on and pulled the microphone down to where she wouldn't have to strain to speak into it.

"My name is Lucritia, and I want to tell you a story. My second-best friend, Blair, was shot in the leg by my daddy. She got hurt real bad, and sometimes she jumps at loud noises. That makes me sad even though my daddy can't hurt her anymore. He was a bad man who had a bad gun. Mama said I shouldn't tell you why he won't hurt anyone else, so I'll leave that part of the story out." Lucritia ventured a side glance at Danella who smiled at her.

She continued her speech. "Some guns are good, and some are bad. My best friend, Mari, taught me to shoot a good gun. Mari and Blair don't agree on guns, but they love each other. I know they agree with me that there are good guns and bad guns. I think it only makes sense that we take away the bad guns and that we don't allow bad people to have any guns. I asked my best friend, Mari, why they allow bad people to have bad guns. She said that not everyone agrees on who should be able to have guns and how they can keep those guns from getting into the hands of the bad people, even if we did agree. She said not everybody agrees on what's a bad gun, either. But I been listening to her talk with Blair, and if they can agree, why can't everyone else? They argue a lot about guns. I don't want anyone else I love to be hurt or be afraid. I would give up my good gun if that meant nobody else got hurt, even though I love shooting with Mari. That's all I gotta say."

The crowd erupted in applause and Lucritia beamed. Maribel gave her the thumbs-up gesture. Blair started to stand again to introduce Emma Bronson, but Maribel touched her shoulder and said, "Lucritia said you shouldn't have to get up so much and asked if she could introduce Emma. She practiced with me. She has this."

Blair nodded and smiled.

"I had to practice this next part with Mari. She said it was good. I know Blair's leg still hurts 'cause I see her make a face. I told Mari I could introduce Emma. She's the big Hollywood actress. I know she's famous 'cause Blair talks about her all the time. She was excited. I was worried at first because I didn't want Emma stealing Blair away from Mari, but Mari said that wouldn't happen because Emma's married already. I told Mari she should ask Blair to marry her so's nobody steals her away."

Maribel started coughing. “Um, I swear this was not what she practiced with me.”

Blair laughed. “Oh, really? It is rather enlightening and given the chuckles in the crowd, this little bit of levity could only be accomplished by an eight-year-old. Although, I think Danella is giving her daughter the sign to move along.”

“Emma’s real famous for her two shows that Mama wouldn’t let me watch. She said they aren’t meant for kids. But Emma has kids of her own, and she’s got stuff to say today.”

Emma offered Lucritia a warm smile and a gentle hug. “Your speech was amazing,” she whispered before making her way to the microphone. “How do I top that?” Emma asked the crowd.

She glanced over at Lucritia and winked. “But this day isn’t about any of us standing out. It’s about each of us standing up. I know what many people will say. Who is Emma Bronson to address gun violence in America? An actress isn’t qualified to speak about serious issues. Emma Bronson is actually Emma Blake. I’m a daughter, a wife, and a mother. I can honestly tell you that when I was Lucritia’s age, I never feared going to school because someone might shoot me. As a mother, the reality that my children have to practice active-shooter drills in their classroom, when they should be practicing multiplication tables or playing kickball at recess, is nothing short of unacceptable. It is incomprehensible to me that we allow lives to be ended and altered every day across this country by gun violence when we have the power to do something about it."

Emma paused and Maribel thought she had every person in the audience hanging onto all her words.

Continuing, she forged ahead. "Lucritia said there are good guns and bad guns. I've heard it said many times that there are good people and bad people. As an actor, it's my job to play characters who are often written as heroes and villains. I have to do research. Part of that research involves spending time with people who resemble the character I'm playing or the characters that surround her. When I was working on *Found*, I spent hours with victims of violent crime. I also spent time with some of the perpetrators of violence. Do you know what I discovered?" Another well-placed pause.

"They are all people. People are capable of creating wonderful things and of inflicting unimaginable hurt. I do know this much; a person with a semi-automatic weapon can inflict immeasurable pain in a few seconds. It doesn't stop with the bullets. Gun violence touches lives in waves, from the victims who die or who spend hours, days, or months in a hospital, to their families, friends, co-workers, and classmates. And that wave only grows in size and scope by the day."

A ghost of a smile appeared on Emma's face, and Maribel could almost see her memories shimmer in the rain as Emma began to share them with the crowd.

"I grew up in Kansas. I was raised in a house with guns. I was brought up to respect the power of a gun. When my brother cheered after shooting a large buck, my father told him to remember that the buck was also a father, a brother, and a son. Life always matters. The power to kill should not be celebrated. I never wanted to hunt with my brothers. I do know that when they take the life of a deer or a duck, they say a prayer for the life that was lost, and they give thanks for what the animal offers them—food for other lives to be sustained. There are people who do not think like my brothers or my father. They do not revere life. A gun in the hands of a person who believes a gun is a toy is dangerous to all of us. I understand that people fear losing their rights."

Emma glanced at Maribel and Blair who sat together with their hands intertwined.

"As a lesbian, I am familiar with that fear. I understand that some argue if we take away the ability to own one type of weapon, gradually people will lose the right to carry any firearm at all. But from the moment we are born, we are taught limits. As a mother, it is my job to teach my children limits. Boundaries are not meant as punishments. They are established as a way to keep us from harm and to ensure that we have the best possible outcomes for our society. That is why we have laws that govern our world."

It wasn't the first time the crowd erupted in spontaneous applause and it wouldn't be the last.

"And, it is time that we implement reasonable boundaries to safeguard our collective future. I'm not a politician. You can be thankful I have no desire to pursue life in that arena. As a human being who loves other human beings, as someone who has been given so much more than I ever could need—I cannot be silent. On this stage, I am not assuming the personality or experience of a character. I am here to play the part of Emma Bronson-Blake—mother, wife, daughter, actress, friend, and citizen. To raise my voice with yours and to call others to join us in paving the way toward a future where our children worry about homework and not active shooters."

"Yes," the crowd shouted their agreement.

"Nothing that we have created could ever be more valuable than the lives of those we love. It's time to revere life over guns. It is time for us to accept reasonable limits and to demand action by our lawmakers to safeguard our communities."

Emma looked over toward Lucritia again. "We can do better and we must. You don't have to be on magazine covers or in celebrity news to matter. We all matter. Our voices matter. Our votes matter," she repeated.

"We are neighbors, not strangers. Thank you so much for inviting me to speak with you today. I know that together our voices and our votes will build the world we imagine for our children—one in which they explore endless possibility and one where they never have to be taught to cower beneath a desk or in a closet. Onward!" She nodded to the throng of people who were clapping and cheering as she stepped to the side.

Maribel's palms began to sweat as the graceful woman left the microphone, and she knew that in a matter of seconds, those thousands of eyes would be focused on her.

Blair stood and touched her arm. "You got this. Don't talk to them, talk to me. Imagine me in the front row."

"I hope you know that even though I believe in the cause, I'm only doing this because I love you."

"I know." Limping to the microphone with Maribel walking beside her, Blair began her introduction.

"I've learned over the past couple of months that if we ever hope to get momentous gun legislation passed, we have to have meaningful conversations about the topic. The next speaker and I don't agree on everything, in fact, when it comes to gun laws, when we first started talking, we didn't agree on anything. As Lucritia so eloquently put, we argue a lot. But I love and respect Maribel Sanders. Regardless of what I believe, one fact is irrefutable: Maribel is a shining example of what a strong, principled woman looks like. She has never been afraid to consider views different from her own and to reassess those perspectives. She's taught me a few things, and I wanted her here because of her unique perspective on this issue."

Maribel leaned in and whispered to Blair, "You love me? Like as in forever love or friend-slash-temporary-lover love?"

"I don't think now is the time to get into that discussion." Blair winked. "Go on, wow this crowd, like you do me every single day." She returned to the chair Maribel had set up for her on the side of the raised platform.

"For those of you who don't know who I am because I haven't ever been asked to be the spokeswoman for Nike or appeared on a box of Wheaties, I'm Maribel Sanders, and

I've made my living off of my talent as a skeet shooter. I have nine gold medals and hope to gather a few more before I stop competing. When I first started shooting, my sponsor was the NRA. I believed in the Second Amendment. I still do. Before you boo me off the stage, I'm not an NRA member anymore. I can't get behind what they stand for now, which is protecting their view of the Second Amendment, no matter what. Guns do kill people. Sure, so do knives, cars, and every other thing that can be weaponized, but the US has more guns than any other nation and as a result we have more mass shootings. One thing I know for sure, there isn't any justifiable reason for a civilian to own a high-capacity firearm. They only do one thing."

Maribel paused and looked at Blair and then continued, "They kill and maim a large number of people. What I've come to understand is that people like Blair who are social activists for reasonable gun control aren't trying to take away our right to have guns. I stopped drinking the Kool-Aid, and when I did, I saw a lot more clearly. Blair is looking for a way to stop the insanity. I don't want to give up my guns, but if by doing so I could stop one innocent child from dying, I'd make that sacrifice. I wonder, if faced with that reality, that choice, to give up your gun, or allow a shooter to kill your son or daughter, who would honestly choose the latter? The inconvenience of waiting for a background check, limitations on the kinds of guns I can purchase, restrictions on ammunition are all small prices to pay if it saves even one life. Why are we throwing up roadblocks? It doesn't make any logical sense. I get it now. I really do. It's not just because I love Blair. If these laws had been in place years ago, several tragedies would never have happened. I may not be the sharpest tool in the box, but even I know that's just common sense. I don't want to be the poster child for the NRA anymore."

Maribel unrolled the poster she'd removed from her former trophy room to show the crowd the big black X across the picture of her as a child with the NRA sponsorship prominently displayed. Tossing the poster aside, she turned away and met Blair's loving eyes.

†

Now that it was Blair's turn to speak, her nerves affected her ability to approach the microphone without stumbling as she used her cane. Maribel rushed to her side and put a protective arm around her waist as she led her to the center of the stage. The crowd was enormous, and Blair felt almost insignificant in comparison.

"I got you, babe. I'll stand right next to you, okay?" Maribel whispered in her ear.

Blair looked out at the sea of people, holding signs and umbrellas. All eyes were on her now, and a surge of energy erupted from deep within.

"On the steps of the Lincoln Memorial fifty-six years ago, Dr. Martin Luther King had a dream," Blair began. "I have a dream, not exactly the same dream as Martin Luther King, but I hope he would approve. This dream is rooted in the same need for America to regain its humanity. To value all human life. I dream of a world where grade school children do not have to pass a metal detector to enter their school. A dream where every school, place of worship or employment in America, no longer has to worry about running active-shooter drills. A dream where my children don't wonder if today is the day someone comes into their school to shoot them. Or that a random bullet doesn't hit them while walking home. It's too late for my little sister because my dream will never erase that nightmare. But I can dream of the future."

She gathered her emotions for the next part. Her voice quivered as she spoke. "They say that lightning never strikes twice," Blair continued. "While that may be true, it isn't true for gun violence. My younger sister, Trina, lost her life on September 7th at the school shooting at Cedarbrook Elementary. Not even one month after that shooting, a man went on a rampage at a store in town. That same man, using his high-capacity shotgun managed to let loose his rage again. Contrary to what you see on TV and the movies, bullets do penetrate vehicles. I have a scar on my leg to prove it. It's not that I don't feel compassion toward the loners or kids who are bullied to the extreme that they feel the need to make a statement through violence. It's just that, there has to be a way to reach them and stop the easy gun access. I know for a fact that a beautiful light was extinguished well before her time, and the world is definitely not a better place for that loss."

Blair looked out at the somber faces. Some of the men and women were wiping their eyes. She forged ahead, determined to complete her speech. “There aren’t simple solutions, but don’t we owe it to the world to try to find them before another beautiful soul is destroyed before his or her time? I know it’s not realistic to remove every single gun from every person’s possession. That’s nearly 400 million in case you wanted to know the numbers. And if you aren’t acknowledging the correlation between the number of guns and the number of mass shootings, you aren’t paying attention to this epidemic that will only get worse. We have to start somewhere, don’t we? Continued pressure on the politicians is essential. On that note, I’d like to introduce my father, Senator Chadwick.”

Blair saw the shocked look on her father’s face when she introduced him as her father. The glistening in his eyes was evidence of how that had affected him. He offered a tentative smile and joined her at the microphone.

“I’m not proud of my previous stance on this issue, or my past voting record, but if I can change…”

Chapter Twenty-four

Blair was exhausted and grateful that Maribel was there to drive them home after the rally. Maribel kept looking at her, but she knew she wouldn't start a serious conversation about their future with Lucritia and Danella sitting in the back of the extended cab. She wasn't going to let the travel time go to waste. The minute they hit the highway, she started her internet search.

Blair almost felt sorry for Maribel. She wasn't trying to ignore her, but she had to find the answers to her dilemma. The silence was clearly eating Maribel up. She hadn't planned on saying anything about loving Maribel today and certainly not in front of a crowd of over a hundred thousand people. The words had snuck out. She knew she should have told Maribel she was in love with her a long time ago. Maribel hadn't been stingy with her emotions, but Blair certainly had been cautious at the very least.

After pulling up to the house, Danella quickly gathered Lucritia and started on the well-worn path to their manufactured home. Lucritia rubbed her eyes and shuffled along, clearly exhausted from the high-energy day.

"Come for breakfast tomorrow," Maribel called out.

Danella waved her acknowledgement of the invitation as she continued down the path with her arm draped around her daughter's shoulder.

Once inside, Maribel asked, "Tea?"

"Sure, that would be lovely." Before Maribel turned toward the kitchen. Blair grabbed her arm and spun her around, kissing her soundly.

"What was that for?"

"I wanted to make sure you felt that, because I know I haven't been great about telling you how I feel."

Maribel grinned. "Okay. Does that mean we can talk about it now? About us?"

"Yup. That's the plan. I had an epiphany today. It's something I've known for some time now but was too preoccupied with the rally. Finally, I've stopped long enough to pick it apart and analyze it to death."

"Two processors. That could be dangerous."

"Or very interesting. But honestly, I'm not the processing type so no real worries there."

"Hold that thought while I put on the water." Maribel filled the teapot and then joined Blair who had taken a seat on the couch.

"I've been selfish and self-absorbed. Why do you love me? I can't quite figure that out."

"Because you have the sort of fire and passion that makes people believe that one person can make a difference in this world. We don't have to be a bunch of sheep, following the flock to our demise. I love that you care enough about this crazy world to do something. Plus, you're good in bed," Maribel joked.

Blair smacked her lightly on the arm. "I realized today that you've been willing all along to do whatever was necessary to make us work. Love and family trumps everything for you. You'd even give up your guns, and that is so much a part of you. Honestly, I don't know that the essence of who you are would remain intact if you did that. I haven't done a single thing to meet you halfway."

"That's not true. I remember you saying you could never live in a house with guns, and yet, knowing there are still guns in the house, you decided to stay. That is the granddaddy of compromises. Besides, I understand why you can't have Squirt and me shooting on the grounds. I get it. I really do. Sometimes, I remember that day and my hands tremble. On those days, I miss every clay disc that machine shoots out, no matter what speed they fly into the air."

"You never told me that."

"Doesn't always happen. I'm trying to work through it. It's like when they say a person should get right back on a horse after they've been thrown."

"See, I should try to find a way to deal. Sometimes I feel so guilty about you leaving your own home to accommodate my issues. It isn't fair to you. Honestly, I've been going back and forth on whether to leave and return to my old life. You'd get back your routines, and I wouldn't have to feel so ashamed about what I'm practically forcing you to do. I've been telling myself every single day that after the rally is over, I'll do it. I'll leave you alone. But when I start to imagine my life without you, it's almost worse. I swear I have a massive panic attack."

Maribel gathered Blair in her arms. "I don't want my old life. I'll never shoot a gun again and give them all away if it means having you stay here. I love you." Maribel let go and swiped at her tears. "Please don't leave."

"See, that's what I realized today. You've been doing all the sacrificing. I also admitted to myself that my panic attacks at the thought of never seeing you again meant I was completely smitten. I'm too in love with you to walk away without a fight. I love you enough to make a few sacrifices of my own. It's time I thought of creative solutions to this dilemma."

The whistling of the teapot halted the conversation, and Maribel hustled to the kitchen to pour the hot water into cups. Returning to the living room, she set the cups on the table to let them cool. "Such as?"

"I did an internet search on the way back home."

Maribel smiled when Blair used the word home. She hadn't realized she'd said that until it slipped out.

"Anyway," Blair continued, "did you know they make suppressors for shotguns? It reduces the noise a lot. I don't know if it affects the accuracy of your shots or somehow distorts things to where you can't use one in practice, but I thought along with noise canceling headphones, we would make it work. I would just need to know when you start. You have a schedule, right?"

"Yeah."

"If that doesn't work, I can find a place to rent an office and go there while you're practicing. I can write grants from anywhere."

Maribel crushed Blair against her chest. "You would do that for me?"

"In a hot minute. I already told work I wasn't going to return in the same position but I would continue to write grants. They were extremely helpful and gave my name to a few other nonprofits. I've decided to be an independent consultant." Blair shrugged. "It will give me the flexibility and time needed to plan more rallies across the country. I sort of committed to doing one in Portland next month. I hope you'll be able to join me. We make a powerful team."

"I'll come with you to every single one. Except I can't plan anything for July and August of next year. I'm hoping to be in Tokyo next summer. And I thought you might want to come with me?"

"I've never been to the Olympics before," Blair answered excitedly. "I'm not sure how I feel about Tokyo, but having excellent sushi will make up for the crowds. Hopefully we'll be able to figure out my aversion to guns before next summer so I can yell and scream in the stands like the other rabid fans."

"It's okay if you don't want to attend my events. Skeet shooting doesn't get a lot of coverage or a lot of fans. It isn't sexy like women's soccer, especially now that the US team took the World Cup. Just having you there will be a treat."

"No way, I'm gonna be there for you, and when you look into the stands, I'll have a sign telling the world I support you. Do you think it would be bad form to add something about gun control, too?" Blair joked.

"Drink your tea, rabble rouser."

"I'll bet you have to sign something that says you won't embarrass the US with a political protest."

"Probably."

Blair grinned. "Do you know how much press—"

"Don't start," Maribel warned.

"There's something else I wanted to do, and I was hoping you'd come with me. It's long overdue. I know that. It's time."

"Anything. You know I'd do anything for you."

"I need to visit Trina's grave. I know you've been there." Blair held her hand up. "It's okay, Sandy told me. I thought it was incredibly sweet. She said you planted flowers and made sure the caretakers attended to the turf."

"I was visiting my pa, and I don't think it's a coincidence that Trina's grave is close to his. I think my pa is looking after Trina. I told him not to teach her things you wouldn't approve of. It just felt right to visit and start talking to her. I've been keeping her up to date on what you've been up to."

Blair couldn't help the tears that began to flow freely, but this time her grief was a little less raw than the day she couldn't muster the energy to go to the gravesite. Maribel didn't stop her from crying. Instead she sat quietly waiting for Blair to respond as she held her hands.

"Now you know I don't believe in an afterlife. But if I did, I'm very glad you instructed your pa not to turn Trina into a far right extremist wearing a red MAGA cap." Blair smiled through her tears.

"How about I take you tomorrow? You can visit with your mother and father afterward."

"Don't push it. Today I had a moment of weakness. Tomorrow I'll likely revert to calling him the Sperm Donor again."

"Some of what he says makes sense to me."

"Seriously? You're bonding with the Sperm Donor? No wonder he approves of you." Blair shook her head. There was no doubt in her mind that life with Maribel would never be boring. She preferred the fireworks that came out of their fiery relationship over the dull, uninteresting day-to-day existence that all too often happened in long-lasting relationships. They had plenty of years to arrive at that stage.

†

Not that Blair thought Maribel had lied, but she didn't realize how close Ray Sander's grave was to Trina's. They had laid Trina to rest in the next row, less than ten feet from Ray's gravesite. Maribel stood a polite distance away, giving Blair a few minutes of privacy, while showing her support at the same time. She'd already visited her father's grave and was waiting for Blair to finish.

Sitting cross-legged on the patch of grass, Blair traced the letters on the marker her mother had picked out.

If love could have saved you,
You would have lived forever.
Beloved Daughter and Sister
Trina Chadwick 2012 -2019

Blair approved of the marker. The words were perfect. She knew that Maribel talked with her father. She also talked with Trina, even though she had never met her. Blair didn't know what to say. Could she convince herself that somehow Trina would hear her if she spoke to her now? Or were the words something that would help Blair find a small amount of peace in the tragedy?

"Hey, Trina. I'm sorry I didn't come earlier. Somehow, I get the feeling you'd understand. Even at seven, you'd developed the capacity for empathy and acceptance to a far greater degree than I've been able to cultivate in my twenty-five years. I wonder if you had anything to do with sending Maribel to me? Good choice if you did. I won't pretend to understand why you were taken from us before you had the chance to live a full life. That's something I don't believe anyone will ever help a non-believer understand. I wish I could believe in God and his plan for a better life for you, but I can't. On the off chance I'm wrong, I hope you're happy wherever you are. Know that I think of you every time I see something beautiful. That's a daily event. Because if I take the time to look around, there's beauty everywhere. I'm going to try not to stay sad. That's hard to do because I miss you every single day. That'll never change. Sandy and Maribel assure me the pain will lesson with time. I'm not gonna lie, I have my doubts, but they've both proven I'm not right about every single thing. So maybe I'll listen. How about if I say see 'ya later, little tater,' like I used to, instead of goodbye. I'll visit again. The next time will probably be a tiny bit easier. At least I think it will be." Blair kissed the tips of her fingers and laid them on the cool marker.

Maribel magically appeared by her side and helped her stand. Blair didn't have closure because that didn't apply. She'd never have closure, but she had faced her grief head on and hadn't completely fallen apart.

With Maribel's arm draped around her shoulder, they walked slowly to Maribel's truck. Maribel kissed her on the temple and then opened the door for her. She knew Maribel would not try to fill the void with nervous chatter. She would let Blair process the visit in her own time and in her own way. When Blair was ready to talk, she would break the silence. But for now, she was content to spend the time driving home in quiet stillness of their individual introspection.

EPILOGUE

Blair sat nervously in the stands. The hard metal seating causing her to wiggle her butt on the cushion she'd brought with her. Lucritia and Danella were sitting on both sides and although she knew Lucritia was squealing in delight, she couldn't hear a thing. The noise-canceling headphones were the best that money could buy, and Blair had already tested their effectiveness.

The section of fans and friends supporting the United States all rose and started clapping when Maribel walked to the spot where she would begin the round. Blair thought she looked so sexy in her baseball hat and eye protection. Blair had joked with her about the cool factor of the safety glasses she wore that would eliminate all glare. Maribel hadn't missed a beat when she retorted that she had a MAGA hat in her pack that she was planning to wear for the big event.

Blair's breathing increased as she focused on the shotgun Maribel was carrying, and Lucritia grabbed her hand and squeezed. Taking deep breaths, Blair channeled her focus on the woman she loved and how important this moment was to her. Maribel had confessed that, although her heart wasn't in the games in the same way as before, she wanted to do well because it would be her last Olympics. Blair was adamant about her not quitting before the summer Olympics. She did not want to be the reason Maribel left the sport. Blair knew it was important to Maribel to overcome the events of almost two years ago that had profoundly affected both of them. It was probably a blessing the 2020 games were postponed to 2021 due to the Coronavirus. There was more time to restore some sense of normalcy. Although the tragedy had brought them together, there were still deep wounds that had not healed completely and perhaps they never would. Neither woman would let those wounds tear them apart. So far, they'd been successful.

Maribel looked back to the stands, and Blair stood up, holding her sign in one hand, while blowing her a kiss with the other hand.

Maribel began laughing when she read the sign. I drank the Kool-Aid, now bring me the gold. I love you now and always.

†

Maribel was looking at the ceiling in the hotel room as Blair drew patterns on her stomach. She was disappointed with her performance. It had been going along so well, and then she let the flash of seeing the blood pouring from Blair's wound distract her in the last round of competition. She'd caught Blair absently rubbing her leg when she'd glanced into the stands, and the videotape played in her head. That had cost her the gold.

"Now don't be a grumpy goose. You got two golds and a bronze. What happened? You were shooting so perfectly until that point."

"I don't want to say."

"Seriously? We don't keep secrets from each other."

"I saw you rubbing your leg. Mini-flashbacks aren't good for my accuracy. Does it hurt?" Maribel asked.

"I don't want to answer. It's embarrassing."

"Come on, I confessed. Now it's your turn."

"I'm a stress eater, and my drug of choice is sticky candy. There was this gooey taffy like candy that I was stuffing into my mouth like it was the last piece of candy I would ever get. It was so sticky, I thought I could rub it off on my shorts." Blair smiled sheepishly.

"You're kidding, right?"

"Nope. Finally, there was this prissy woman in our row who looked at me with disgust and gave me a hand wipe. It was a bit too late for my shorts, but that didn't stop me from trying to remove the stickiness I'd just created. So, you were either watching me trying to clean my shorts or my hand." Blair turned on her side and propped her head in her hand.

"I can't believe I missed that many shots," Maribel complained.

"Neither one of us missed the shot that counts."

"You've never shot a gun in all your life. What are you talking about?"

"My one shot at love. At least I wasn't stupid enough to miss on that. You weren't either. I'm betting if I hadn't called to ask you to coffee after I was shot, you would have started your stalking routine again, and I would have given in, because I knew I loved you, even then."

"I prefer to call it persistence, not stalking. And yes, you were, are, my one shot at love. I'll never love anyone as much as I do you."

"You say the sweetest things. You better start thinking hard because I want something even more special when you recite your vows. Lucritia helped me with mine."

"No fair, she was supposed to write mine and now you stripped her of all the good lines." Maribel turned on her side and began kissing Blair. "I could make up for it on the honeymoon. I've been perfecting this one move that is sure to make you purr."

"Ooh. I can't wait. You know, I also have three holes," Blair teased. "I love you, Maribel Sanders."

"More than I can ever express with words, I love you right back, Blair Chadwick."

About the Author

Annette Mori

Annette is an award-winning author, published by Affinity Rainbow Publications, who lives in the beautiful Pacific Northwest with her wife and their five furry kids. With nineteen published novels and the Goldie Award for her fourth novel, *Locked Inside,* she finally feels like a real author. Annette is as much a reader as a writer and is always looking for the next lesfic novel to queue up. She came up with the One Fan at a Time tagline, because it rolled off the tongue much better than One Reader at a Time. After pondering who she was at her core, it was all about connecting to each reader on a personal level. Annette would be the first to admit she doesn't do well with the masses. If someone picks up her book and it touches them, she believes she has achieved what she wants with her writing by reaching each reader. It is who she is at her core. Drop her a line, she loves to hear from readers: annettemori0859@gmail.com.

Sign up for her mailing list: http://eepurl.com/cS7nr9

Check out her blog: Everyday Occurrences:

https://annettemori0859.wordpress.com/

Visit the Affinity Rainbow Publications website for her books and those of many other outstanding authors:

https://www.affinityebooks.com

Other Affinity Books

The Mountain Whispers by Ali Spooner
Arriving home and discovering the betrayal by her best friend and lover, Eli Fortner leaves to run off her anger and hurt. A chance stop at a convenience store and the purchase of lottery tickets sends Eli's life into a whirlwind of change. Able to now pursue her dreams, Eli heads off to see what else fate has in store for her.
Whit Brewer, Eli's neighbor, is everything Eli never knew she needed and wanted. But can she let go of the betrayal long enough to let Whit in? Thirteen black cats, a baby goat, and Cruz, her furry best friend, join Eli on her adventure, new life, and the possibility of real love.

Charlie by Erin O'Reilly
At fourteen, Hannah Garvin met 'the one,' Charlene Gaines, and her life was never the same. They were inseparable and spent every moment they could together. One day, Charlie left without a word and again, Hannah's life took a dramatic change. Hannah vowed to never fall in love again. When she meets Mick, a new arrival to the small Texas panhandle town near her family's farm, her heart remembers what being in love was like, and yearns for more. Will Hannah let the memory of Charlie go so she can start a new life with Mick? Or will her heart betray her and hold on to her love for Charlie?

Misha's Promise by Renee MacKenzie
Misha Wyatt has settled into a peaceful existence as a healer in Karst, New America. When an airplane crashes in the meadow outside of Karst, Misha hurries to help the pilot. Misha is not expecting the pilot to be alive…or so beautiful. Will her uncontrollable desire to keep the pilot safe be her downfall? Can *they* survive their journey? The last book in the Karst series brings our characters to their physical and emotional limits. Don't miss the culmination of this exciting series!

Heart Strings Attached by Ali Spooner & Annette Mori
Socialite Remy has her world shaken. Bartender Chancy has her orderly life turned around. A mutually beneficial business agreement between Remy and Chancy turns into

undeniable attraction. Will the two ignore culture norms to explore their intense desire for each other?

The Panty Thief by Annette Mori
Someone is stealing panties, but who? And why? Joey Hartford is a fourth-year medical student who insists she doesn't have time for a relationship. A new tenant in her apartment building is proving too tempting to ignore. Sabrina is in her final year of her doctoral program and focused on completing her dissertation. Meeting Joey is dangerous for so many reasons. Add a suicidal ex-girlfriend who suddenly reappears in Sabrina's life and Joey's jealous friend-with-benefits, and things get complicated quickly.

Country Living by Jen Silver
Peri Sanderson achieves her dream of moving from London to a cottage in the English countryside with her wife, Karla. Peri sees their future as pastoral while chatting with the locals in a quaint village pub. Sexy urbanite, Karla, has other ideas. Secrets are everywhere. Peri quickly senses something not quite right among her rural neighbours and also with Karla. Temptation, betrayal, and intrigue combine to change the lives of both women beyond anything they could have imagined.

Before the Light by Samantha Hicks
One year after her long-time partner Meredith's abduction and their subsequent break-up, Kathleen Bowden-Scott's life is spiralling out of control. She meets Bethany Jones and

despite an instant attraction Kathleen shies away. In this fast-paced, romantic suspense, lies are exposed and hearts unite as Kathleen and Beth fight for their future.

Wanted for Christmas by JM Dragon
Belle Farrow knew what she wanted for Christmas–work. She had little to offer but a minor degree in cookery and household management. Certainly not enough for a decent chef or housekeeper position. Then she saw an advert in the local newspaper. Wanted: Housekeeper/cook/nanny for the period of Christmas until the New Year. This is Christmas. Perhaps Santa reads the ad column too and pushes a little spirit of the season to that request.

Dreams in a Jar by JM Dragon
When you believe your life is a never-ending spiral of despair and the only personal joy you have is inside of a novel, would you grab a chance to hide away in the local bookstore and dream of adventures? Thea's life is about to embark on a journey she never envisioned when local bookstore owner, Marion, is taken ill. Her niece, Sheryl Appleby, takes over the reins and her presence provides Thea the courage to take a leap of faith. Can she embrace the butterfly effect, or are Thea's dreams bottled in a jar forever?

Pleasure Workers by Annette Mori
Alex Cortez is accomplished at two things, fixing broken equipment and pleasuring women. She is happily doing both at the Ranch in Nevada. Danna Nichols, newly widowed,

feels lost and alone. When her good friend Lindy invites her to check out the newly established Trophy Wives Club, it awakens dormant feelings and desires. An instant attraction happens and the two form a bond under unlikely circumstances. Will the challenges of their social status tear them apart before they can enjoy the pleasures of their new love?

The Trophy Wives Club by Ali Spooner
What happens when under-appreciated professional women are offered their dream jobs? When one of Atlanta's elite businesswomen and wife of a prominent judge sets her sights on a goal, life begins to change for these women. Friendships and romance bloom in a unique fitness club on the outskirts of Atlanta, where more than a workout is offered.

Unknown Forces by Samantha Hicks
Jennifer Wilson spent the last seventeen years raising her younger sister Kelsey after a boating accident killed their parents. Riley hasn't had an easy life either and her friendship with Kelsey is the only thing steadfast in her life. When tragedy and secrets emerge, Jennifer and Riley must learn to lean on each other. The growing attraction between them only complicates matters. When events conspire to keep them apart, will they trust the unknown forces that keep pushing them together, or hide from their feelings forever?

A Window to Love by Annette Mori

Two life events, two paths colliding, two souls destined to meet. Mandie Carter lives an uninspired life. No passion, no romance, and just when she thought things couldn't get worse, life throws her a curve. Gail Forrester is barely hanging on. Buried under mountains of debt, only her much in demand architectural designs keep her afloat. Now, they must find a way forward together through what life and destiny has in store for them. Only then can they hope to step into that window to love.

Free Spirit by Erica Lawson
Priory McAllister has fought off boardroom sharks, handled high-pressure jobs, and thought she'd seen it all. She found her dream home and couldn't wait to move in. Unknown to Priory, two ghosts…Rhee and a mischievous Dylan…have inhabited the house since 1935. They have no intention of leaving. Jacey Ryder, Priory's long-suffering secretary, gets to play referee between her boss and a bossy ghost, as each side try to lay claim to the house. What can she do when an unstoppable force, (her boss) meets an immovable object, (the ghost) besides hope for a peaceful solution? They are like two peas in a pod—two *angry, stubborn* peas in a pod.

Addicted to You by Erin O'Reilly
Elin Prescot's dream to be a top fashion designer is finally within her reach—then Marissa Banks enters her life. Snared by her first taste of passion, Elin is consumed by desire for more. Her life spirals out of control until she meets Doctor Aimee Sullivan, who understands all too well what Elin is

going through. Can Elin let Aimee into her heart? Or will her addiction keep her enthralled with Marissa? This story explores first love, intense passion, manipulation of emotions, and the gentleness of real love and true romance.

Affinity
Rainbow Publications

eBooks, Print, Free eBooks

Visit our website for more publications available online.

www.affinityrainbowpublications.com

Published by Affinity Rainbow Publications
A Division of Affinity eBook Press NZ LTD
Canterbury, New Zealand

Registered Company 2517228

www.ingramcontent.com/pod-product-compliance
Lightning Source LLC
Chambersburg PA
CBHW050700290626
47170CB00016B/2507
* 9 7 8 1 9 8 8 5 8 8 7 7 3 *